GUIDE
TO THE
HUNGER
GAMES

CAROLINE CARPENTER

PLEXUS LONDON

**Character and muttation illustrations by
Veronica Kantorovitch**

All rights reserved including the right of
reproduction in whole or in part in any form
Copyright © 2012 by Plexus Publishing Limited
Published by Plexus Publishing Limited
25 Mallinson Road
London SW11 1BW
www.plexusbooks.com

British Library Cataloguing in Publication Data

Carpenter, Caroline.
  Guide to the Hunger Games.
  1. Collins, Suzanne. Hunger games.
  I. Title
  813.6-dc23

ISBN-13: 978-0-85965-486-9

Cover and book design by Coco Wake-Porter.
Printed in Great Britain by Bell & Bain Ltd

Acknowledgements
Thanks to all my family and friends for their love and support, especially Leisha – who gave me my first copy of *The Hunger Games* – and my parents for always believing in me.
This book was written by a tribute for other tributes to enjoy. Your dedication, creativity and enthusiasm in *Hunger Games* discussions, forums, artwork and fansites inspired me to write this guide.
    I would like to thank everyone at Plexus whose hard work and help made this book come together, especially: Sandra Wake for taking a risk on this book and giving me the chance to write it; Laura Slater for her insightful suggestions and feedback; Laura Coulman for guiding me through this process with excellent advice and fantastic editing; and Coco Wake-Porter, whose innovative designs have brought the text to life. Special thanks also goes to Veronika Kantorovitch, a wonderful friend and very talented artist, who took the time out of her busy schedule to share my vision and contribute her beautiful illustrations.
    The following books, magazines, and websites proved invaluable in writing this book. The author and editors would like to give special thanks to: *The Hunger Games* by Suzanne Collins; *Catching Fire* by Suzanne Collins; *Mockingjay* by Suzanne Collins, *Romeo and Juliet* by William Shakespeare; *Wuthering Heights* by Emily Brontë; *Brave New World* by Aldous Huxley; *Nineteen Eighty-Four* by George Orwell; *The Hunger Games Companion* by Louis H. Gresh; *The Machine Stops* by E. M. Forster; *The Time Machine* by H. G. Wells; *Fahrenheit 451* by Ray Bradbury; *The Tragedy of Julius Caesar* by William Shakespeare; *Battle Royale* by Koushun Takami; *The Girl who was on Fire* by various authors, edited by Leah Wilson; *Vanity Fair*; *Entertainment Weekly*; suzannecollinsbooks.com; wikipedia.com; imdb.com; thehungergames.co.uk; thehungergamesmovie.com scholastic.com/thehungergames; deviantart.com; mtv.com; hungergamesmovie.org; mockingjay.net; thehungergames.wikia.com; thehob.org; jabberjays.com; hggirlonfire.com; hungergamesdwtc.net; hungergamestrilogy.net; myhungergames.com.

CONTENTS

Introduction 5

BOOK 1: THE HUNGER GAMES

Welcome to Panem 11

Main Players 22

The 74th Hunger Games 43

Tribute Test 68

Muttations 69

BOOK 2: CATCHING FIRE

Navigating the Capitol 81

Growing Inferno 86

Quarter Quell 96

Cinna's Creations 121

BOOK 3: MOCKINGJAY

District 13 127

Old Order versus New Order 133

Gale or Peeta? 151

Panem Personal Ads 167

Becoming the Mockingjay 169

War of the Words 180

How to Survive the Hunger Games 183

Quiz 189

Personal Review 191

INTRODUCTION

With *The Hunger Games* trilogy, Suzanne Collins has created something truly special. So, just what's the inspiration behind her string of wildly successful books? Collins says that the idea came to her one night when she was channel-surfing between a reality TV competition and actual war footage. 'The lines began to blur in this very unsettling way,' recalls Collins. And, from here, the seed of her creation was sown; which shouldn't come as a surprise. So many elements of the story – the surgically enhanced people of the Capitol and their obsession with reality TV – mirror the Western world (albeit a very extreme version). *The Hunger Games* is clearly very much a product of our own troubled times.

However, Collins' writing is shaped by more than just current affairs, drawing on a rich array of classical references besides. The timeless story of Theseus and the Minotaur is particularly important for the development of Collins' protagonist, Katniss. Mentioned by Collins on numerous occasions, this Greek myth recounts how, in a bid to stop King Minos of Crete from attacking his land, King Aegeus of Athens agreed to a deal whereby, every nine years, seven Athenian boys and seven Athenian girls would be sent to Crete to be eaten by the Minotaur, a monstrous half-man, half-bull kept by Minos in a maze on the island. However, after this ritual had taken place a couple of times, King Aegeus' son Theseus volunteered to be one of the youths sacrificed to the Minotaur, with the intention of killing the beast and ending the atrocity once and for all. When he arrived in Crete, King Minos' daughter Ariadne fell in love with him. Desperate to help him overcome the Minotaur, she provided him with string and a sword. As he wandered deeper into the labyrinth, Theseus unravelled the string to leave a trail behind him. Using the sword given to him by his sweetheart, he somehow managed to slay the monster. Then it was simply a question of following the thread he'd laid to find his way back to Ariadne.

Theseus' story had a profound impact upon Suzanne Collins as a child. She was deeply affected by the ruthless way that the children's deaths were used as a form of punishment. The parallels between this myth and *The Hunger Games* – a tale of young people chosen to die, within a society that is powerless to stop it – are immediately evident. Both stories are centred on the terrible bargains made to appease an all-powerful, dominant force. In the ancient myth, the human sacrifice stops the Cretans unleashing further destruction on the Athenians; in *The Hunger Games*, the tradition is payback for a much earlier failed rebellion against the ruling power. But perhaps the clearest comparison to be drawn is between the heroes at the heart of each narrative. Theseus proves he is admirably fearless and selfless when he volunteers to face the Minotaur; likewise, Katniss stands out when she puts herself forward to take part in the dangerous Hunger Games in place of her younger sister. This element of self-sacrifice is fundamental to both characters and, while Katniss does not set out to overthrow the practice that threatens the children of her nation (the Hunger Games) in the same way that Theseus does, her actions ultimately lead to the same conclusion.

Another source of classical inspiration within Collins' books is that of the Roman Empire. She has said herself that, 'the world of Panem, particularly the Capitol, is loaded with Roman references'. Not only are many words in the book derived from Latin (the name of the nation itself, Panem; Avox; tessera), but several of the Capitol-dwelling characters have traditionally Roman names, such as Octavia, Seneca, Venia, Flavius and Portia. Even more significant is the use of gladiatorial games as a form of entertainment. When the Roman Empire was at its height, these games – in which fighters battled to the death in an arena, often with dangerous animals thrown in – were incredibly popular and watched by huge audiences. The Hunger Games are essentially an updated form of these events – an assortment of kids forced to fight to the death by a sadistic government, in the name of an exciting 'show'. A marked difference is that the Hunger Games are not watched by a live audience, but through television screens (in an eerie echo of the hugely popular reality TV shows that dominate the airwaves today). Nevertheless, the reaction of the crowd remains paramount. With the makers of the games constantly seeking new ways to keep things 'interesting', the viewers' response can play a vital role in how the action unfolds, for tributes and gladiators alike.

As well as ancient history, Collins drew ideas from her own upbringing. Her father – a military specialist, historian and doctor of political science – was also an Air Force officer who fought in the Vietnam War for an entire year of her childhood, meaning that, from a young age, she was taught the consequences of war, poverty and starvation. Her father's absence (echoed by that of Katniss' dead father years later) meant that stories such as Theseus and the Minotaur, telling of families torn apart by destructive forces beyond their control, hit young Suzanne especially hard. However, her father never shielded her from the harsh realities of war and tried to explain things in a way that was appropriate for her age, whilst also trusting that his daughter could cope with a certain amount of truth – in much the same way that Collins herself would come to write about serious and complex issues for her young audience.

Mr Collins also provided some of the background to the survival techniques employed by Katniss and Gale. He grew up during the Depression – a time when his family had to resort to hunting for food – and even as an adult he would forage in the woods for edible mushrooms. Again, we can see a parallel here with Mr Everdeen, who taught Katniss how to hunt and distinguish between edible and poisonous plants.

Despite the range of factors behind Collins' creation of Panem and the Hunger Games – from the strikingly apparent to the deeply personal – some people have been quick to draw comparisons between *The Hunger Games* and a number of seemingly similar texts. *Battle Royale*, for example, is a Japanese novel, Manga series and film depicting a totalitarian state that forces high-school students to participate in an annual program in which they must kill each other, with the purpose of scaring the wider population so badly that they do not rebel against their oppressors. On the surface, the two stories seem almost identical, yet they are very different. What is it about Collins' story, referencing familiar ideas and age-old fears, that makes it so fresh and appealing to the teenagers (and adults) of today?

First and foremost, it is almost unnecessary to say that the books are fantastic adventure stories. They are fast-paced, filled with action and Collins constantly builds up suspense with infuriatingly intriguing chapter endings that practically force you to read on. Yet, despite the focus on a thrilling narrative, characterisation is not lost. All of the characters are vividly portrayed (in the first book, Gale isn't given more than a few pages' space, but somehow this is enough to completely convey the essence of who he is) and they are nearly all made to feel 'real', rather than two-dimensional. Katniss, for example, is not shown to be a perfect heroine. She can be moody, aggressive and unforgiving as well as brave, compassionate and resourceful. Her mother is not a caring angel, but neither is she a cruel witch. She is someone who has had her heart broken and become selfish as a result, but is still forever trying to be stronger for her family – in short, she is human. And so are the rest of the characters in Collins' books – similarly complex creations with fully-formed personalities that we can truly 'believe' in.

Equally important as this personal connection with the characters are the universal themes that Collins touches upon. Inequality, corruption, exploitation and morality are always going to be important concerns and they are dealt with so cleverly within *The Hunger Games* trilogy. Rather than telling us what to think, Collins shows many different perspectives on these complicated topics (most clearly shown in the distance that grows between Gale and Katniss in *Mockingkay* because of their different outlooks on how the war should be won). Through the characters, we see the effects of their struggle for equality . . . a struggle we can believe in because Panem reflects the flawed world around us.

Despite the obvious distinctions to be made between our own society and that of Panem, there are enough similarities to resonate with readers everywhere. We too seem to have a strange obsession with reality TV programmes that see people put in ever more awkward and sometimes unpleasant situations in the name of entertainment. We enjoy luxury goods shipped in from other countries without ever really considering the working environments of people who produced them. Though we're not quite on the same level as the vacuous citizens of the Capitol just yet, alongside the fantastical elements of Panem (with its shocking developments in cosmetic enhancement, genetic engineering and lethal weaponry), there is enough truth in the stories to make them feel real and relevant.

Another aspect of the books that feels real is the inner turmoil experienced by Katniss. As well as an action hero, she's also a fairly typical adolescent girl. Though the Hunger Games arena provides an extreme backdrop to say the least, virtually everyone can relate to the worries experienced by Katniss whilst she's in there – apart from her main concern of fighting to stay alive, of course! Constantly stressing over the impression that you're making and whether or not you're being judged are standard adolescent anxieties experienced by almost everyone at some point in their lives – whether you happen to be facing a pack of ruthless teen tributes, or just another day at high school. As Katniss must do later in the series, we have all grappled with trying to define who we really are, if only we could know ourselves a little better. For Katniss, this is of course made all the more complicated by the presence of the two boys in her life.

While by no means the main storyline, the love triangle between Katniss, Peeta and Gale is highly intriguing. Suspense is increased by the fact that Katniss seems no clearer about who she should be with than the reader. Collins certainly hasn't given her (or the reader) an easy choice. Gale, the ruggedly handsome best friend, would surely have been Katniss' first choice if she hadn't been thrown into the Hunger Games arena and forced to pair up with the charming, selfless Peeta. Wanting to find out who she'll choose in the end is just another reason why we all keep turning the pages.

However, *The Hunger Games* never strays too far into the territory of soppy romance. There's plenty of blood, action and gore to balance the love story out. In fact, it's morbidly fascinating to find out how the tributes will defeat each other and to see which devices and creatures the Capitol will unleash on its subjects next. Though few readers would be rushing to volunteer on reaping day, you can't help but wonder as you read what kind of tribute you'd be and the strategy you'd adopt to stay alive. Through the character of Katniss, we all get to feel like an action hero for a little while and it's a thrilling experience!

Ultimately, to try to pin the addictive appeal of these novels down to any single aspect is a pointless exercise. It's Collins' expert combination of genres and issues that makes them so unique and enthralling. Elements of our modern society are amplified and mixed with Ancient Roman practices in a way that makes the story feel timeless. Adolescent angst and the struggle to stay true to your own self are contextualised within age-old tales of heroes overcoming evil and wider social issues, so that everyone can find something to relate to within this epic and varied trilogy. Panem is a dark and mystical place pulled from the depths of Collins' wonderful imagination, but it bears enough resemblance to our world for the story to make a genuine impact on audiences in this century (and any other). Suspense and adventure run throughout the series, however there are also softer moments where the pace slows and relationships between the characters can truly develop. For every romantic or humorous moment, there is one filled with tragedy or danger. In short, there's something for everyone in *The Hunger Games*.

That is also what I hope you will find in this book. Offering comprehensive profiles of each of the main characters, detailed descriptions of the main settings, complete coverage of the 74th and 75th

Hunger Games and much more, it provides an in-depth introduction for anyone who's yet to discover the trilogy. For those who are already fully-fledged tributes, I hope it'll be an opportunity to revisit all your favourite characters and moments from the books, offering a fresh new perspective on Collins' richly imaginative universe. With extra information about the inspiration, context and parallels with our own society, I hope to illuminate some of the complex issues surrounding *The Hunger Games*, engaging with Collins' world in exciting new ways with the aid of quizzes, guides and illustrations. Whether you want to learn about the true-life histories that influenced Collins' writing, get to grips with a particular species of muttation, or pick up strategic tips for surviving the Hunger Games, it's all here. I hope you enjoy reading this guidebook as much as I enjoyed writing it!

WELCOME TO PANEM

To understand *The Hunger Games*, you need to understand the world in which the action unfolds. Like many great writers before her, Suzanne Collins has created a whole universe in her books – a nightmarish dystopian vision of what our society could become in the future.

Part of what makes Panem feel so real is the fact that it shares some similarities with our own world. However, there are still a lot of things in Collins' imaginary state that are different and new to discover.

The Capitol doesn't let people speak their mind about what life is really like in Panem (as the poor Avoxes would tell you, if only they could), but they can't keep everyone silent. Luckily, we've found an old resident of District 12 who's willing to share their knowledge of Panem – as long as you promise to keep it confidential and check there are no jabberjays around to report back!

DYSTOPIA DEFINED

A dystopia is a fictional society that is very controlled and repressed. It is the opposite of a utopia – an ideal society with perfect legal, social and political systems. *The Hunger Games* comes from a long tradition of dystopian novels, such as Aldous Huxley's *Brave New World* and George Orwell's *Nineteen Eighty-Four*. While Huxley's imaginary state is divided into strict social castes, Orwell's citizens – or 'Proles' – are ruled over by Big Brother, an all-powerful leader who keeps them under constant surveillance. Panem has many characteristics of a typical dystopia (see the next page). Like other writers, Collins has exaggerated elements of the real world to create her own vision of what the future could bring if our culture were to collapse. For example, climate change, the use of plastic surgery, the inequality of wealth and resources in the world and the popularity of reality TV are all very real concerns indeed. According to Collins, it could only take between 100 and 999 years for our world to become Panem!

DYSTOPIAS COMMONLY FEATURE:

- A futuristic setting with amazing technological advancements
- A back story involving war, revolution or some variety of natural disaster which changed the old systems so the new dictatorship could take over
- A hero from this society who feels there is something wrong with the way it is run and fights to change the accepted order
- A figure of conflict who represents everything that the dystopia promotes
- A group of people who are not under the state's control; the hero puts his (or her) hopes in this band of rebels
- A climax followed by the sense that everything is not completely resolved in the end

Can you recognise any of these elements in *The Hunger Games*?

'So, you want to learn all about Panem? I can't imagine why, but I'll fill you in. Be warned though – this won't be a Capitol-approved account! And you didn't hear it from me, ok?

'I suppose I should start with the history of how Panem was created. Well, it used to be a country called North America, but it suffered many natural disasters. The sea crept higher and higher, until it came to cover most of the Earth. There was a fierce battle for the remaining land on the north-western side and what was left after that became our nation of Panem – a Capitol city in the Rocky Mountains with thirteen surrounding districts. We're told that everyone worked in harmony then, but that all changed about seventy-five years ago, when what is now known as the Dark Days began.

'I guess everyone wasn't quite as happy with the way Panem was run as the Capitol says now, because people in the districts started to rebel. It was a tough war and both sides had big losses, but in the end, the Capitol's greater numbers, superior resources and geographical advantage of the mountains separating them from the rest of Panem, meant that the rebels lost the battle. The Capitol claims that two rebels died for every one of their citizens. Twelve of the districts were defeated and punished by the Capitol, but I suppose we got off lightly compared to District 13 – that was completely destroyed by the Capitol's toxic bombs, which left the whole place nothing more than burnt rubble.

BREAD AND CIRCUSES

Panem's name comes from the Latin expression, *panem et circenses* (meaning 'bread and circuses'), which describes the frivolity of the Roman Empire before its decline. It was first used by the Roman poet Juvenal around AD 100 to describe a strategy used by Roman politicians to win votes from the poor by providing circus games as a form of entertainment and a constant supply of wheat grain. This way, politicians rose to power and the Roman people were kept happy without ever really questioning how they were being ruled.

There is quite a clear link between this idea and the society of Panem. (The very name of the 'Hunger Games' references food and entertainment, and how the Capitol uses both to control people. Also harking back to Roman times is the rule that children can earn extra tesserae by entering their names into the reaping more than once a year.) The people of the Capitol never question the unfair way that their nation is governed because they live in luxury and are kept entertained by lethal gladiator-style battles, presented as 'games'.

Panem et circenses is also about ignoring your moral duty to others, which we can certainly see in the thoughtless citizens of the Capitol. Viewing the Hunger Games as nothing more than a bit of fun, they've no appreciation for the lives of the children killed on-screen.

'Not that anyone in the other twelve districts feels particularly lucky now. You see, after we'd signed the Treaty of Treason stating the new laws to keep the peace, the Capitol proposed the Hunger Games. It's promoted as nothing more than entertainment in the Capitol – the highlight of their TV viewing – but its real purpose is to remind us in the districts of the Capitol's power over us and to stop us from ever challenging it again. The Hunger Games are a yearly event, in which two children from each district are "reaped" (their names are picked out from all the others in the district aged between twelve and eighteen) to fight in an arena to the death. Reaping days are terrible. The whole district must go to the town centre to see whose son or daughter will become one of that year's "tributes". As well as punishing everyone in the districts, it's another way for the Capitol to keep an eye on the population there, you see. The tension is unbearable – especially when you're of reaping age, just waiting to see if you or one of your family or friends will be called. It's even worse if you're older because your name is automatically entered in once more with every passing year, or if you're poor and had to exchange more entries for extra tesserae rations to feed your family. Although it's been years since I was entered, I still feel a chill down my spine when the piece of paper bearing someone's name is picked and I find out which of the town's children I've seen growing up will be going off to face his or her death.

> **Tessera = a year's supply of grain and oil for one person.**

'Even after the reaping, we can't escape the Games. Cameras film the whole thing and broadcast it to the rest of Panem, where it is obligatory viewing. Every year the Gamemakers come up with new ways to keep the Games "interesting". For example, one year the only weapons available were spiked maces. Another time, the whole arena was flooded. If the action ever lulls, they always have some new twist – like a fire, or a wild beast – to throw in and keep the bloodthirsty audience happy. Every twenty-five years, they like to push the madness to the next level with a Quarter Quell – an extra big Hunger Games marked with huge celebrations in the Capitol and an added obstacle for those in the arena. In the 25th Games, the districts had to choose which two tributes they sent to their likely deaths and in the 50th, twice the amount of contestants were subjected to the carnage. I dread to think of what the Gamemakers will come up with for the next one . . . However the game plays out, the ending is always the same: only one tribute survives. As punishments go, it's certainly stopped anyone I know from even thinking about standing up to the Capitol.

'So, I suppose Panem's pretty much gone back to how it was before the Dark Days, except now the Capitol rules over twelve districts instead of thirteen. And the man who creates those rules is President Coriolanus Snow, who has governed Panem for as long as I can remember. Of course, this means that the Capitol standard of living is far higher than in the districts. They live in luxury – with more money, more food and more possessions than the rest of us put together. Everything they own is state of the art, powered by technology like you wouldn't believe. Somehow though, even these perks wouldn't make me want to be one of the silly fools, with their affected accents and ridiculous fashions – they're so blinded by their nice things that they can't see the suffering that their lifestyle causes. As tough as it is living in the districts and working hard just to have all your goods taken by the Capitol, I couldn't live the way they do. Though, if you asked me in the middle of winter when I've an empty belly and I can see them feasting on-screen, I might change my mind!

'Each district has its own Mayor, but in reality we're all controlled by the Capitol. They send their trained guards called "Peacekeepers" into each district to watch over us all and stop any law-breaking. I've never been outside of District 12, but I've heard that Peacekeepers in other places can be quite harsh when they're enforcing the rules; luckily here, ours act almost the same as other citizens. That's typical of the way things work in Panem. The districts are all very separate as the Capitol makes sure that we rarely come into contact or learn much about each other. Most of what we know about the other districts is based on what we've seen in the Hunger Games. Therefore, we have all developed our own cultures and traditions. This is also because each district has its own major industry, which greatly influences our respective ways of life. The standard of living and wealth can vary a lot from district to district, depending on what they produce.

'District 1, for example, is one of the richest districts in Panem because it's where all the Capitol's luxury items are made – including their beloved precious gems. This means that their tributes are always well-fed and well-trained. They're also usually good-looking, with strange names that reflect their luxurious backgrounds, like "Cashmere" and "Glimmer". District 1 takes the Hunger Games very seriously and their tributes are always in the Career Pack, along with anyone from Districts 2 and 4. Of course, it makes sense for the strongest, healthiest tributes to join forces in the beginning. Fighting as a team, they soon kill off the weaker competition. It happens every damned year and I hate to see it. Really, what chance do the others stand against the Capitol's lapdogs? Those kids are always the most vicious and ruthless in the arena – they're killers born and bred.

'If anything, District 2 is even more of a threat in the Games than 1. It's actually the closest district to the Capitol because, although known for its stone quarries, it's also where most of our Peacekeepers come from. I've heard that, since the Capitol had to stop using District 13 as their military base (it hasn't been that way since the Dark Days), they keep a lot of their hovercrafts in District 2's old mining mountain. This link to the Capitol means that kids from District 2 are raised to consider taking part in the Hunger Games as the highest honour. I mean, as soon as they can walk they start training for it and many of them even volunteer to go into the arena! I suppose it's no surprise that their tributes have a reputation for being the most aggressive. I'll never forget this one year when their girl tribute actually ripped her rival's throat open with her bare teeth!

'The other Career District, 4, is by the sea so it is also our fishing district . . . although it's only the Capitol that benefits from what they catch. All the same, District 4's industry often comes in handy in the Hunger Games because their tributes can produce fishhooks and nets out of the plants in the arena. They also know which sea creatures are edible and – unlike most of the competition – they can swim. It seems like the sea influences their whole way of life; their bread is made with seaweed and shaped like a fish and even their wedding ceremony involves touching sea water to each other's lips! (Ours in District 12 is very simple and has nothing to do with mining; there is just a "toasting" ceremony, where the bride and groom share a piece of bread and then toss it into a fire they made together.)

'Holed up in the Hunger Games arena, the tributes can't help but give away secrets of the lives they lead back home and some details of the other districts' cultures can be seen in the way they play the game. For example, District 3 mainly manufactures electronic products like televisions, cars and explosives, so their tributes usually do best when they can get hold of wire or some kind of explosive – in their expert hands, it can become a lethal weapon. District 7 has a lot of woodland and provides lumber, which is why it's safe to assume that any tribute from there is going to be a natural with an axe. District 10 raises livestock and, since tributes' costumes for the opening ceremonies are supposed to reflect the industry of their home district, this causes their Hunger Games stylists no end of problems! Industrial districts like 9 and 8 – a cold, god-forsaken place that's all run-down houses and textile factories – don't have much of an advantage in the Games and so their tributes are usually knocked out of the competition early on, the poor souls.

'Apart from those from my district, of course, District 11's tributes are probably at the biggest disadvantage. Eleven may be the largest district, but it's also one of the poorest. Apparently, their houses are more like shacks and the open fields there stretch on for miles and miles. The district is known for agriculture and is filled with orchards and meadows, though almost all the farmers' produce goes to the Capitol. Everyone works in the orchards; even the children have to miss school to work during the harvest and sometimes they toil through the night. I've heard that their government is quite strict and cruel; they get whipped publicly if they try to take so much as a handful of the crops they've grown to eat. One of their boys was killed for trying to pocket a pair of the night-vision glasses that they wear when they have to farm in the dark. The only time those starving folk are given more to eat is when they need to work longer hours through harvest-time. They don't have much of a city centre and the whole district is surrounded by a huge barbed-wire fence lined with watchtowers and armed guards. Though District 11's tributes are underfed, they're stronger than you'd think from years of hard labour in the fields. Another advantage of theirs is a good knowledge of which plants are edible and which are not – given the Gamemakers' tendency to place poisonous decoys in the arena, this skill can literally be a lifesaver!

SOUTHERN SIMILARITIES

Most of the people from District 11 are described as having dark hair and skin, shedding little light on their ethnic origins. However, Suzanne Collins has confirmed that this district was once America's Deep South (a sweltering region of cotton and tobacco plantations, built on slavery and bigoted values) and much of what Rue reveals about life in District 11 mirrors the abominable treatment of black slaves there in the past – all of which suggests that they are of African-American descent.

Like the African-American slaves, the people of District 11 work long unpaid hours in the fields with very little food to go around. Another important similarity between the two groups is their use of music. In the days before slavery was abolished, work songs helped to lift the spirits of the slaves as they laboured in the fields. They were also used to synchronise daily tasks in much the same way that Rue tells Katniss the mockingjay call is used to herald the end of the working day in the orchards of District 11.

'Then there's my home, District 12. Along with 11, we are one of the least wealthy districts and the rest of Panem sees us as a bit of a joke. I suppose it's not too surprising considering our terrible performances in the Hunger Games; we haven't won since the 50th Games! Even our only living victor (Haymitch Abernathy) is an embarrassing drunk.

'Around 8,000 people live in District 12 and our main industry is coal mining. The district is split into three different areas: the Seam, the merchant area and the Hob. (Of course, like every other district, we have a Victor's Village, where the people who have won the Hunger Games can live in large, luxurious houses. As you can imagine, ours is pretty empty!)

'The Seam lies on the border of 12 next to the forest and it's where the poorest people live. Nearly everyone here works in the coal mines and the streets, lined with shabby grey houses, are black as cinder. You can usually tell who's from the Seam by the way that they look – you see, we all tend to have black hair, grey eyes and olive skin as most of the families here are distantly related. Those from the merchant class are fairer, with blond hair and blue eyes and, of course, they have that healthier, better-fed look you can only get from having a little more money. They've never had to go hunting illegally or to enter their names into the Hunger Games extra times to earn their families more tesserae, like some of us from the Seam have had to. The merchant area of town is where the shops are, like the bakery and the apothecary. In the middle of town, in between the shops, we have a large square where we have public market days. It can be quite nice there, but it's also where we hold the Hunger-Games reapings, so I can never enjoy it too much.

'The merchant area is where officials and Peacekeepers go shopping. The Seam residents go here when we can afford to, but we tend to mostly go to the Hob for the things we need. The Hob is our black market, set up in an old warehouse which used to store coal. You can get pretty much anything you want here, from paraffin for your fire to white liquor sold by Ripper, who had to start selling on the black market after losing one of her arms in a mining accident. Some of what's sold there is obviously not legitimate (I'm sure Greasy Sae puts wild dog in her "beef soup"!) but the Peacekeepers here in 12 are quite relaxed and more than willing to turn a blind eye. I suppose we're luckier than most districts in that our leader, Mayor Undersee, isn't too strict and the Capitol mostly ignores us just as long as we provide them with enough coal. Our Head Peacekeeper, Cray, is also easy to keep happy; he's usually too busy bribing poor young Seam girls into his bed to notice what anyone else in the district is up to!

'Surrounding our district is a high fence designed to keep wild animals out. It's supposed to be constantly electrified, but seeing as we don't get much more than a couple of hours of electricity each evening, it's pretty safe to get past. During the autumn, some people crawl under the fence to gather apples and everyone knows that Gale Hawthorne and Katniss Everdeen go out hunting in the woods every week, but I suppose the Peacekeepers need the game they catch just as much as the rest of us, so they're not going to be the ones to stop them. That's one of the reasons why our tributes never do well in the Hunger Games – they're just so underfed and weak. It doesn't help that their mentor, who is meant to be guiding them through the Games, can't stay sober for more than five minutes! But I guess Haymitch is just like everyone else in District 12 – trying to do whatever he can to get by. Although as a Hunger Games victor, he certainly has more money to buy liquor . . .

'That pretty much sums up life in Panem – great if you live in the Capitol and not so great if you don't. If you're staying in the districts take my advice: do what you're supposed to and try not to step out of line. I think nearly everyone in the districts wishes things could change, but no one is prepared to face the only thing worse than the Hunger Games – becoming the next District 13. So, I doubt things around here will change anytime soon . . .'

PANEM POP QUIZ!

Now that you've been introduced to Panem by a local, you should know it like the back of your hand, right? Let's put your knowledge to the test!

1. If you wanted to buy strong white liquor in District 12, where would you go?
   a) To Mrs Everdeen – she uses it for medicinal purposes in her role as a healer
   b) The liquor store in the merchant part of town
   c) Ripper's stall in the Hob

2. What does the marriage ceremony in District 4 traditionally include?
   a) Salt water
   b) Roses
   c) Toasted bread

3. Which district is responsible for producing livestock?
   a) District 7
   b) District 10
   c) District 3

4. How was District 13 destroyed during the first rebellion?
   a) By natural disasters such as floods and fires
   b) By the Capitol's toxic bombs
   c) By the Capitol unleashing a pack of mutts which killed
      the whole population

5. Which special secret ingredient that can sometimes be found in Greasy Sae's 'beef stew'?
   a) Wild squirrel caught by Katniss Everdeen and Gale
      Hawthorne in the woods beyond the fence
   b) A mix of herbs and spices to make up for the
      lack of meat
   c) Wild dog when no beef is available

6. Tributes from which three districts are normally in the Career Pack?
   a) 1, 2 and 4
   b) 1, 2 and 3
   c) 2, 9 and 11

7. How can you recognise if someone is from the Seam area of District 12?
   a) They have dark hair and eyes, and tanned skin
   b) They are usually very tall
   c) They speak with a different accent to everyone else in
      District 12

8. You meet two girls called Shimmer and Satin – which district are they most likely to be from and why?
   a) They must be from the Capitol with such silly names!
   b) District 8, where they make textiles -- hence their names
   c) District 1, where their names reflect the luxury items
      they produce

Now add up your scores using the table below to see how well you'd survive if you were left on your own in Panem . . .

1. a – 0, b – 0, c – 5
2. a – 5, b – 0, c – 0
3. a – 0, b – 5, c – 0
4. a – 0, b – 5, c – 0
5. a – 0, b – 0, c – 5
6. a – 5, b – 0, c – 0
7. a – 5, b – 0, c – 0
8. a – 0, b – 0, c – 5

If you scored:

0-15: You are AN IDIOT ABROAD
Oh dear, you really need to do your homework. I'd say you should explore Panem a little more to increase your knowledge, but you'd probably end up getting lost!

20-30: You are a SAVVY SIGHTSEER
You've obviously been paying attention. You could probably pass for a Panem resident, as long as you aren't expected to work down the mines or swim like a District 4 native.

30-40: You are PANEM PERFECT
Wow, you really know your stuff! With this score you must have lived in Panem in another life and would fit right in cavorting in the Capitol or haggling down at the Hob.

MAIN PLAYERS

KATNISS EVERDEEN

Age: Sixteen.

From: The Seam, District 12.

Occupation: Student, illegal hunter and trader.

Appearance: With her olive skin, grey eyes and long, straight, black hair (usually tied back in a braid), Katniss is a typical Seam girl who's never paid much attention to how she looks. However, with all eyes on the girl tribute from District 12, she'd better start taking an interest. If she wants to be noticed, (attracting life-saving sponsors in the process), she'll need to put on a captivating show for the crowds. Luckily she has a first-class stylist and preparation team on-hand to help turn her from a Seam tomboy to a flaming stunner!

Background: Katniss' father died in a mining accident when she was just eleven. Since then, Katniss has been looking after her mother and sister. She is used to living in poverty and going hungry, but has learned to survive by hunting and trading her catches. Neither is she afraid to enter her name into the reaping ball extra times in exchange for precious tesserae. Katniss' need to care for and protect her loved ones is an instinct which never leaves her, even when she is separated from them in the Hunger Games. In fact, this is what gets her drawn into the Games in the first place – inspiring her to leap on-stage and take Prim's place as female tribute!

Characteristics: Katniss is extremely independent, having had to fend for herself from a young age. She doesn't trust others easily and is a loner at school, choosing not to mix with the other children, except for Madge Undersee, the mayor's daughter, who also keeps to herself.

Naturally rebellious, Katniss rejects authority and doesn't play by the rules. However, before being thrown into the Hunger Games arena, she avoids any direct challenge to the Capitol's power as she doesn't believe there's anything that can be done to change her life. Despite her toughness, she has a softer side and can be caring – especially towards her little sister. Ironically, even though she is an experienced hunter, Katniss is squeamish and hates the sight of blood or injuries that her mother and sister take in their stride.

Important relationships:

Primrose – sister. Katniss loves Primrose more than anyone else in the world and her main goal in life is to protect and provide for her younger sister. Katniss would readily risk her own life to save Prim's, as she proves by volunteering to take her sister's place in the Hunger Games. Such self-sacrificing acts are rarely seen on reaping day, highlighting the close bond that the sisters share. Although Katniss worries that this decision may be viewed as a sign of weakness by her rivals in the Games, this is certainly not the case. Yet, her love for her sister shows that there is certainly a heart beneath Katniss' tough exterior.

Mrs Everdeen – mother. Katniss has a difficult relationship with her mother. Ever since Mr Everdeen died, her mother has retreated into a private world of her own, leaving it to the adolescent Katniss to take care of the family. Though she knows how hard the loss of her husband must have been, Katniss resents her mother's behaviour and feels let down by her. Despite Mrs Everdeen's tentative attempts to make amends, Katniss does not find it easy to let her mother in. It's not until Katniss experiences losses of her own – and a string of difficult moral choices in the arena – that she comes to understand her mother better and can start to build a relationship with her again.

Mr Everdeen – father. Katniss inherited her dark Seam looks from her coal-miner father. She also has his singing voice, which was apparently so beautiful it made the birds fall silent to listen. It was Mr Everdeen who taught Katniss nearly everything she knows about hunting and finding food in the wild. He made her first bow and even taught her how to swim in a secret lake, hidden away in the woods! Though he died when she was only eleven, his lessons have stayed with her as a vital part of her day-to-day survival and much of Mr Everdeen lives on through Katniss.

Gale – best friend. Gale and Katniss have grown up together in District 12's Seam area. Gale's father died in the same mining accident as Mr Everdeen and, like Katniss, as the eldest child in his family he received the Medal of Valour from the Mayor at the memorial ceremony. They met again when they were both hunting in the woods to find extra food for their families, at which time Katniss was twelve and Gale was fourteen. They decided they would be more effective hunters if they worked together and, after spending every Sunday in the woods together, soon became best friends. Gale even has a special nickname for Katniss – 'Catnip', chosen because this is what he genuinely thought she'd said when she shyly introduced herself on their first meeting. Due to their similarities, Gale is the only person Katniss can be herself around and so she ignores the idea of anything other than friendship with him. Even though she admits she is jealous of the way girls whisper about his good looks, she insists this is down to the thought of losing him as a hunting partner – but is this worry purely practical or could there be something more about her relationship with Gale that she is not ready to admit, even to herself?

Haymitch – mentor. Haymitch is Katniss' mentor in the Hunger Games. Katniss starts off thinking that Haymitch is nothing more than a useless drunk, but once she's proved that she stands a chance in the arena she starts to see a different side to him. Haymitch is able to communicate with her while she is in the arena (hinting at Katniss' next move through the gifts he does or doesn't send to her) and, even though their relationship remains volatile, they come to understand each other. Peeta even suggests that they find it so hard to get on because of their similarities: both grew up in the Seam and they share a smart survival instinct as well as a rebellious nature.

Peeta – friend/fellow tribute. Katniss and Peeta have known each other since their first day at school, but have never mixed or really talked to each other. Lonely, starving Seam girls and popular, well-to-do bakers' sons aren't the most likely of friends! Thus, the only direct interaction these two have shared is by a chance meeting. Shortly after her father's death, Peeta happened upon a shivering eleven-year-old Katniss cowering by the bins behind his father's bakery – on the brink of starvation. Rather than chasing her away, he gave her some bread from his family's bakery. This random act of kindness – one that likely saved Katniss' life – has stuck with her. Since she has never been able to pay him back for it, she is uncomfortable when his name is picked out as her rival at the Hunger Games reaping. Knowing that only one of them can leave the arena alive, Katniss is determined to keep her distance from him, even when he confesses his love for her live on television! However, as the Games continue, Peeta proves he can be trusted and she reluctantly begins to accept him as an ally and love interest in the arena in order to increase the public's interest in them and the odds of them making it out alive. When the Games are over and the cameras stop rolling, Katniss is left wondering if their relationship was all for show or if there is something real beneath the charade . . .

PRIMROSE EVERDEEN

Age: Twelve.

From: The Seam, District 12.

Occupation: Student, assists her mother with healing.

Appearance: Unlike Katniss, little Prim takes after her mother and possesses the fair skin, blond hair and blue eyes of District 12's merchant class.

Background: Prim was seven when her father died, leaving her mother depressed and unable to take proper care of her children. Although Prim realises only too well how tough life can be in the Seam, she has been protected from the worst by her older sister Katniss.

Characteristics: Primrose lives up to her sweet name by being very good-natured and loving. She is also very caring and nurturing, taking in and looking after animals, helping her mother with her healing duties and later training to be a doctor. Prim is wise beyond her years and can often see things in a clear and simple way. She looks beyond appearances and circumstances to try to find the good in everyone. All of these traits mean that Prim is loved by everyone who meets her!

Important relationships:
Katniss – sister. In the years since their father was killed, Katniss has been more like a mother than an older sister to Primrose: looking out for her, making sure she is fed and generally shielding her from the harsh realities of life in the Seam. While Katniss is very protective of Prim, this is far from a one-way relationship. In return, Prim is often Katniss' voice of reason and her symbol of hope. Katniss proves her love for Prim when she volunteers to take her place in the Hunger Games and throughout the competition, her main reason to keep going is the promise she made her little sister – that she'd come back alive.

Mrs Everdeen – mother. Primrose seems to take after her mother in terms of her looks and in her role as a healer. Despite her mother's withdrawn behaviour after the girls' father's death, Prim forgives her and seems closer to her than Katniss is.

Buttercup – pet. When Prim finds an ugly stray kitten suffering from all kinds of diseases, she takes him home to cure him – just as she loves and cares for all living creatures. Despite his surly character, Buttercup – just like everyone else who meets her – is won over by Prim and even tries to protect her in times of danger. Not even the hardest heart can resist Primrose's kind nature and pure spirit!

MRS EVERDEEN

Age: Mrs Everdeen is around 40 years old.

From: She was raised in the merchant area of District 12, but now lives in the Seam.

Occupation: She previously worked in her family's apothecary business and is now a healer. This is a sort of unofficial doctor who uses mainly herbal remedies to cure the illnesses of people who can't afford to go to a proper hospital.

Appearance: Unlike most Seam residents, Mrs Everdeen has blond hair and blue eyes because she was born into the merchant class. She was very beautiful when she was younger, catching the eye of Peeta's father when they were growing up (apparently, a soft-spot for the Everdeen women runs in Peeta's family). However, years of depression, poverty and heartache have left her looking sadly worn-down.

Background: Mrs Everdeen grew up in the relatively wealthy merchant area of District 12, but left this life behind to marry the poor coal miner, Mr Everdeen. As a teenager, she was a close friend of Maysilee Donner, one of District 12's female tributes in the 50th Hunger Games. Sadly, Maysilee died in these Games. Watching her own daughter face the arena years later can scarcely have been easy for Mrs Everdeen. After all, history has a habit of repeating itself . . .

Characteristics: Once a happily married woman, in the years since her husband died, Mrs Everdeen has been so consumed by grief that she has neglected her children, leaving it to her oldest daughter Katniss to provide for the family. Despite this, as a healer Mrs Everdeen is extremely brave and caring – anyone injured in District 12 is brought straight to her door and if she can't help them, no one can. When Katniss becomes a tribute in the Hunger Games, Mrs Everdeen is forced to take on more responsibility, becoming a real mother to her daughters again.

Important relationships:
Mr Everdeen – husband. Mrs Everdeen clearly loved her husband very much. She gave up her nice home, job and family life to move to the poor Seam area with him, apparently charmed by his singing voice, so captivating it could make even the birds stop to listen. After he was killed in a mining accident, Mrs Everdeen was devastated and retreated into herself, unable to deal with everyday life properly for years afterwards.

Katniss and Primrose – daughters. Mrs Everdeen has a complicated relationship with her daughters because her depression has prevented her from looking after them as a mother should since their father died. Although she shares an affectionate relationship with Primrose, her oldest daughter cannot forgive her for what she sees as weakness when her family needed her to stay strong. Ironically, the thing that distances Mrs Everdeen from Katniss – her ability to love her husband so strongly that she struggles to carry on living without him – is a trait she seems to have passed on to her daughter, who risks her life to save her sister without a second thought.

GALE HAWTHORNE

Age: Eighteen.

From: The Seam, District 12.

Occupation: Student, illegal hunter and trader, miner.

Appearance: Gale could pass for Katniss' cousin as he shares her olive skin, straight black hair and grey eyes. He is also tall, muscular and handsome, with the kind of classic good looks that attract attention from many of the local girls.

Background: Gale's father was killed in the same mining accident as Katniss' and he too has been providing for his mother and three younger siblings ever since by hunting and trading illegally and entering his name into the reaping several times a year to receive extra tesserae.

Characteristics: Like Katniss, Gale is rebellious and breaks the rules. He is protective and constantly looking out for his family and Katniss. He is strong, practical and a good hunter which, combined with his good looks, makes him a desirable partner for any girl his age. He is also brave and reliable, as he proves while Katniss is away taking part in the Hunger Games. With Katniss herself out of the picture, Gale ensures that her family want for nothing. However, Gale can be short-tempered, often having angry outbursts on his hunts in the woods about the Capitol's tyrannical reign over the districts. With his ruthless, end-justifies-the-means attitude, he can seem cold-hearted at times – even to Katniss – as he's willing to do almost anything to overthrow the Capitol, no matter what it costs him.

Important relationships:

Katniss – best friend. Katniss and Gale are hunting partners who've become extremely close as they have so much in common. The fact that they have both had to take on responsibilities that people of their age should never have had to shoulder means that they can understand each other very well. They are able to relax and joke with each other like they can with no one else. Gale has romantic feelings towards Katniss, although he knows enough to keep them to himself. When Katniss becomes a tribute, she knows she can trust Gale to look out for her family while she is away. Despite their similar backgrounds, the two have different outlooks on how to fight the systems that oppress them. Whereas Katniss is reluctant to take any action against the Capitol (feeling powerless to stand up to them, she doesn't see the point), Gale is much more eager to fight back.

Gale is very protective of his **mother, Hazelle**, his two younger **brothers, Rory and Vick** and his little **sister, Posy**.

PEETA MELLARK

Age: Sixteen.

From: The town, District 12.

Occupation: Student and baker.

Appearance: A typical member of District 12's merchant class, Peeta has pale skin, blue eyes and ashy blond hair that falls in waves over his forehead. He is of medium height and stocky build from his hands-on work at the bakery.

Background: Although Peeta is also from District 12, he has led a more privileged life than Katniss and Gale and has never gone without food because his father is a baker. He is the youngest of three boys and helps his father in the bakery, his speciality being frosting the cakes.

Characteristics: Kind and courageous, Peeta is constantly putting other people before himself. He has a special way with words that means he can win over an audience easily with his natural charm and humour. He finds it easy to get on with people and is quite popular. Like Gale, he's keen to rebel against the Capitol and hopes to prove he is more than just a pawn in their Games, but as he does so he never loses sight of his strong moral values.

Important relationships:
Katniss – friend/fellow tribute. Peeta noticed Katniss on their first day of school when his father pointed her out. After hearing her sing he was smitten but, apart from providing her with a couple of loaves of bread when she was on the brink of starvation, he never truly gets a chance to get close to her until they are pitted against each other in the 74th Hunger Games. Peeta surprises Katniss with his confession of love during his pre-Game interview and they are cast by the Gamemakers as star-crossed lovers. In the arena, Katniss plays on their romance to keep them in favour (with sponsors and viewers alike), but Peeta isn't faking his emotions. Although Katniss is not sure if her feelings for Peeta are more than friendly, their shared experiences in the arena certainly create a strong bond between them.

WRITTEN IN THE STARS

The term 'star-crossed lovers' is often used to describe a couple that destiny seems determined to keep apart. Commentators in the Capitol apply this idea to Katniss and Peeta because, though they are supposedly in love, the rules of the Games state that only one of them can live; tragically, they can never be together. The phrase was first used by William Shakespeare in his play, *Romeo and Juliet.* This link to the original star-crossed lovers hints at the ending of *The Hunger Games.* Desperate to escape the Capulet household, Juliet concocts a secret plan to fake her own death, despatching a note to warn Romeo of the 'bad news' coming his way. Yet, her message goes awry and Romeo's left to believe she is really dead. Wild with grief, he breaks into the family vault and drinks a deadly dose of poison. Upon waking to find his body, Juliet stabs herself. Luckily, Katniss and Peeta's threat of double suicide by poison berries has a much happier outcome.

Haymitch – mentor. Whereas Katniss doesn't appear to get on particularly well with her mentor, Haymitch and Peeta generally have a much less rocky relationship. There are times in the arena when Peeta thinks Haymitch is favouring Katniss but, whilst it's her who Haymitch sends bread and burn medicine to, this is no indication of his regard for the boy tribute. When Katniss and Peeta become engaged, Haymitch proves that he thinks very highly of Peeta, telling her bluntly that she could live a hundred lifetimes and not deserve his affections.

Although Peeta has quite a large family, he does not seem very close to them. Neither of his **older brothers** volunteer to take his place in the Hunger Games and his bad-tempered **mother** believes more in Katniss' chances of surviving the Games than her son's!

HAYMITCH ABERNATHY

Age: Forty.

From: District 12.

Occupation: Victor of the 50th Hunger Games and Mentor to the tributes of District 12.

Appearance: Despite being strong and good-looking with bright grey Seam eyes and curly dark hair when he was a teenager, Haymitch is now scruffy and carrying extra weight.

Background: Aged sixteen, Haymitch was reaped for the 50th Hunger Games, in which there were twice as many tributes as usual in honour of it being a Quarter Quell. By managing to outsmart his fellow tributes and forming an alliance with Maysilee Donner, Haymitch lasted until the very end of the Games. To defeat his last opponent, he made use of the force-field surrounding the arena. Flouting the Gamemakers' rules (to President Snow's mind at least), Haymitch dodged the axe she threw at him; the weapon fell into the force-field and then rebounded to hit her in the head. Before the Games, Haymitch had been living happily in the Seam with his mother, younger brother and girlfriend. Yet, his trick of using the arena itself as a weapon cost him dearly. Though it won him the Games, those he cared for were killed in retaliation. Since then, Haymitch has been forced to mentor the tributes of District 12 – all of whom have died. Drinking lots of alcohol to block everything out is Haymitch's only way of coping with the reality of his lonely life as a so-called 'victor'.

Characteristics: Haymitch is largely anti-social, mostly drunk and often rude or sarcastic. At first glance, he seems to be just another incoherent alcoholic, but he is actually very smart. It is his ability to think on his feet that helps him – and later Katniss and Peeta – to survive the Hunger Games. Although he rarely shows it, he does love Katniss and Peeta, but finds it hard to express his emotions after years of trying to repress the pain brought on by his part in the Hunger Games. Haymitch can be understanding and funny at times, although his morbid sense of humour is not to everyone's taste. On the rare occasions that he is parted from his alcohol supply (a lethal white liquor sold by Ripper on the Hob), he suffers withdrawal symptoms and becomes even more grouchy than usual!

Important relationships:
Katniss and Peeta – tributes he's obliged to mentor. Haymitch does not take much notice of his tributes at first and they are not impressed by their lazy, drunken mentor. This changes when they confront him for his seeming indifference, despite the deadly challenge they face. Realising that they have a better shot of winning than the District 12 tributes he's mentored in previous years, he agrees to work with them – but only on his terms. Haymitch has a 'tough love' approach to being a mentor and is brutally honest, but always with the survival of his protégés in mind. Haymitch warms to Peeta, but his relationship with Katniss is more complex. Perhaps because they have similarly short tempers and they are both used to being in control, they often clash. Nonetheless, Haymitch admires Katniss' courage and the two reach a mutual understanding when she is in the arena, communicating through the gifts Haymitch sends to her and Peeta.

Maysilee Donner – fellow tribute. Maysilee was the other District 12 tribute in the 50th Hunger Games and joined forces with Haymitch for a while. They parted ways towards the end as they did not want to have to kill each other. Shortly afterwards, however, Haymitch heard Maysilee cry out and went running back to her rescue. He saw her being attacked by pink bird muttations and held her hand as she died. This is very similar to Katniss' experience with Rue years later and highlights more of the characteristics that they share – strong loyalties and good hearts (however gruff or tough the exterior).

EFFIE TRINKET

Age: Unknown, although her frequent references to getting promoted to a better district suggest that she is still new to her career and so relatively young.

From: The Capitol.

Occupation: Escort to the tributes of District 12 en route to the Hunger Games; it is also her duty to draw the names of the tributes at the reaping.

Appearance: With her colourful clothes, Effie embodies the garish 'style' of the Capitol, but her defining feature is surely her hair. For the 74th Hunger Games, she opts for a bright pink wig. This is later changed to orange and then gold, to match Katniss' mockingjay pin, which becomes a popular fashion statement in the Capitol.

Background: From the way that Gale and Katniss talk about Effie before the reaping, this is clearly not her first year as an escort for District 12's tributes – much to her disappointment! Effie is evidently unimpressed at being landed with the drab district which hasn't produced a victor in twenty-four years, and wants to be promoted to somewhere more renowned.

Characteristics: Initially, Effie can come across as no more than a typical Capitol resident – insincere, stupid and over the top. However, there is more to her than meets the eye. She is good at her job and works hard to keep the rest of the District 12 party motivated and punctual for their appointments, as she wants to give Katniss and Peeta the best shot at victory possible. Effie is also a stickler for manners, very organised and ambitious.

Important relationships:
Katniss and Peeta – District 12 tributes she must escort in the 74th Hunger Games. Before they get to know her, Katniss and Peeta have little time for Effie and her condescending pep talks – as far as they're concerned, she's just another shallow supporter of the cruel Hunger Games. However, as the Games progress, Effie becomes increasingly attached to her young charges, perhaps realising that they have more potential to win than previous District 12 tributes, and she proves herself by doing all she can to improve their chances in the arena.

Haymitch – fellow member of the District 12 Hunger Games party. Effie and Haymitch are opposites: Effie is well-presented, polite and always upbeat while Haymitch is scruffy, ill-mannered and grumpy. When Haymitch causes a scene with Effie at the 74th Hunger Games reaping, she is clearly disgusted. Later, she becomes frustrated by his drunkenness and lack of interest in his role as mentor. To her credit, Effie manages to persuade Haymitch to meet with Hunger Games sponsors and they start to work together to help Katniss and Peeta.

CINNA

Age: Unknown, but as this is his first year as a Hunger Games stylist he is probably quite young.

From: The Capitol.

Occupation: Katniss' stylist for the 74th Hunger Games, the public tour that follows her victory and the 75th Hunger Games.

Appearance: Katniss is surprised by how 'normal' Cinna looks compared to other Capitol stylists who are usually surgically altered or ridiculously made-up. In contrast, Cinna has short, natural brown hair and dresses in simple black outfits, his only enhancement being the lightest touch of metallic eyeliner to highlight the hints of gold in his green eyes.

Background: A first-time Hunger Games stylist, Cinna put in a special request to work with the tributes of District 12, rather than just being lumbered with the least glamorous district because he was a newcomer. This could be because he was impressed with Katniss' self-sacrifice on reaping day, or maybe he was already part of the rebellion against the Capitol at this early stage. Discreet as ever, Cinna never reveals the true reason for this.

Characteristics: Cinna is obviously amazingly talented and creative. His innovative designs put an exciting twist on the traditional costumes of District 12 tributes and make Katniss stand out from her competitors. Indeed, the intelligence of the designer behind them never fails to shine through. His creations play a large part in creating Katniss' public image in the Games and as the figurehead of the rebellion. Despite being a Capitol resident, he does not follow their flamboyant fashions and shows an appreciation for more simple styles, such as the braid Mrs Everdeen puts in Katniss' hair at the reaping. Cinna's rejection of the Capitol way of thinking is all the more unusual because he lives there and has been taught that their ideas are normal, so he must be very strong and independent to question this. Cinna also proves himself to be a good friend as he is very supportive and helpful to Katniss, always believing in her. In the end, Cinna shows that he is extremely brave as he criticises the Capitol through his designs with little thought for the consequences for himself . . .

Important relationships:
Katniss – tribute to be styled/friend. Cinna is given the role of creating Katniss' costumes throughout her time as a Hunger Games tribute. He helps her to create the best impression possible at the 74th Hunger Games opening ceremony with his eye-catching 'girl on fire' design. Though this breathtaking outfit (consisting of a black unitard, fiery-coloured cape and matching head-dress lit with synthetic fire) makes her unforgettable, it also shows the essence of who she is in its simplicity, with the fire illustrating her burning resentment towards the Capitol. As well as being her stylist, Cinna is a true friend to Katniss.

He helps her to stay calm throughout the publicity surrounding the competition and urges her to believe in her own abilities. He is one of the few people she trusts in the Capitol. When Katniss is called on to present a 'talent' during her victory tour, Cinna helps her by passing off his designs as her own. Even after Cinna has paid the ultimate price for his courageous stand against the Capitol, Katniss can feel his support through the personalised outfits he made for her to wear during the rebellion, left behind for her with a note, stating that he would still bet on her surviving any challenge she faces.

Octavia, Venia and Flavius – prep team. Although Cinna is very different from his shallow and silly prep team, he treats them with tact and decorum, encouraging them to be less selfish and more mature.

Portia – fellow stylist. Cinna works with Peeta's stylist, Portia, to create a wardrobe of memorable matching outfits for the District 12 tributes. Cinna and Portia also advise Peeta and Katniss on how to carry themselves. Thus, they are partly responsible for the public image of the victors.

PRESIDENT CORIOLANUS SNOW

Age: His exact age is unknown, but he is obviously fairly old, given his wizened appearance and how long he has been in power.

From: City Circle, the Capitol.

Occupation: Snow has been the President of Panem for at least twenty-five years.

Appearance: President Snow is a small, thin, elderly man with white hair. At first glance he might seem grandfatherly but a closer look reveals that he is actually quite menacing. Unnaturally pulled across his face, his lips look as though they may have been enhanced to make them fuller and he has snake-like eyes. He always wears a white rose and his breath smells of roses and blood hinting that, like the Capitol he runs, underneath a respectable façade, there is a hard brutality.

Background: President Snow showed his ruthless cruelty early on in life – working his way to the top by poisoning anyone he considered to be a threat to his authority. So as not to arouse suspicion, he drank a dose of the same poison that killed his victims . . . followed by an antidote. However, he was left with bleeding sores in his mouth and still uses the smell of perfumed roses to disguise them, hence his distinctive fragrance. President Snow has a family which includes an adolescent granddaughter.

Characteristics: True to his name, Snow is a cold-hearted, ruthless leader. Intent on maintaining his power over the people of Panem, he'll stop at nothing to achieve this. He promotes the Hunger Games as a demonstration of his superiority and blackmails the victors into fulfilling his demands afterwards. President Snow will crush anyone who openly criticises his rule and manipulate anyone else who could be a useful tool to him.

Important relationships:

Though President Snow does not form important relationships with others in the same way that most people do, among his many adversaries there are some who stand out and come to have a significant impact upon him and his rule:

Katniss – 74th Hunger Games co-victor. When Katniss and Peeta threaten to commit double suicide rather than kill each other, President Snow is furious at their public challenge to his rules. Knowing that he can't kill two such popular public figures, he demands that Katniss make it appear that their behaviour was an act of love rather than defiance – the kind of gesture which may just spark a rebellion. He threatens to hurt her loved ones if she doesn't comply.

Peeta – 74th Hunger Games co-victor. After the arena is blown apart at the end of the 75th Hunger Games, Peeta is captured by the Capitol and used as a weapon against Katniss. President Snow forces him to dissuade the rebels from fighting the Capitol and 'hijacks' Peeta's mind; using tracker-jacker venom, he distorts Peeta's memories to turn him against Katniss.

Finnick Odair – 65th Hunger Games victor. After good-looking and hugely popular Finnick wins the Hunger Games, President Snow sells his body to rich Capitol residents. During the second rebellion, Finnick reveals this and many more scandalous secrets of the Capitol's high society and President Snow.

WHAT IS IN A NAME?

We already know from Collins' chosen setting for *The Hunger Games* – the Latin word for bread, 'Panem' speaks volumes about decadent Capitol politics – that she selects her place-names very carefully indeed. This is also true of the names of her characters, many of which are loaded with significance and well worth a second look.

It is no secret that Katniss herself is named after a plant. At the roots of this particular plant are edible blue tubers and Katniss remembers an occasion when they served her well. Shortly after the death of her father, she cooked them up to feed her starving family. This says something about why Collins chose the name for her plucky protagonist – from a young age Katniss learns that survival is all about self-sufficiency. Though Gale and Prim are dear to her, she's a resourceful young woman who's learned to rely on no one but herself. And 'Katniss' certainly suits a girl so closely connected to nature that she feels most at home in the forest . . . but, why this particular plant? Growing in a shape that resembles an arrowhead, its pointed leaves seem especially appropriate for such an accomplished archer as Katniss. Not only does this re-affirm her survival instinct (she primarily shoots game to feed her family), but it signals that Katniss is a true warrior, with the inner-strength to spearhead the rebellion.

Katniss' little sister Prim is obviously also named after a plant: the primrose. This small flower with pale yellow petals is a perfect symbol for pale and pretty Primrose Everdeen. It blooms in the early spring (*prim* means 'first' in Latin, so its name translates as 'first rose'), representing Prim's youthful innocence. The fact that she is named after a blossom also reflects her beautiful, pure nature. Like Katniss, Prim is aligned with nature. Although she does not engage with the natural world in the same hands-on way as her older sister, she must often use plant-based medicines to help her mother heal patients and has a real affinity with animals, proven by the pet goat she keeps and her cat, Buttercup (named after a flower, just like her mistress).

Gale is another character whose name is closely linked with nature. Not only does his first name mean 'a strong wind' (which fits the forceful character of the boy himself, while conjuring images of movement and change – things he is forever pushing for), but his surname, Hawthorne, is borrowed from a small species of tree known as the 'hawthorn'. Again, this suits Gale's character down to the ground, as he spends a lot of time out in the forest. The fact that Gale and Katniss both have nature-themed names strengthens the bond between these two fatherless teens, reflecting their similar backgrounds and all that they already share in common.

Peeta's name can be interpreted in a couple of ways. Firstly, it sounds like 'pitta', which is a type of bread and relates to his family business (his father runs a bakery where Peeta regularly helps out). The name is also a variation on 'Peter'. This means 'rock' and seems appropriate for the second boy in Katniss' life. Strong, reliable and always there for her to lean on, he is more than willing to be her rock. Probably the most famous person with this name is Saint Peter, the most prominent of Jesus' twelve apostles and regarded by some as the first Pope. Perhaps this connection explains Peeta's saint-like personality. Saint Peter was also considered the spokesman for the apostles – which is very relevant to Peeta, who is a charming and articulate public speaker.

Haymitch also seems to be an alternative spelling of a more well-known name – in this case, Hamish. Hamish itself is the Scottish form of James and it means 'supplanter'. This is someone who takes the place of another, often through trickery or force. Haymitch also shares his surname with Ralph Abernathy, who was a leader of the Civil Rights Movement in the 1960s and worked closely with Martin Luther King Jr in the fight for racial equality in America. Therefore, both of Haymitch's names give hints of his importance as a revolutionary figure, battling for equality and civil rights in Panem by plotting to overthrow the corrupt Capitol government.

Effie is a shortening of the name Euphemia, meaning 'good speech' (in Ancient Greek, *eu* means good and *phemi* means voice), which makes sense because a large part of Effie's role as a tribute escort is public speaking. Interestingly, this name is also associated with a saint. Saint Euphemia lived in the third century AD at a time when it was decreed that everyone must take part in pagan sacrifices. Euphemia refused to do so because she was a Christian, and as a result she was tortured for days before the Emperior threw her into an arena with with a bear, which fatally wounded her. Isn't it strange to think of Effie as a rebel against the government put in the place of a Hunger Games tribute? Striking a completely different tone, her second name, 'trinket', is a small ornament or piece of jewellery, which captures Effie's vain, image-conscious nature perfectly.

Cinna shares his name with two characters from Shakespeare's play, *The Tragedy of Julius Caesar,* based on actual events in Ancient Roman history. One of them, Lucius Cornelius Cinna, was part of the conspiracy to overthrow the Roman emperor, Julius Caesar. The second, Gaius Helvius Cinna, was a poet, mistakenly killed in retaliation for Caesar's murder – a grave error caused by the fact that he too bore the name Cinna. Collins' stylist Cinna is a combination of both these figures. Like the poet, he is extremely creative and expresses himself through art and, like the conspirator, he takes part in a plan to overthrow a dictator. Unfortunately, Cinna's fate follows that of his poet namesake and he is killed as punishment for daring to make a stand against President Snow.

President Coriolanus Snow, in keeping with all the Capitol residents, has a Roman first name. Gaius Marcius Coriolanus was a famous general who represented the Roman aristocracy and earned the support of politicians after defeating enemies of the empire. However, his opposition to the idea of democracy made him unpopular. This seems just the right name for the power-hungry president of Panem. Only truly concerned with keeping the rich and influential citizens of the Capitol happy, equality is clearly not on his list of priorities. Certainly, President Snow does not care about the rights of his starving subjects in the districts. His last name mirrors his cold, unfeeling personality, setting him in direct contrast to Katniss, the 'girl on fire'. Let's hope that, as fire melts snow, she can overcome him.

There are plenty of other characters whose names hint at some deeper significance, especially as regards their district of origin. For example, people from District 11 are given names with agricultural associations, in keeping with that district's industry. Thresh (a method of separating grain that involves beating it forcefully; hinting at Thresh's strength and power), Chaff (the dry husks of grains separated from wheat during threshing – this certainly reflects Chaff's rough edge), Rue (which means to feel regret or sorrow – as Katniss does when she dies – is also the name of a plant; another bond between her and Katniss) and Seeder are all inspired by farm life. As has already been touched upon, the inhabitants of District 1 are often named after the luxurious items that they produce, whilst Capitol citizens all have traditionally Roman names to signify that their decadent way of life is very similar to that of the Ancients.

So, we can see that with regards to the question 'what's in a name?' when it comes to Suzanne Collins and the world of *The Hunger Games*, the answer is 'quite a lot'!

THE 74TH HUNGER GAMES

The Hunger Games have been running for seventy-four years, ever since the Capitol defeated the rebels and put an end to the Dark Days. So, everyone in Panem pretty much knows what to expect from them by now (although the Gamemakers always have new surprises to throw into the mix). Many citizens even try to predict the outcome and place bets on certain tributes' chances.

For those of you who are a little less familiar with how the Games work, we have managed to recruit a canny Capitol-based bookmaker to provide his own commentary in the run-up to the 74th Games. Hopefully his unique perspective on the tributes and their strengths and weaknesses, with a little added help from the yearly Capitol magazine, *Games Gossip*, will bring you straight up to speed with the rollercoaster ride that is the Hunger Games!

'Hello! I hear you want filling in on this year's Hunger Games? Well you've certainly come to the right place – Capitol Chances is the best bookmakers in all of Panem to find the odds that could be in *your* favour. And I'm the man who keeps on top of everything to do with the Games. I've been following every twist and turn, and probably know these tributes better than their mentors by now! So, stick with old Prosperus and you can't go wrong . . .

'As usual, it all started with the reaping. I don't usually take bets at this stage – miles away in the Capitol, who can say which kids are going to be up next? – but I've heard some district-based bookies make a killing on reaping day, taking bets on who people think will get picked. I always take a real interest in reapings because they're the first glimpse you'll have of the future tributes and it helps to be prepared. Even though I've never attended one myself, I've seen enough on television to tell you exactly how it goes.

'Once a year, the whole population of each district gathers in their city centre at two in the afternoon (apart from in districts like 11, where there are so many people that I think they must hold draws beforehand to narrow down the numbers in attendance – otherwise they'd never fit everyone in). By this time, they'll have set up a stage, along with a podium and two large glass balls – one holding slips with the girls' names on them and the other holding slips with the boys'. That district's mayor, the Capitol escort who has been assigned to look after the tributes and the mentor(s) to the tributes (former Hunger Games victors themselves, also from that district) all sit together on the stage.

'The mayor takes the podium. He explains why the Hunger Games started in the first place and reads a list of past victors from that district – which takes a lot longer to do in District 1 than District 12! Then it gets to the good part. The escort pulls one name out of each ball and announces which boy and girl will be that year's tributes. From the kids' reactions alone, I can start putting together a picture of what kind of competitor they're going to be – brave or scared, strong or weak. The smartest ones don't react at all; they don't want to give anything away. After the new tributes take the stage, the escort asks if anyone wants to volunteer to take their place.

'This year we had two volunteers. The first wasn't too surprising; in District 2, a big brute of a boy named Cato stepped forward, looking ready to jump into the arena there and then. I've seen his type before – so hungry for glory, they'll do anything to get a piece of the action. Lots of people put their money down on him winning straightaway. The second volunteer was something else, though . . . a little girl – couldn't have been more than twelve – was originally picked from the crowd, but before she could even reach the stage, another older girl cried out to take her place – her sister, apparently, Katniss Everdeen.

'You could tell she was shaky, but she put on a brave face, so now she's my "one to watch". First time in years that it's been someone from District 12; they have a terrible record in the Hunger Games. Given that I doubt anyone in 12 actually wants to enter the arena, it's been years since they last had a volunteer. Effie Trinket actually looked like she might be lost for words – and that's got to be a first! Still, she held it together better than Haymitch Abernathy. That man's a drunken wreck; for a former victor, he's really in a sorry state . . . it's awful to see him come to that.

'Anyway, the reaping finishes with the mayor reading out the Treaty of Treason, the tributes shaking hands and the anthem of Panem playing out. Straight after, the tributes are whisked off to their district's Justice Building to say their goodbyes to friends and family. Then it's on to the Capitol for opening ceremonies, which you certainly won't want to miss. Clad in extravagant costumes and riding in chariots, you'll see all the tributes take a twenty-minute tour through the packed streets of the Capitol. They end up in the City Circle, where President Snow gives his official welcome speech. Then they're brought to the Training Centre, where they'll live and prepare for battle until the Games begin.

GAMES GOSSIP

The only place to get your fix of all the latest goings-on in the Hunger Games! FIRST LOOK! Look out ladies, because District 12's Haymitch Abernathy is off the wagon and on the prowl. Clearly inebriated, the mental mentor lunged at this year's girl tribute, Katniss Everdeen, bellowing some nonsense about what a spunky young lady she is. He then took to pointing wildly at the camera, before dropping off-stage like a drunken bear. That man never fails to make us giggle!

'The night of the opening ceremonies is when everyone in the Capitol starts getting really excited. It's the first chance you'll have to get a proper look at the tributes and the atmosphere in the crowd is something electrifying. Take it from me, you can't help but be swept away by the spectacle of it all. I always book my seats in advance to make sure I'm right at the front. Well, I have to keep a close eye on my money-spinning tributes, don't I?

'Anyway, this year's tributes and stylists certainly didn't disappoint. (I've heard that an incredible amount of preparation goes into getting the tributes ready for this event, which isn't surprising considering the starved, grubby appearance of some of the poor specimens plucked from the crowd at reaping stage. Apparently it can takes hours of waxing, plucking, smoothing, coiffing and makeup to make them Capitol-worthy!)

'As usual, District 1 got things off to a breathtaking start. Who knew those naturally stunning tributes could look even better painted silver? Dressed in jewel-embellished tunics, in chariots drawn by pure white horses, they were really something to behold. There's no denying, though, the stars of this year's show were the tributes of District 12 – without a doubt. They must have new stylists or something, because usually their tributes are painted black like coal or shoved into miners' outfits. This year those kids were on fire – *literally*! The whole crowd was cheering for them as they passed by in their flaming capes. I bet the other tributes saw their odds decreasing right in front of their eyes.

OLYMPIC OVERTONES

Possibly the nearest thing we have in our world to compare with the Hunger Games is the Olympic Games, in which the best athletes from all over the world come together every four years to compete against each other in various sporting activities. Unlike the tributes, Olympic contenders are only striving to be the best and win medals rather than fighting for their lives! The original Olympic Games – athletic races and tournaments held in a stadium – were started by the Ancient Greeks back in 776 BC (they are named after Mount Olympus, a Greek mountain and the home of that civilisation's mythical gods). The games ended when the Romans seized power over Greece, but were revived again in the late 1800s and have continued ever since, being hosted by a different country each time.

As with the Hunger Games, an important event in the run-up to the Olympics is the opening ceremony. This starts with the host country's flag being flown and a rendition of its national anthem, followed by traditional musical, dance and theatrical performances from native artists and then the entrance of the athletes from every nation. These processions have become grander over time, as each new host country raises the standard a little higher – wanting their own display to be remembered . . . in much the same competitive spirit as the Hunger Games tributes!

Another pre-games ritual in our world is the lighting of the Olympic Flame, a torch lit in Olympia months in advance and carried by relay runners to the Olympic stadium in the host city. Again, this tradition originates in Ancient Greece, where a fire was kept burning throughout the original games in honour of the myth in which Prometheus stole fire from the god Zeus. The opening ceremony of the Olympic Games ends with the final torch bearer – usually a famous and successful athlete from the host country – lighting the Olympic Flame in the stadium. Bringing up the rear of the 74th Hunger Games opening-ceremony procession in their flaming outfits, Katniss and Peeta shine as brightly as two Olympic Flames!

'Well, the opening ceremonies are great for making an impression on the audience, but I suppose the Training Centre is where the tributes really start sizing each other up. This is where they spend their days in the run-up to the Games, training at various work stations. There, they can brush up on their existing skills, or even learn new ones with the help of experts in each field. Archery, weightlifting, climbing, hand-to-hand combat and boxing are the essentials, of course, along with other more specialist stations teaching the kids how to handle some pretty serious weaponry – we're talking axes, slingshots, knives, spears and the like. Then there are those which aren't so physical (but come in just as useful in the arena), where tributes can learn how to camouflage themselves, build shelters, start fires, make knots and distinguish which plants are edible and which are deadly.

'Tributes with smart mentors don't showcase all of their skills in the Training Centre; they save that for their private session with the Gamemakers. This is where they can really let loose and show what they're made of to try to snag the top training scores. You see, after they present their skills individually in front of the Gamemakers, they'll be awarded a mark out of twelve as an assessment of their chances of winning. The higher the better (unless they happen to be trying to hoodwink everyone – just like that girl tribute, Johanna Mason, did one year. Deliberately scoring low, she certainly gave all the others who'd underestimated her abilities a nasty shock in the arena!), because those who score the most usually also gain the most sponsors – rich patrons who can afford to send them gifts of food, medicine, tools or even weapons in the arena that can be the difference between life and death.

'Before the scores are announced, people place bets on who will get the highest. This year, most people went for the Career Tributes or that gigantic lad, Thresh from District 11 ... but there were more than a few upset customers! Those guys certainly did well (I suppose Thresh earned his ten just by turning up), as did the boy from District 12 with his eight. But the real shockers were the girls. That little slip of a girl from District 11 somehow scored a seven, whilst Katniss Everdeen proved that my instincts are never wrong by getting a mighty eleven. I knew that girl was a firecracker in more than just the wardrobe department! I bet the boy from District 2 is just fuming ...

'After the scores are announced, the tributes' last chance to impress comes the night before the Games, when they'll film their TV interview with our long-time Hunger Games host, Caesar Flickerman. In conversation with the old charmer, the tributes usually try to play up a certain angle, and so we'll certainly get to see if they have that little bit of spark or not. Last-minute bets are always placed depending on the tributes' interview performances. This year, the sexy girl tribute from District 1, Glimmer, got things off to a great start in a see-through gold dress. Cato from 2 came across about as bloodthirsty and brutal as you might expect. That girl from District 5 – you know, the one with the foxy features – is another interesting one. She was being very mysterious and I think she could be a dark horse. The high-scoring young girl from 11 looked like a little fairy on the stage. She plans on not being caught by the others and is so tiny she might just get away with it! Her district partner, Thresh, answered all Caesar's questions with simple, "yes" or "no", which only made him look tougher. He's a real favourite among my clients . . . then came my girl, Katniss, who didn't give too much away but certainly looked amazing in her fire-themed dress!

'Right at the end was District 12's male tribute, Peeta Mellark. I have to say, I don't think anyone was expecting anything much from him, but he blew us all away by confessing his love for Katniss. What an angle! Bets on him shot through the roof after that; people in the Capitol can't get enough of a doomed romance it seems.

GAMES GOSSIP

The only place to get your fix of all the latest goings-on in the Hunger Games! OMG! It seems like the District 12 tributes haven't been out of the limelight since they were reaped . . . first those fiery costumes, then the sky-high scores in training. Next, Peeta Mellark's busy confessing his love for district partner, Katniss Everdeen, live on-air! Oh, we do just love a pair of star-crossed lovers! Katniss is one lucky lady if you ask us. Too bad it can't end well for the lovebirds of District 12. Still, if Peeta comes home a broken-hearted victor, we'll be more than happy to pick up the pieces. What a cutie that boy is!

'So, now they're all set to go into the arena. Tomorrow they'll slip on their uniforms (I've a friend on the inside – it keeps me one step ahead of the punters! – who reliably informs me that they'll be wearing tawny-coloured trousers, a light green blouse and a black hooded jacket made of some thin material that reflects body heat, with a brown belt and leather boots that are good for running. They've been luckier than some of their predecessors!) and be pushed up into the arena with nothing more than their tribute tokens for good luck. Of course, one of them was hoping hers would bring a little more than just luck . . . I heard that Glimmer from District 1 tried to sneak a ring with a poisoned spike hidden inside as her tribute token! No harm in trying I suppose, but she had it confiscated, of course.

'Once they're in the arena, who knows what will happen? I suppose it will start with a bloodbath at the Cornucopia as usual. The Cornucopia is a huge horn filled with weapons, food and supplies in the centre of the arena. The tributes enter the arena on metal plates circling the Cornucopia, each of them an equal distance away from the prize. They must stand still for 60 seconds (anyone who moves from their spot will have their legs blown off by landmines immediately), before a gong sounds telling them the game has begun. Naturally, many kids run straight for the Cornucopia, in the hope of pocketing something from it that'll help them survive. The problem with this strategy is that the Career Tributes, who are the fittest and have had most training, usually get there first and start using their newly-acquired weapons against their rivals, working in a pack to eliminate as much of the competition as possible right from the start. The Gamemakers don't even bother to sound the cannon to announce a death, or start collecting bodies until the initial carnage is over and done with . . . otherwise it would get too complicated. Given this, several tributes completely forgo their chance to lift anything from the Cornucopia. For them, the only objective is to get well out of harm's way before the bloodshed begins. I'd say that's the safest bet (although if it were me in there, I'd be sure to try and grab one of the less precious items left strewn on the ground around the Cornucopia on my way out).

> **Tribute Token**
>
> Each tribute is allowed to bring something into the arena that reminds them of home – as long as it cannot be used to help them in the Games. Katniss' tribute token is the mockingjay pin given to her by her friend, Madge Undersee.

> **Cornucopia** derives from a Latin word meaning, 'horn of plenty'. It describes a large horn-shaped container filled with food or goods. A classical symbol of nourishment and abundance, it is still used in Western art today and is associated with the American holiday of Thanksgiving.

'The safety of that plan also depends on the terrain . . . and that's something that can vary greatly from year to year. Of course, I need to be aware of this; it can be a deciding factor in who becomes the gamblers' top choice. If the arena is filled with water, for example, you can be sure everyone will be betting on District 4's tributes – kids who've been swimming their whole lives – to come out on top. Some years there's nothing more than a few shrubs and rocks in there, which makes for pretty boring viewing. Thankfully, I have it on good authority that this year the arena has a more varied landscape, with a forest filled with plants and animals, a field of grain, some caves and water in the form of ponds, a stream and a lake. There's so many ways for the Gamemakers to make something interesting happen with all that lot at their disposal!

'We'll just have to wait until tomorrow to see how things will play out. After paying close attention to every stage of the run-up, I think I've got a fairly good idea of who my money would be on, but that could all change depending on how the tributes react when they realise what they're up against. Until then, all bets are off!'

DISTRICT 1
INDUSTRY: LUXURY ITEMS

GLIMMER Female Tribute

Defining characteristics: Glimmer is shown to be a serious contender in the Games before they even start. Her attempt to smuggle a weapon into the arena (a poisoned spike disguised as a harmless ring) is as risky as it is underhand. Katniss also notes that Glimmer is very attractive, describing her as tall with flowing blond hair and emerald eyes. Even in mutt form, these striking features make her instantly recognisable.

Weapon of choice: Glimmer obtains a bow and arrows at the Cornucopia. And though she's clearly not comfortable using them, she doesn't let that stop her causing some serious harm.

Strengths: As a District 1 tribute, Glimmer follows tradition and becomes part of the Career Pack. She also plays on her beauty in interview with Caesar Flickerman, clad in a revealing dress that's sure to attract attention.

Weaknesses: Glimmer isn't a natural with a bow and arrow and does not display the same quick-thinking as her allies when stung by the tracker jacker mutts.

Allies: Marvel (district partner); Cato and Clove (District 2); District 3 male; District 4 female and Peeta (District 12).

Kills: Though no kills are attributed to Glimmer specifically, it's safe to assume she was responsible for some deaths in the initial bloodbath at the Cornucopia.

Death: Trapped in a tree, Katniss drops a tracker-jacker nest on the Career Pack awaiting her on the ground. Glimmer is fatally stung and dies a gruesome death almost immediately. After her body has been removed from the arena, her DNA is mixed with that of a wolf to create a ferocious species of mutt, which is also slain by Katniss with a well-aimed arrow.

Ranking: Eleventh.

MARVEL Male Tribute

Defining characteristics: Typically for a Career Tribute, Marvel is strong and ruthless. A smooth-talking member of the Career Pack, he takes a reasoned, strategic approach to winning the Games and is even able to calm Cato in moments of rage.

Weapon of choice: At the Training Centre, Marvel proves himself to be very handy with a spear.

Strengths: Marvel is at an advantage from the start, as he manages to get his weapon of choice at the Cornucopia. He is also a key component in the formidable Career Pack, showing more intelligence than certain others members when he suggests they keep Peeta in their alliance to help them gain access to Katniss. He also successfully rigs up a net to catch other tributes.

Weaknesses: Marvel doesn't show many weaknesses, but he makes a fatal mistake in underestimating Katniss.

Allies: Glimmer (district partner), Cato and Clove (District 2), District 3 male (originally), District 4 female, Peeta (District 12, originally).

Kills: Rue (District 11) and undoubtedly others at the Cornucopia.

Death: Ensnared in Marvel's net, Rue begins to panic. Katniss follows her little ally's cries and arrives just in time to see Marvel deal Rue a deadly wound to the stomach with his spear. In retaliation, Katniss instantly shoots Marvel in the neck. He pulls the arrow out and quickly bleeds to death.

Ranking: Eighth.

DISTRICT 2
INDUSTRY: WEAPONRY
MANUFACTURE/TRAINS
PEACEKEEPERS

CLOVE Female Tribute

Defining characteristics: Clove is the first tribute to make a kill when she throws a knife into the back of District 9's male tribute at the Cornucopia. She then aims for Katniss, but a supplies pack gets in the way. Nevertheless, Clove proves early on that she is playing to win.

Weapon of choice: Callous Clove arms herself with a fearsome selection of knives in the arena – and she certainly knows how to use them.

Strengths: As well as her expert knife-throwing skills, Clove benefits from being part of the Career Pack, meaning she has pre-Games training, better resources, and stronger allies. In particular, Clove shares a strong bond with her fellow District 2 tribute Cato, one of the year's most fearsome competitors.

Weaknesses: While Clove doesn't display many physical weaknesses, like Marvel, her downfall is brought about by her own overconfidence.

Allies: Glimmer and Marvel (District 1); Cato (district partner); District 3 male (originally); District 4 female, Peeta (District 12, originally).

Kills: District 9's male tribute and probably more at the Cornucopia.

Death: Towards the end of the Games, the remaining tributes are drawn together by the Gamemakers' tantalising promise of a feast at the Cornucopia. In the chaos that follows, Clove attacks Katniss. As she sits on top of her rival, nonchalantly playing with the knives she's about to use, she taunts Katniss about the death of her friend Rue, unaware that District 11's gigantic Thresh is approaching. Hearing her gloat over the killing of his district partner, Thresh assumes that Clove is responsible for the murder. Despite Clove's protests of innocence, Thresh crushes her skull with a large rock and she dies soon after.

Ranking: Sixth.

CATO Male Tribute

Defining characteristics: As a Career Tribute, Cato has been trained to fight in the Games since birth and sees winning as the highest honour. His determined bloodlust is evident from the start, marking him out as the one to beat.

Weapon of choice: Cato has acquired a sword and protective armour by the end of the Games, but both accessories seem superfluous to say the least. More often than not, he relies on brute strength alone.

Strengths: Although not quite as large as Thresh, Cato is physically very powerful. Furthermore, his brutal mindset gives him an intimidating edge. This, combined with his fearlessness and the support of the other Careers, makes him an almost unstoppable force in the arena.

Weaknesses: Potentially, Cato's violent fits of rage could prove a weakness, but Clove and Marvel prevent him from making stupid mistakes . . . while they're still alive.

Allies: Glimmer and Marvel (District 1), District 3 male (originally), District 4 female and initially Peeta (District 12). Cato is especially close to his District 2 partner, Clove. Enraged by her death, he immediately sets about hunting down her murderer – the unfortunate Thresh – for vengeance.

Kills: District 3's male tribute, Thresh (District 11) and almost certainly more. Cato also severely wounds District 8's female tribute (although Peeta has to go back and finish the job) and Peeta, cutting deep into his thigh. The blood poisoning Peeta suffers as a result would surely have killed him, had Katniss not been able to get him medicine in time.

Death: Cato is one of the final three tributes left when the Gamemakers unleash a pack of ferocious wolf muttations in to the arena. Along with Katniss and Peeta, Cato struggles to climb the Cornucopia, out of reach of the deadly mutts. Katniss gets there first, but relentless Cato's not ready to go down without a fight. Grasping Peeta in a headlock, he leaves Katniss unable to shoot him to the ground, unless she wants to watch him take Peeta with him. Yet, Cato never figured on Katniss aiming for his hand. True to form, she pierces the skin, forcing him to let go and drop down to face the mutts. Armed with a sword and covered in protective armour, Cato manages to hold off the wolves for hours . . . but at the sound of his deathly, agonising cries, Katniss shoots him out of pity. The human quality that Cato gains in these final moments proves that it is not the tributes who should be blamed for the terrible acts committed in the arena, but those who continue the barbaric tradition of the Games.

Ranking: Third.

DISTRICT 3
INDUSTRY: ELECTRONICS

The **female tribute** from District 3 is killed in the Cornucopia bloodbath on day one.

Male Tribute
Defining characteristics: The District 3 male survives the Cornucopia and, unusually for a tribute from his district, lives to join the Career Pack.
Weapon of choice: His greatest weapons are his intelligence and his knowledge of electronics – rare attributes which convince the Careers to keep him alive.
Strengths: This tribute earns his place in the Career Pack by reactivating the mines around the Cornucopia and cleverly constructing a booby-trapped minefield around their hoard of food and vital supplies. His quick-thinking and technological skills win him protection, for a time at least.
Weaknesses: With neither the strength nor the speed of his fellow Careers, District 3's boy tribute is highly vulnerable to attack. As he is not a traditional Career ally, his position in the group is tenuous to say the least.
Allies: The District 3 male joins the Career Pack along with Glimmer and Marvel (District 1); Cato and Clove (District 2); District 4 female and Peeta (District 12, originally). This arrangement ends when the mines protecting their food and supplies are blown up and he is no longer useful to the Careers.
Kills: Whether or not this boy has killed is unknown. Though he's part of the ruthless Career Pack rampaging through the arena, it's safe to say that most of the damage was inflicted by the more aggressive members of the alliance. However, it's certainly possible that he played a part in the carnage at the Cornucopia and he was certainly aiming to kill with his explosive trap.
Death: Realising that the only way to stop the Careers is to cut off their food supply (something they cannot handle due to their privileged upbringings), Katniss travels back to the Cornucopia. She watches silently as District 5's crafty female tribute, Foxface, carefully navigates the surrounding area. Stepping painstakingly between the safe spots, she manages to steal from the Careers' stash of supplies. In this moment,

Katniss realises that the entire area has been booby-trapped. To test her theory, she shoots an arrow at a bag of hanging apples, causing them to fall and set the mines off. When the Careers realise what has happened, Cato is furious. The boy from District 3 tries to run away, but Cato snaps his neck in a fit of rage, killing him instantly.
Ranking: Ninth.

DISTRICT 4
INDUSTRY: FISHING

In an unexpected twist, the **District 4 male** is killed in the Cornucopia bloodbath on day one of the competition.

Female Tribute
Defining characteristics: The District 4 female survives the Cornucopia bloodbath and follows tradition by joining the Career-tribute alliance.
Weapon of choice: Her specific weapon isn't mentioned, but she could have taken her pick from the resources at the Cornucopia.
Strengths: As a Career Tribute, she would have received training to make her a stronger competitor long before the reaping. She also has the support and protection of the rest of the Career Pack.
Weaknesses: The District 4 female does not appear to have sharp instincts or even much common sense, as she does not react to the tracker-jacker attack with the same urgency as the rest of her Pack.
Allies: Glimmer and Marvel (District 1); Cato and Clove (District 2); District 3 male and Peeta (District 12).
Kills: In the thick of the initial conflict at the Cornucopia, it is likely she murdered some of her fellow tributes, but her victims are never identified for sure.
Death: When Katniss was trapped in a tree by the Careers, Rue materialised to point out a tracker-jacker nest hanging inches above. In desperation, Katniss dropped the nest on her pursuers. Along with Glimmer, the girl from District 4 received the worst stings. Unlike her allies, she could not make it to the lake to soothe the stings and died straightaway from their poisonous venom.
Ranking: Twelfth.

DISTRICT 5
INDUSTRY: POWER
AND ELECTRICITY

The **District 5 male** is killed in the Cornucopia bloodbath on his very first day in the arena.

'FOXFACE' Female Tribute

Defining characteristics: Due to her coming across as sly and elusive during the interview stage, Katniss starts to call her District 5 rival 'Foxface' – a nickname that matches her sharp features, as well as her sneaky character. The wolf mutt that is created with a sample of her DNA at the end of the Games shares her fiery-red hair and amber eyes.

Weapon of choice: For much of the tournament, Foxface does not appear to be armed at all – until she picks up a knife from the ruins of the Career Pack's exploded camp. However, her cunning is surely her greatest asset.

Strengths: Katniss predicts that Foxface is the smartest tribute and would easily win if the Games were merely a test of intelligence. Foxface uses her craftiness to gain food, outwitting the Career Pack time and time again. For a time, she spies on them from a safe hiding place. As soon as they leave their stash unguarded, she invades their camp and easily picks her way through a lethal minefield to steal their food – lifting amounts so small that they go unnoticed. She also hides in the Cornucopia at the Gamemakers' feast so that, when the supplies are dropped into the arena, she can flee the scene before any of the others can attack her. It is carefully plotted acts like this that ensure Foxface obtains resources whilst avoiding confrontation with her rivals.

Weaknesses: Foxface is quite small so she probably wouldn't do well in physical combat – but she is unlikely to let herself get into that situation! Additionally, her lack of hunting skills and the fact that she couldn't fight to win herself more supplies at the Cornucopia mean she has to rely on staying dangerously close to her opponents to survive.

Allies: Foxface works alone, only venturing near the other tributes to steal from them.

Kills: Though we do not know for sure, it seems likely that Foxface escaped the battle at the Cornucopia altogether and spends the rest of her time in the arena avoiding the others rather than killing them.

Death: Foxface lasts long into the Games by hiding and stealing food from her fellow tributes. Unfortunately, this plan backfires when she eats some poisonous nightlock berries that Peeta has accidentally picked. When her body is taken away by the Gamemakers, Katniss is shocked to see how emaciated she's become, suggesting that she was struggling to survive by this point anyway.

Ranking: Fourth.

DISTRICT 6
INDUSTRY: TRANSPORTATION

Both tributes from District 6 are killed in the Cornucopia bloodbath on day one.

DISTRICT 7
INDUSTRY: LUMBER AND PAPER

Both tributes from District 7 are killed in the Cornucopia bloodbath on day one.

DISTRICT 8
INDUSTRY: TEXTILE PRODUCTION

The **male tribute** from District 8 is killed in the Cornucopia bloodbath on day one.

The **female tribute** from District 8 has the skills – or sheer luck – to survive the battle at the Cornucopia and subsequently flees into the forest. On the second morning she makes the fatal mistake of starting a fire, which leads the Career Tributes straight to her. Cato seriously wounds her, but the cannon to announce her death does not fire straightaway, so Peeta goes back to finish the job.

Ranking: Thirteenth.

DISTRICT 9
INDUSTRY: GRAIN

Both tributes from District 9 are killed in the Cornucopia bloodbath on day one, neither of them having the strength or skill to overcome the fiercer, stronger, healthier tributes from wealthier districts.

While the **District 9 male** is still tussling with Katniss (over a tiny backpack's worth of supplies), District 2's Clove has already reached the horn and recovered half a dozen knives. With deadly accuracy, she tosses one into his back, putting a decisive end to his struggle with Katniss. At the end of the Games, Katniss picks out his mutt as the one with hazel eyes and ashen hair.
Ranking: Twenty-fourth.

DISTRICT 10
INDUSTRY: LIVESTOCK

The **female tribute** from District 10 is killed in the Cornucopia bloodbath on day one. Coming from the third poorest district in all of Panem (after 11 and 12), District 10's deprived tributes are unlikely to have the strength to face tougher competitors at the Cornucopia. In the fight for supplies, the odds are certainly not in their favour . . . and it will have surprised no one to learn that District 10's female tribute was amongst the first casualties of the year.

Their pitiable **male tribute** caught Katniss' attention before the Games even began. Not only has his crippled foot left him with a chronic limp, he's also rather quiet in interview with Caesar Flickerman. Despite this apparent disadvantage – and against all odds – he outlasts many of his opponents by surviving the fight at the Cornucopia. It is not known how he does this or how he manages to stay in the Game for another week. We do know that by day eight, his luck's run out – the Career Pack track him down and kill him.
Ranking: Tenth.

DISTRICT 11
INDUSTRY: AGRICULTURE

RUE Female Tribute

Defining characteristics: At twelve, Rue is the youngest of all the competitors in the 74th Hunger Games. Described by Katniss as bird-like, she is physically tiny, with dark eyes and brown skin. Rue comes from a large family in a poor district, so she is underfed and used to working in the orchards, where she sings to the mockingjays to announce the end of each hard day in the fields. Despite her size, she warns her tributes not to underestimate her in conversation with Caesar Flickerman and surprisingly scores a fairly high seven out of a possible twelve from the Gamemakers after the pre-Games training sessions. Heartbreakingly, Rue's wolf muttation is the smallest of the pack and has a woven-grass collar similar to the tribute token worn by Rue in life.

Weapon of choice: Rue's special talent is jumping from tree to tree – a skill perfected at work in the orchards back home. It is presumably this ability that earns her a seven in training, though Katniss thinks she deserves even higher.

Strengths: Rue's tree-climbing means that she can stay out of harm's way for most of the game by avoiding confrontations with other tributes. She can also move swiftly from tree to tree, whilst keeping an eye on the others' movements. Katniss also notices in training that Rue knows a lot about plants and has a very accurate aim with a slingshot. The detailed knowledge plants and their properties that Rue has gained from her agricultural background keeps her fed in the arena and means she is also able to help Katniss relieve her burns.

Weaknesses: If drawn into a physical confrontation, then tiny bird-like Rue is at an obvious disadvantage.

Allies: A few days after Rue helps Katniss escape from the Career Pack, they cross paths again. Katniss suggests that they form an alliance and Rue accepts, trusting Katniss because of her mockingjay – a familiar creature from District 11. Rue reminds Katniss of her little sister and the girls gain comfort from each other's company, as well as sharing knowledge and resources. Rue teaches Katniss more about the useful plants in the arena and informs her that the glasses she picked up in her supplies pack have night-vision, whilst Katniss catches game for them and feeds Rue well. The girls then start devising a plan to destroy the Career Pack's supplies, as they know the well-fed tributes won't be used to finding their own food, and their elimination will mean a better chance at survival. Whilst they never form an official alliance, Rue's district partner, Thresh, seems to feel a duty towards Katniss when he kills Clove in response to Rue's murder.

Kills: Although Rue is not directly responsible for the deaths of any of her fellow tributes, she is the one who suggests that Katniss drops the tracker-jacker nest on the Career Pack, a move which kills Glimmer and the District 4 female.

Death: While Katniss goes to the Careers' camp to sabotage their stash of food, Rue sets fires in the forest as a decoy. The plan is working well until Rue gets caught in a trap set by Marvel. Rue calls out to Katniss, but her ally only manages to get there in time to see Marvel plunge a spear into her stomach. Katniss kills Marvel with an instant arrow to the neck and cradles Rue in her arms. As her dying wish, Rue asks for Katniss to sing to her and the older girl fulfils this request with a lullaby. When Rue dies Katniss covers her body in flowers to prove that she is not just a dead body – she was a little girl, beloved by her family and friends – and gives her a respectful farewell salute. Shortly afterwards, Katniss receives bread from District 11 – the first time a district has awarded a present to any tribute but their own – as a thank you for her kind treatment of Rue and to honour their allegiance.

Ranking: Seventh.

THRESH Male Tribute

Defining characteristics: Despite his considerable bulk – clearly making him one of this year's major threats – Thresh does not seem to seek confrontation in the way that the Careers do. Instead, he retreats into a field of long grain by the Cornucopia for most of the Games, only emerging to attend the Gamemakers' feast. Katniss immediately identifies Thresh's wolf mutt as it the largest, with the ability to jump the highest, and its colouring reflects his dark brown skin and golden-brown eyes.

Weapon of choice: Thresh does not appear to have picked up a weapon, which suggests that he did not participate in the Cornucopia bloodbath, but headed straight into the cover of the field. Nevertheless, his incredible power means he is just as deadly unarmed – as he proves when he brutally attacks the District 2 female, Clove, with a rock.

Strengths: With large muscles and standing at six and a half feet tall, Thresh is the biggest of the tributes in this year's Games. As well as the physical power this gives him, his stature is a source of intimidation to the other tributes, even the Careers. Thresh's decision to remain in the grain field means he has a constant supply of food (indeed, he's the only tribute who seems to have gained weight in the arena) and also keeps other tributes away, as they are frightened of their huge rival lurking in the long grain, which provides the perfect hiding-place for him.

Weaknesses: Thresh makes no attempt to arm himself, which could be why he was eventually defeated by Cato. His tactic of remaining in the field and his apparent reluctance to fight his competitors means that he has to rely on them not wanting to face him, as they could easily locate him if necessary. Luckily his colossal presence means they do avoid him, until he crosses Cato . . .

Allies: Despite being approached by the Career Tributes in training, Thresh stays out of any alliances and works alone. However, he does show some loyalty to his district partner, Rue. He is incensed to hear Clove mocking her death and kills her in retaliation.

Kills: Thresh's only known victim is Clove, whose skull he crushes with a heavy rock. Whether he could be responsible for more deaths is an interesting question . . . yet, we do see Thresh avoid murdering at least one person. After slaying Clove at the feast, a vulnerable Katniss asks him to deal with her quickly but, upon learning about her friendship with Rue, he lets her run away instead.

Death: When Thresh kills Clove and leaves the Cornucopia with the backpack sent for the District 2 tributes, Cato is furious and runs after him into the field. A day later Thresh's image is sent into the sky during a thunderstorm, after what was probably a long and bloody battle with Cato.

Ranking: Fifth.

DISTRICT 12
INDUSTRY: COAL MINING

KATNISS Female Tribute

Defining characteristics: Going into the competition, Katniss – a non-Career, she's not nearly the biggest or richest of the tributes – is at both at a disadvantage and an advantage. The highest scorer in training, she's also the desirable young woman at the heart of the 74th Hunger Games love story, thus everyone has their eyes on her from the very beginning. An accomplished archer, she has hunting experience and bravery on her side, but she also has to overcome her revulsion at the very idea of the Games and the bloodthirsty Career Pack who see her as a major threat to be annihilated.

Weapon of choice: Katniss' weapon of choice is undoubtedly a bow and arrow, with which she is very familiar from her years of hunting in the forest surrounding District 12 with Gale. However, in her haste to get away from the Cornucopia before the bloodbath begins, she only manages to pick up a pack of supplies. Needless to say, she doesn't find a bow and arrows inside and has nothing of the sort until she takes them from Glimmer's body. Until then Katniss copes by using the survival skills her father taught her (which she's often put use to provide for her family), the items in her backpack (a packet of crackers, a packet of dried beef strips, a thin sleeping bag, a bottle of iodine, a large empty plastic bottle, a coil of wire and night-vision glasses) and all the resources that the arena has to offer, including a deadly tracker-jacker nest.

Strengths: Despite the unfairness of Katniss having to be the one to feed her family since the age of eleven, this experience proves extremely useful to her in the Hunger Games arena. Not only do her archery abilities mean she has a strong method of attack against the other tributes, but she can also hunt for game and she has good knowledge of traps, tracking and edible plants. Katniss' high training score and strong survival instinct help her earn valuable gifts from sponsors, such as burn medicine. Another edge that Katniss has over her competition comes when Peeta confesses his love for her in Caesar Flickerman's interview. This makes them both stand out and as the competition continues and they play out a love story, the public interest is clear from the increased number of sponsor's gifts they receive.

Weaknesses: Throughout the first part of the Games, Katniss is frustrated not to have a bow and arrow. Additionally, the fact that she does not want to hunt down her opponents means the threat that they will find and kill her is always looming. Ironically, the fact that Katniss scored so highly in training with an unknown talent and that she showed a fighting spirit when she replaced her sister at the reaping, make the chances of the others perceiving her as a contender they need to eliminate even higher. In a sense, Katniss' partnership with Peeta weakens her chances because it urges her to put herself in dangerous positions that she could otherwise avoid, such as the feast at the Cornucopia.

Allies: Despite being determined to work alone, Katniss ends up forming three alliances in the arena. The first is with Rue. Katniss notices Rue before the Games, touched by how small and young she is and Rue's likeness to her own younger sister, Primrose. Katniss is also impressed by Rue's performance in the Training Centre and the high score she is awarded by the Gamemakers, thinking that she would make a good ally if Katniss weren't so determined to work independently. When Katniss is stuck in a tree with the Career Pack waiting for her at the bottom and Rue helps her escape, she realises that an alliance might be beneficial. The two girls are happy to join forces and naturally slip into sisterly roles, providing each other with some welcome companionship as well as teaching each other about their lives at home and sharing survival tips. Katniss is heartbroken by how difficult Rue's life has been, even compared to her own, and feels very protective of the younger girl. When Marvel kills Rue, not only does Katniss instinctively murder him in return, she also holds Rue in her arms and serenades her until she dies and then covers her in flowers; a mourning ceremony that is completely uncharacteristic of the bloodthirsty Hunger Games.

When Katniss and Peeta first arrive in the Capitol, according to Haymitch's rules they conduct their mentoring sessions with him and their lessons in the Training Centre together, but before their televised interviews Peeta requests that they work separately. Although Katniss has been reluctant to form a bond with him anyway because she knows one of them will have to die for the other to survive, she is annoyed by his move, but decides it will make it easier for her to detach herself from him. In his interview with Caesar Flickerman, Peeta confesses his secret love for Katniss since childhood. Katniss is furious that Peeta has put her in such an embarrassing situation for what she thinks is just a tactical attempt to make himself stand out. Haymitch calms her down by pointing out that at least this has drawn public attention to Katniss, giving her a mysterious and desirable edge that she never had before. In the arena, Katniss is once again shocked by Peeta's behaviour when he joins the Career Pack. In District 12, Career Tributes are considered brutal and inhumane so she decides that Peeta must be a manipulative liar, who was only ever pretending to be decent around her. After the Careers corner Katniss and she escapes by dropping a tracker-jacker nest onto them, she is confused when Peeta returns to the camp and urges her to run before Cato finds her. She cannot decide if the venom from the tracker jackers has made her imagine this or if Peeta was really trying to protect her, but she later sees that Peeta is no longer with the Careers after fighting with Cato. At the Gamemakers' rule change, stating that two tributes from the same district can both be victors, Katniss sets out to find Peeta. She discovers that he is injured and very weak, but she nurses him back to health, risking a meeting with the other tributes by attending the Gamemakers' feast to get him medicine. She also agrees (albeit reluctantly) to feign a romance with Peeta, kissing him as if she loves him back – a show of affection which earns them gifts from sponsors.

Katniss' third 'alliance' during the 74th Hunger Games is with someone who is not even another tribute but her mentor, Haymitch. Before going into the arena, Katniss and Haymitch do not always see eye to eye, but once the Games begin she has to learn to trust him. Early on, she is extremely dehydrated and wishes he would send her some water, but realises that he probably hasn't because she is so close to finding some for herself – making water a wasted gift. When her theory is proved right, Katniss and Haymitch start to 'communicate' through his gifts. Haymitch sends Katniss cream to relieve her burns after she gets caught in the Gamemakers' fire. When she is reunited with Peeta and they kiss, Haymitch rewards them with a pot of broth. From this, Katniss understands tacitly that she will have to be more affectionate towards Peeta in order to win more public interest and therefore more gifts. Later on in the game, Haymitch provides Katniss with a sleeping draught to use on Peeta, allowing her to attend the Gamemakers' feast (unconscious Peeta could do little to stop or accompany her) and pick up medicine to cure his blood poisoning. As the romance between Katniss and Peeta picks up, Haymitch shows his approval through a large food parcel.

Kills: Katniss makes a number of kills throughout the Games, but none of them are purely out of bloodlust. Katniss drops a nest of deadly tracker-jacker wasps on the Career Pack to escape from the tree they have her trapped in, killing District 1's Glimmer and the female District 4 tribute in the process. Yet, her next kill is not out of necessity, but revenge, after Marvel fatally stabs her little friend Rue. She fires one arrow straight into his neck. Marvel speeds up his death by pulling it out, effectively drowning himself in his own blood. Katniss' final kill is Cato. Surprisingly, given that he has been the most aggressive tribute in the competition, her arrow shot to his head is not the result of a fierce battle between them, but an act of pity. Horrifically mauled by a pack of wolf muttations, Cato's agonising death drags on for hours.

Hearing his agonised pleading for the relief of death, Katniss finally makes up her mind to put an end to his suffering.

Ranking: Joint victor.

PEETA Male Tribute

Defining characteristics: Before the Games start, Peeta casts himself as a romantic, hopelessly in love with his district partner, Katniss, but in the arena he takes a different approach, joining up with the vicious Career Pack. Peeta's new alliance doesn't last long, however, and he is left on his own fighting for his life after his attempt to protect Katniss angers District 2's Cato. However, 'the boy with the bread' from District 12 has many more tricks up his sleeve, proving to be a much stronger, smarter tribute than he first appears.

Weapon of choice: During his time as part of the Career Pack, Peeta is armed with a knife. He is also strong and an expert at camouflage.

Strengths: Years of carrying heavy loads at his father's bakery mean that Peeta has physical strength, enabling him to face the brutish Cato and survive (just!). Despite Katniss mocking Peeta's interest in the camouflage station at the Training Centre – it is similar to the work he does at home, frosting cakes – this proves to be a very useful tool when he is weak and injured, as it allows him to hide for days without being discovered. Peeta's budding relationship with Katniss is also of major benefit to both of them because the romance keeps the Capitol interested in them, earning the star-crossed lovers much-needed sponsors. Most important, though, is Peeta's resilience. His determination to protect Katniss from harm is what keeps him fighting to stay in the Game.

Weaknesses: As the privileged son of a baker, Peeta isn't used to fending for himself and if he hadn't allied with Katniss or the Careers, there's a chance he would have either starved to death, or poisoned himself trying to eat nightlock berries! Undoubtedly, Peeta's greatest weakness in the arena is his desire to protect Katniss. Many times he proves he's willing to put his own life at risk to save hers, making the Careers turn against him.

Allies: In a distinct break from District 12 tradition, Peeta joins forces with the Career Pack at the start of the game. He is with them when they rampage through the arena, killing any tributes that they find. Katniss is disgusted with Peeta's apparent abandonment of decency in favour of this alliance with the bloodthirsty Careers, who are unpopular in District 12 to say the least. However, when the Careers find Katniss and she attacks them with the tracker-jacker nest, Peeta's true allegiances become clear. As Katniss is wrestling the bow and arrows from Glimmer's dead body, Peeta comes back. When he sees her there, rather than kill her, he tells her to flee because Cato is coming and will kill her on sight. In fact, Cato witnesses Peeta's protection of his district partner and they fight as a result, leaving Peeta severely wounded.

When the Gamemakers broadcast the rule change that district partners can win the Games together, Katniss finds Peeta and they become a team. Peeta is on the verge of death due to the deep cut in his thigh inflicted by Cato, which has turned septic. Despite her phobia of blood and gore, Katniss nurses Peeta and they start to bond. At the Gamemakers' announcement that they will supply essential items for the remaining tributes at the feast, Katniss realises that they will surely provide medicine to cure Peeta. Peeta is against her putting herself at risk by facing the other tributes but she tricks him into taking a sleeping draught and leaves to secure him his only chance of survival.

Kills: Peeta accidentally kills the District 5 female tribute Foxface when she steals some of the poisonous nightlock berries that he had picked to eat. Peeta is also partially responsible for the death of the District 8 female tribute; after Cato seriously injures her, her body is not lifted from the arena, so Peeta goes back to ensure she is dead. Aside from these two known kills, it is possible that Peeta is responsible for more as he was part of the Cornucopia bloodbath and with the Careers when they went on their killing spree through the arena.

Ranking: Joint victor.

VICTORY

Among the final three remaining tributes, Katniss and Peeta wait through the night in the Cornucopia, the unspeakably awful sounds of Cato being attacked by the wolf mutts resounding in their ears and Peeta's health deteriorating fast. After Katniss finally shoots Cato with an arrow to relieve him of any more pain, they expect to hear the cannon sound, announcing his death and their victory. Instead, there is only silence. They move away from the Cornucopia, thinking that they might be too close to Cato's body, when Claudius Templesmith's voice booms out across the arena once more. He tells them that the previous rule change is now void and there can in fact be only one winner of the Hunger Games, a cruel move to force the star-crossed lovers to kill each other.

At the announcement, Katniss sees Peeta move and instinctively reaches for her weapon, but is ashamed of her behaviour when she realises that Peeta was acting innocently. He tries to persuade her to kill him, as he wants her to survive. Katniss does not want to and knows that her life in District 12 would be hellish even if she did survive because the citizens would regard her as a traitor for killing her district partner. Instead, she hits upon an idea that she hopes will save them both.

She picks some poisonous nightlock berries and hands some to Peeta. They count to three and put the berries into their mouths at the same time in an apparent suicide pact. Luckily, their gamble pays off as the Head Gamemaker, Seneca Crane, panics at the thought of having no victor at all and allows them both to be crowned as such. Thus, for the first time in Panem's history there are two winners and Peeta and Katniss prove that they are more than just pieces in the Games.

In choosing to die rather than kill each other, they outwit the Gamemakers, rejecting the whole premise of the Hunger Games – an act of rebellion that proves to have far greater consequences than they could ever have imagined . . .

TRIBUTE TEST

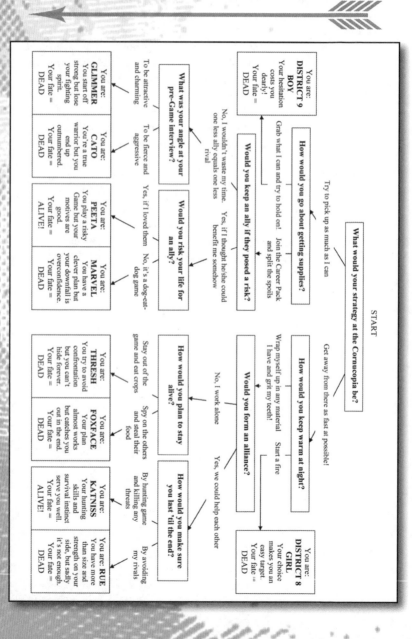

START

What would your strategy at the Cornucopia be?
- Try to pick up as much as I can
- Get away from there as fast as I possible!

How would you go about getting supplies?
- Grab what I can and try to hold on!
- Join the Career Pack and split the spoils

Would you keep an ally if they posed a risk?
- No, I wouldn't waste my time. one less ally equals one less rival
- Yes, if I thought he/she could benefit me somehow

You are: **DISTRICT 9 BOY**
Your hesitation costs you dearly!
Your fate = DEAD

Would you risk your life for an ally?
- Yes, if I loved them
- No, it's a dog-eat-dog game

What was your angle at your pre-Game interview?
- To be attractive and charming
- To be fierce and aggressive

You are: **GLIMMER**
You start off strong but lose your fighting spirit.
Your fate = DEAD

You are: **CATO**
You're a true warrior but you end up outnumbered.
Your fate = DEAD

You are: **PEETA**
You play a risky Game but your motives are good.
Your fate = ALIVE!

You are: **MARVEL**
You have a clever plan but your downfall is overconfidence.
Your fate = DEAD

How would you keep warm at night?
- Wrap myself up in any material I have and grit my teeth!
- Start a fire

Would you form an alliance?
- No, I work alone
- Yes, we could help each other

You are: **DISTRICT 8 GIRL**
Your choice makes you an easy target.
Your fate = DEAD

How would you plan to stay alive?
- Stay out of the game and eat crops
- Spy on the others and steal their food

How would you make sure you last 'til the end?
- By hunting game and killing any threats
- By avoiding my rivals

You are: **THRESH**
You try to avoid confrontation but you can't hide forever.
Your fate = DEAD

You are: **FOXFACE**
Your plan almost works but catches you out in the end.
Your fate = DEAD

You are: **KATNISS**
Your hunting skills and survival instinct serve you well.
Your fate = ALIVE!

You are: **RUE**
You have more than size and strength on your side, but sadly it's not enough.
Your fate = DEAD

MUTTATIONS

Muttations, or mutts, are animals that the Capitol has genetically modified to serve their own sinister ends. They were originally created during the Dark Days, when they were a crucial weapon against the rebel uprising, acting as the eyes and ears of the Capitol. Now they're a regular feature of the Hunger Games, often unleashed upon the unsuspecting tributes, imprisoned within the arena, as a way to spice up the competition whenever things get a little dull for the viewers' liking.

Some muttations pose an obvious physical threat, while others are designed to get inside your mind – altering opinions, thought processes, and even memories. Some look vicious, while others are deceptively fragile. The one common trait that all muttations share is the threat they pose to anyone who crosses their path. To the weakened tributes, mutts may look the same as any other innocent woodland animal, but recognising that they are in fact creatures engineered to cause pain and suffering could be the difference between life and death!

Let's take a closer look at the weird and wild creatures that have been let loose in Panem (but not too close a look!) . . .

FEARING ENGINEERING

Genetic engineering is the deliberate changing of a living organism's characteristics by manipulating its genetic material. This might allow a plant or animal to carry out a new function or produce a useful substance. While the muttations that the Capitol's scientists have created seem totally futuristic and far-fetched, genetic engineering is actually very present in our world today.

Genetic engineering is vital to medical research, where it enables scientists to alter genes that cause disease, to produce hormones or medicines, and to recreate the symptoms of a disease (usually in an animal, such as a mouse) in order to test potential cures. It is also used in agriculture where some crops are genetically modified to make them resistant to pesticides, plant viruses, and drought.

In spite of the potential benefits, as the science behind genetic engineering advances, there are several objections to this process.

Many people do not like the idea of humans being able to override nature and have control over the characteristics of animals or, even worse, humans! So with her muttated creatures, which are extreme examples of the unnatural effects genetic engineering could have in the future, Suzanne Collins is playing on very real human fears and making them a horrifying reality!

'BEAST'

Purpose: In the 75th Hunger Games the arena was designed to resemble a clock, with each twelfth containing a different threat to the tributes, which was revealed at different times of the day. One of these came in the form of the 'beast'!

Features: Though Katniss and her pack never saw the brute that Peeta named 'beast', the fact that it ripped one of their fellow competitors to pieces assured them that it was a creature to avoid! From the damage that it did, it can be assumed that the monster is very large and has razor-sharp claws and/or teeth.

In action: This terrifying muttation prowled the six-to-seven-o'clock sector of the arena, just waiting for an unfortunate tribute to pounce on. When one of the victors made the mistake of straying into its territory, the predator tore him or her apart in what must have been a violent (and probably quick) attack that gave the victim no chance of escape.

Victims: On the second day of the Games, both the District 5 female victor and the District 10 male victor died in unknown circumstances – one of them was taken out by the tidal wave in the ten-to-eleven-o'clock sector of the arena, and the other fell victim to the mutt monster, but Katniss never found out who suffered which fate. All she did know was that whoever faced the 'beast' met a gruesome end, as their body was removed from the arena in five parts . . .

BUTTERFLIES

Purpose: These muttations were used in the 50th Hunger Games, when the whole arena was designed to be stunning but toxic. Despite the picturesque setting of a fresh green meadow beneath a clear blue sky, everything turned out to be harmful to the contestants, down to the poisonous flowers, the streams, and even the butterflies!

Features: Whilst they appear to be nothing more than pretty butterflies, in fact they have painful and potentially deadly stings.

In action: These beautiful insects are as lethal as their surroundings in the Hunger Games, as the tributes soon find out to their peril!

Victims: Their exact count is unknown, but it's safe to say that more than a few of the tributes felt their sting that year!

GOLDEN SQUIRRELS

Purpose: Despite being no bigger than an average squirrel, these muttations have the power to kill and were sent into the Hunger Games arena to do just that.

Features: Fluffy golden squirrels might sound adorable, but forget the fairytales you've read; with their penchant for hunting down human prey in packs, these carnivorous critters are anything but cute!

In action: Featured before Katniss' time, Haymitch and his competitors had to face these nightmarish squirrels in the 50th Hunger Games. Unfortunately, it took the confused tributes a while to work out that these seemingly harmless animals were actually threats!

Victims: The squirrel mutts killed and ate at least one unknown tribute in these Games and probably more.

INSECT MUTTATIONS

Purpose: These muttations were another of the Gamemakers' creations, used to torment contestants in the 75th Hunger Games. Although Katniss steered well clear of them, the insects certainly made their presence felt!

Features: Though they are small individually, these insect-like creatures move as a cloud and are a force to be reckoned with. Though she's never actually set eyes on them, Katniss suspects they are some kind of beetle. She is tormented by the sound of their clicking pincers

– so loud that they can be heard from some distance – and feels sure they could strip human flesh to the bone. They get even noisier when people are close, as if they can sense potential victims . . .

In action: A swarm of these insect muttations inhabited the eleven-to-twelve-o'clock sector in the 75th Hunger Games arena. What they lacked in size, they made up for in numbers and sheer ferocity. They never got a chance to unleash their bloodlust on a victim – perhaps the sound of their clicks was too clear a warning to the wary tributes – but imagine the effect of thousands of vicious little pincers on defenceless human flesh and you can picture the damage they could have done quite clearly!

Victims: Luckily, none of the past victors made the mistake of wandering into the way of the insects – if they had, they would surely have been stripped to bare bones before they could even scream!

JABBERJAYS

Purpose: The Capitol first created jabberjays during the Dark Days as a way of intercepting the rebels' plans.

Features: Small, crested black birds, there is nothing about the physical appearance of jabberjays which exposes them as muttations. However, this all-male species has the ability to remember and repeat human speech in extremely lifelike tones.

In action: During the Dark Days, the homing birds were released wherever rebels were known to be hiding. Disastrously for the rebels, the birds were able to memorise some of their private conversations, before flying back to centres where all of this information could be recorded and used against them. However, the rebels eventually caught on to what was happening and began to feed the jabberjays lies. Once the Capitol realised their birds were of no further use, they left them to die off in the wild, but the resilient species lived on regardless . . .

The Capitol decided to give these troublesome mutts a second outing in the 75th Hunger Games. They were placed in the four-to-five-o'clock section of the clock-design arena where they unleashed a horrifyingly personal form of torture on the tributes, including Katniss and Finnick Odair, by replicating the tortured screams of their loved ones for a whole hour. When the birds begin to mimic the cries of Katniss' beloved little sister, Prim – followed by her best friend Gale and his entire family – it's almost more than she can stand. On the other hand, it probably makes great viewing for the sadistic audience!

Victims: The jabberjays' original victims were the rebels whose plans were revealed to the Capitol; however, they soon became a problem for the Capitol too, once the rebels worked out how to manipulate their spies! Later victims of the jabberjays were the tributes in the 75th Hunger Games, such as Katniss and Finnick, who were very shaken by their encounter with the creatures, even after they were persuaded by Beetee that the screams the jabberjays were repeating were not real and just altered recordings of human speech.

LIZARD MUTTS

Purpose: The Capitol released these muttations for one reason only: to kill Katniss and the rest of Squad 451.

Features: When Katniss heard her name being hissed repeatedly she wondered what could be making the sound, but when she found out she was even more scared! The lizard/human hybrids are the size of full-grown adults with tight white skin, long reptilian tails, clawed hands and feet, arched backs, and facial features that resemble both of the species they are derived from. They can stand upright with their heads jutting forward or scurry along on all four of their limbs. Although these mutts can be killed, it takes dozens of bullets to achieve this and there always seem to be more to replace those that fall.

For Katniss, their scent – a mixture of blood and roses, just like President Snow's breath – is particularly terrifying. For everyone else, their worst feature is the fact that they kill their victims instantly by biting into their necks and ripping their heads right off!

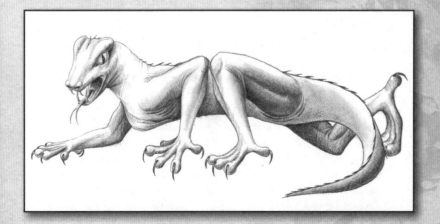

In action: During the second rebellion of the districts against the Capitol, President Snow realised that some of Squad 451 had escaped his bombings and gone underground, so he sent a huge group of lizard muttations into the sewers to finish them off.

Victims: All but invincible, and in massive numbers, the reptiles meant certain death for anyone who crossed their paths. Although programmed to track down Katniss and her crew, they had no problem killing anyone else who got in the way. So, several Peacekeepers and Avoxes working in the sewers were decapitated during their attack, as well as Jackson, Leeg 1, Castor, Holmes and Finnick Odair from Squad 451.

The lizard mutts were only stopped when Katniss detonated her Holo and blew up the whole sewer.

> **Squad 451** = District 13's special, highly-trained team of rebels who were sent on a mission to the Capitol during the second rebellion and were the on-screen faces of the war against the Capitol.

> **Holo** = a device used by District 13's rebels during the second rebellion to see where the Capitol's dangerous pods are hidden. They are only activated by a specific commander's voice and blow up everything in a five-yard radius if someone in the squadron repeats the word 'nightlock' three times.

MONKEY MUTTS

Purpose: These ferocious primates were put into the 75th Hunger Games arena to attack, and potentially kill, some of the tributes.

Features: Almost half the size of a human adult, these creatures have orange fur and converge in trees like real monkeys, but the slightest glance from a human is all it takes for them to prove they are actually lab-bred killing machines. With their fangs and claws bared, they can jump huge distances from tree to tree, and slide down them as fast as lightning. They can even somersault through the air to avoid arrows!

In action: In the clock-like 75th Hunger Games arena, these monkey-like muttations inhabited the jungle in the three-to-four-o'clock sector. At first, the tributes took their presence to be a sign that the air was

good, but the mutts soon showed their deadly side as the Gamemakers set them to attack mode. Once the monkeys had inflicted sufficient damage, those that were alive retreated back into the trees and the carcasses of the rest were covered by the jungle vines and vanished.

Victims: The monkeys had the potential to harm any of the Quarter Quell tributes, but they certainly had one fatal victim. When Katniss, Peeta, and Finnick were locked in a battle with the horde of mutts, one looked set to finish Peeta off – until the female from District 6 jumped in the way! The monkey sunk its fangs into her chest before Peeta could stab it, causing internal damage beneath her shallow wounds, and she died a few minutes later. The mutts may also have been used by the Capitol in other Games.

PINK BIRD MUTTATIONS

Purpose: The candy-coloured birds were part of the beautiful but deadly 50th Hunger Games arena.

Features: A pastel-pink colour with long, thin beaks that they use as deadly weapons, they gather in a flock.

In action: Like all the mutts released into the Hunger Games, these birds were able to kill, or at least seriously injure, the tributes.

Victims: Although they may have killed more, their one known victim was District 12 tribute Maysilee Donner, who died after one of the birds stabbed her through the neck with its beak during the 50th Hunger Games. At the sound of her screams, Haymitch was on the scene and running to her rescue. Tragically, though, the damage had already been done. The most Haymitch could do was to take the hand of his former ally and watch her life slip away.

TRACKER JACKERS

Purpose: Tracker jackers are a type of wasp introduced by the Capitol during the Dark Days to harm the rebels as they are able to kill or, at the very least, send people mad with their stings.

Features: Larger than normal wasps, tracker jackers have solid gold bodies and stings filled with poisonous venom. If you have the misfortune to be stung by one, you will immediately develop a plum-sized swelling in the spot where you received the sting, and you will instantly feel the effects of the venom kicking in. These can vary depending on how many times you are stung, if you have the sense to remove the stings straight away, and if you happen to have any healing leaves or medicine to hand. One thing that is guaranteed is that you will suffer terrifying hallucinations that will make you question your sanity.

The other feature of tracker jackers is hinted at by the first part of their name: if you are unwise or careless enough to disturb their nests, they will track you down and try to kill you!

In action: Tracker-jacker nests were planted around the districts by the Capitol during the rebellion. Some of these nests still exist throughout Panem. The deadly wasps also made a big impact in the 74th Hunger Games, where a large nest of them was hidden in a tree.

Victims: With nests spread throughout Panem, countless people must have fallen victim to tracker jackers – in and out of the Hunger Games arena. Certainly the outcome of the 74th Hunger Games would not have been the same without them! When Katniss Everdeen got trapped up a tree by the deadly Career Pack, she thought her chances of escape were slim. Luckily for her (and very unluckily for them) her fellow tribute Rue pointed out that she was sharing the tree with a tracker-jacker nest. Knowing it was her only chance of making it down from the tree alive, Katniss dropped the nest on the unsuspecting Careers beneath her. Though she suffered a few nasty stings in the process, Katniss herself got off relatively lightly (suffering gruesome hallucinations for two days only) as she had the good sense to remove the stings quickly. While some of the others also escaped a worse fate by running straight towards water to ease their pain, the girls from Districts 1 and 4 were fatally stung.

After the 75th Hunger Games, the Capitol captured Peeta Mellark and used tracker-jacker venom to 'hijack' him. They altered his memories of Katniss by recalling her to his mind before injecting him with a small amount of venom, which raised feelings of fear and doubt in him. By the time they were finished, he was left with nothing but negative thoughts towards Katniss. A changed man, he looked upon the girl he once loved and saw a deadly mutt who needed to be killed! He had to work hard with District 13's doctors to learn which of his memories were real and which had been distorted by the tracker jackers, and ended up feeling like he himself was a mutt being used by the Capitol.

WOLF MUTTS

Purpose: As the 74th Hunger Games were drawing to a close, the Gamemakers decided to spice up the competition by releasing a pack of genetically-altered wolves into the arena. Perhaps the wolves were sent in to force the final three tributes into the same area of the arena, or to reduce their numbers – in the end, they did both!

Features: At first glance, these mutts just look like huge wolves with ten-centimetre-long, razor-sharp claws. However, a closer look shows that they have many unnatural abilities. They can stand on their very powerful hind legs, which also allow them to jump extremely high, and they move their paws as if they have wrists. They seem to communicate through high-pitched yelps as they work out the best way to attack their prey.

There is something even more unnerving about these mutts, though. Their numbered collars, thick coats of varying colour and texture, and distinctive eyes can only mean one thing – each wolf represents one of the dead tributes from the competition! The big mutt with silky waves of blond fur, green eyes, a collar with a jewelled number 1 on it (to reflect District 1's industry) is Glimmer, while the small red one with amber eyes is District 5's Foxface. One of the wolves has the same ashen hair and hazel eyes as the boy from District 9, the one who jumps the highest is Thresh, and the littlest, snarling one with big brown eyes, dark glossy fur and a woven collar numbered 11 (which resembles her woven tribute token) is Rue. Their eyes look so human that they may actually belong to the dead tributes, or perhaps the DNA of the fallen tributes has been mixed with the wolves to create the creepy look. Either way, it's clearly another of the Gamemakers' cruel tricks to spook the surviving tributes, and it has the desired effect!

In action: These muttations were used in the 74th Hunger Games and their specific features, relating to the tributes from this year, suggests that they probably weren't used again, although the Capitol may have created versions of them at another time.

Victims: These mutts affected each of the last trio of tributes in different ways. One wolf harmed Peeta physically by ripping a deep gash into his leg – he lost so much blood he wasn't sure he'd make it to the end of the Games. Katniss was affected psychologically as she was left with nightmares for months afterwards about the way her fellow tributes had been turned into evil creatures. Without a doubt, Cato was the main victim of the wolf mutts as they tortured him, and used him to torture the other tributes. In the struggle between the final three to stay on the Cornucopia – and out of reach of the jumping wolves – Cato lost. However, the warrior from District 2 was not prepared to go down without a fight! Covered in armour and wielding a sword, Cato was able to battle the mutts throughout the night, hanging on until he was just a bloody mess. The sound of his moans as the wolves attacked him haunted his rivals. In the end, Katniss decided it would be kindest to kill him with one of her arrows. The remaining wolf mutts subsequently retreated into a hole in the ground with their mission achieved.

MOCKINGJAYS

Purpose: Mockingjays were not created intentionally; these birds are 'accidental muttations', born when male jabberjays, abandoned in the wild after they ceased to be of use to the Capitol, mated with female mockingbirds.

Features: Mockingjays are mostly black in colour, like their forefather jabberjays, with white patches on their wings from their mockingbird mothers. Though mockingjays can't repeat human speech in the same way that jabberjays do, they can mimic the songs of birds and humans. They copy the tone of a singer's voice and repeat several verses if they like a voice.

In action: Mockingjays bred after the end of the Dark Days and still remain in some of the districts. They are mostly treated as songbirds, except in District 11, where they are used to pass a tune throughout the orchards to signal the end of the day to the workers. After Katniss wears a mockingjay pin (given to her by her friend Madge Undersee) as her token in the 74th Hunger Games, accessories in the shape of the bird become all the rage in the Capitol. More importantly, the mockingjay becomes the symbol of the rebellion in the districts, fuelled by Cinna's mockingjay-inspired outfits, worn by Katniss before the 75th Hunger Games and during her rebellion broadcasts.

Victims: The Capitol! The Capitol never intended for mockingjays to exist, yet they are creatures born out of the Capitol's own mistakes (breeding jabberjays to spy on the rebels). This is why the mockingjay becomes such an important symbol to those fighting against the Capitol in the second rebellion. Just as the mockingjays pass on messages in the orchards of District 11, their image is used to spread the spirit of the uprising.

NAVIGATING
THE CAPITOL

A fter winning the 74th Hunger Games, Katniss and Peeta thought they had waved goodbye to the Capitol, but it seems they just can't escape it! After travelling through the rest of Panem on their Victory Tour, they end up back in the silly and surreal city, and they find it just as strange as before. Here, with the help of a very 'informative' local guide*, we take a look at the bizarre trends and over-the-top culture of the Capitol . . .

Disclaimer: the views and opinions expressed by your tour guide are not our own!

CAPITOL CONNECTIONS

Suzanne Collins has said that she wants *The Hunger Games* trilogy to make readers ask themselves 'questions about how elements of the book might be relevant in their own lives. And, if they're disturbing, what they might do about them.' The unusual spelling of Panem's Capitol city seems to link it to the United States Capitol. This is the meeting place of the United States Congress, the legislative (or law-making) branch of the US government. Maybe Collins is comparing the rich Capitol to America (and other wealthy countries in the western world) and she is asking us to think about how our lifestyles are supported by, and affect, poorer and developing countries (represented by the other, poorer districts in Panem).

'Hello there! First time in the Capitol? Well, let me show you around then!

'Welcome to the largest, richest and most exciting city in Panem! You probably already know that the Capitol governs the twelve surrounding districts, so it really is *the* place to be. Here in City Circle is where all the big decisions are made – that huge mansion over there is where President Snow lives! All around us you'll notice the brightly coloured houses, so different from the drab dull buildings in the districts. We simply love bright colours here, the brighter the better!

'In fact, we try to make everything as vivid as possible – our clothes, our hair, even our skin. It's all about standing out! You should try one of our "enhancements" while you're here; you could get a nice face tattoo or dye yourself a lovely shade of green, or perhaps you'd like to get something even more exciting, such as whiskers or gem implants. You'd be the talk of the town among all the plainly presented people back home – they might even mistake you for a genuine Capitol citizen! If you really want to fit in here though, you should get yourself a mockingjay accessory; they're all the rage ever since Katniss Everdeen won the Hunger Games.

'We've got mockingjay watches, belt buckles . . . you can even get a mockingjay tattoo if you want to be really cutting edge. I think the mockingjay will be in fashion for quite some time – at least a couple of months. This year's Games were so fun, weren't they? A classic year, I'd say, what with the romance and the twist at the end, and the next one is guaranteed to be just as good – a Quarter Quell! It's just a shame that we'll have to wait so long for it; the Hunger Games are always the highlight of our social calendar here. Everyone gets so excited to see what the Gamemakers will do next, and we all support our favourites (mine's District 4, even though they didn't do very well last year. Finnick Odair is just *so* dreamy!). Also, Games season is when all the best parties take place – not that we need much of an excuse to throw a party in the Capitol!

'When you get a chance, you should really attend one of our celebrations. If you think our buildings are beautiful, you should see the decorations that some people have at their parties. There are rooms transformed into "flower gardens" with big dance floors in the middle for the performers. A friend of mine, Venia, was in Katniss' prep team for the Hunger Games, so she was lucky enough to go to the engagement party President Snow held at his house for her and Peeta at the end of their Victory Tour. She said that the ceiling was designed to look like a starry night sky, and the musicians were floating on clouds! Can you imagine?

'And the food . . . as you've probably noticed, we love our food here in the Capitol – you can get anything you want at the press of a button. Katniss Everdeen even said her favourite thing about the Capitol was our rich lamb stew with dried plums, although I'm sure she must have been joking. At parties, we take the cooking to another level with tables piled with all sorts of dishes, from roasted meats and fresh seafood to tureens of soup and, of course, fountains of alcohol. I know what you're thinking: how do we manage to eat it all? Well, we have a great way of solving that problem – alongside the food we have a clear liquid drink that makes us throw up what we've already had to make room for more! Genius, isn't it?

ROMAN ROOTS

There is a very clear link between the Capitol and Ancient Roman society. Suzanne Collins herself has said that 'the world of Panem, particularly the Capitol, is loaded with Roman references'. Not only do the people of the Capitol live the sort of extravagant lifestyles rich Romans were famous for – including watching people fight to the death in gladiatorial games, and making themselves vomit during feasts so they can eat more – but many of the characters from the Capitol have traditionally Roman names (Octavia, Seneca, Flavius, Portia) and lots of the words they use come from Latin, such as 'avox' meaning 'without voice'.

'You will probably have noticed that the city is shaped like a big square, split into smaller squares. Under the ground we have a complex sewer system – but don't worry, I won't be taking you to see it! Only the Avoxes go down there, and rats. I'm sure you've seen the Avoxes all around the city, there must be some in your hotel. (Gorgeous place you're staying in, by the way. I love all the different oils and scents they use in their showers and the way the windows can focus on any part of the city you want them to. After staying there, I even got myself one of those machines that detangles your hair; I just don't know how I'd cope without it now!) Anyway, Avoxes get all the worst jobs as part of their punishment for their terrible crimes – the other part, of course, is having their tongues cut off. Some visitors from the districts seem to have a problem with being served by them, but you don't need to worry about that – it's what they're there for after all!

REALITY BITES

It may be hard for us to understand how inconsiderate the Capitol inhabitants are, but if we look at the reality TV appeal of the Hunger Games – broadcast live throughout Panem – we can see a little of our own culture. In the 'reality' shows that we all watch, there is usually a competition element, as in the Hunger Games, which makes us want to find out who'll win. More worryingly, these shows often also involve embarrassment or rejection for some participants, yet they are a very popular form of entertainment. Obviously, there is still a long way to go before we think that watching real people die for the sake of a contest is fun, but this is the path we walk when we separate what happens on 'reality' TV shows from the true reality of the contestants' lives. The people of the Capitol simply don't understand the impact of the horrible things that happen in their world because they don't see or feel the negative results. It is interesting that when President Snow announces that past victors will have to compete in the Quarter Quell, many Capitol residents are upset. Finally, the cruelty of the Games affects them because the victors they have become attached to over the years are in danger. It seems that there may be a little compassion and empathy beneath their silly wigs and makeup after all!

'Now, if you look to the east you'll see the mountains, which form a barrier between here and the eastern region of Panem. This natural barrier is part of the reason why it was so easy for the Capitol to overcome the rebels during their uprising (besides our obvious superiority!), because our air forces could target them more easily. It's a shame that the districts had to start a rebellion for no reason but I suppose if they hadn't, we wouldn't have the entertainment of the Hunger Games now! At least we all get on much better these days! The districts provide us with all our products: we get our luxury items from District 1, and seafood from District 4; really, it's a wonder that they have anything left for themselves!

'Well, we're coming back to the City Centre now so sadly our tour is nearly over. I hope you learnt a lot about our beautiful city and that you enjoy the rest of your time in the Capitol! Like I said, try to attend a party and get yourself a makeover, even if you just buy a colourful wig like mine. Another great thing to do while you're here is to check out one of the past Hunger Games arenas – we have them all preserved as tourist attractions. You can re-watch the Games, take part in re-enactments, and even visit the sites of all the deaths – it's amazing! (I recommend the arena for the 50th Hunger Games; it's *so* pretty. The snow-capped mountain and the flower-filled meadow look just as good up-close as they did on the screen. Just be careful not to smell any of the blossoms!) Whatever you do in the Capitol, have fun!'

GROWING INFERNO

When Katniss and Peeta threatened to commit suicide by eating nightlock berries rather than attempting to kill one another to win the 74th Hunger Games, they were only trying to stay alive. They did not think that their refusal would be seen as an act of defiance that would ignite a rebellion. But that's exactly what it did.

After winning the Games, Haymitch warned them both that the Capitol was not happy with their refusal to follow the Gamemaker's rules, so they continued to act as star-crossed lovers and claim they were only acting out of desperation. Just before their Victory Tour, President Snow pays Katniss a visit to tell her that in the districts her behaviour has been interpreted as a protest against the Capitol, and it could lead to a full-scale rebellion. To stop this happening, and protect her family and friends from being hurt by the President, she must keep up the act and continue to profess her love for Peeta. Katniss is both excited and scared by the possibility that some of the districts may be staging uprisings against the Capitol's rule. As she takes part in the Victory Tour through Panem, she begins to see the real effect of her actions on the people who were watching her in the Games.

With the help of pieces of evidence from the districts, let's take a look at how the rebellion is spreading throughout Panem . . .

An article from the underground rebel newspaper
Mockingjay Murmurs *about Katniss and Peeta's trip to District 11*

MOCKINGJAY MURMURS

**The only newspaper in Panem bringing you the *real* news!
Limited distribution**

The Victory Tour – the second chance for the Capitol to rub the cruelty of the Hunger Games in our faces – has begun, and the

first stop was District 11. Yesterday Katniss Everdeen and Peeta Mellark appeared in the city square. Also present were the families of their fellow tributes, Rue and Thresh. In the arena, we watched Everdeen and Mellark act with more dignity and humanity than most of the other tributes put together. Never more so than when they refused to follow instructions and kill each other, preferring to die instead. We were therefore expecting a lot from them, and they certainly didn't disappoint.

Mellark spoke first, honouring District 11's dead tributes and promising to donate one month's worth of the victors' yearly winnings to their grieving families. If the Captiol allows it, this will surely keep the recipients from falling into poverty, and may go some way in easing their loss. Never before has a Hunger Games victor offered to do such a thing, and the crowd in District 11 was very appreciative. But there was another surprise to come. At the ceremony's conclusion, Everdeen stepped forward and gave a touching speech about Thresh and Rue, which obviously came straight from the heart.

This was the cue that the good people of District 11 had been waiting for. At the sound of old Cropper's whistle, the whole crowd gave the traditional signal of respect from District 12 to the girl who had befriended their tributes. (The gesture consists of pressing the three middle fingers of your left hand to your lips and holding them out in front of you, in the same way that Katniss saluted Rue's body as it was lifted out of the Hunger Games arena.) Following this, the Mayor quickly rushed to finish the ceremony and the guests were hurried out of the square, which was when the real show began.

The Peacekeepers picked old Cropper out of the crowd, dragged him to the stage, forced him to kneel down and shot him through the head. That's right, *they killed him for whistling*. Then, just for good measure, they fired a couple of shots into the air to warn the rest of the crowd to stay subdued, and not to protest about this outrageous act of violence against an old man – or else they would be the next ones to find themselves with a bullet in their skulls.

Their tactics may have worked for now, but any Peacekeepers who get their hands on this, be warned: we will not be kept silent for much longer.

Keep the spirit of the mockingjay alive and spread the word. Long live the revolution!

As they travel through the rest of the districts, Katniss notices that there is discontent brewing throughout Panem. She can feel the anger of the crowds she sees. They are starting to push back against the Capitol and she knows that it is too late for her and Peeta to stop things changing with their desperate lovers act. Katniss highlights Districts 3, 4 and 8 as being particularly defiant.

Back in District 12, Katniss stumbles across a news report from District 8 while at the home of her friend Madge. The report is meant only for the eyes of Madge's father, District 12's Mayor, but when she sees the television screen showing a full-blown riot taking place in District 8's main square, with screaming citizens throwing bricks and burning down buildings while Peacekeepers shoot at random in an attempt to stop them, Katniss knows the rebellion has begun.

A coded message passed between the factory workers in District 8

eeoplP fo tistricD 8, rof oot gonl ew eavh dubmittes ot het sapitol'C lvie eegimr. satnisK dna aeetP dhowes su that eht lapitoC nac eb dhallengec dna won st'i eimt ot wollof rheit deal. set'L eakt kacb lontroc fo ruo nwo tistricd!

ruO nlap si eimpls – ew eisr pu dna eeizs lontroc fo eht naim sentrec ni tistricD 8. Eht seacekeeperP ton'w eb dreparep rof ti dna fi hnouge fo su eakt tarp ew nac evercomo mhet yasile. set'L ees woh yhet eikl that!

texN keew eht yictorV rouT sassep hhrougt eerh. sA ew era lla dequirer ot dttena, ew lilw esu ti sa a lehearsar rof eht nevolutior. Everyone lilw eb dlacep ni a meat dna that meat lilw eb dssignea a guildinb. gurinD eht yeremonc, hace meat nac nositiop ftseli rean sti dpecifies guildinb ot eracticp woh ti lilw korw nhew eht eimt somec rof eht rropep gprisinu. nheT, ta eht texn yandatorm cublip tvene, ew nac tup eht nlap onti nctioa rof lear!

nisteL tuo nt eht yactorf rof rurthef srrangementa.

Can you crack the code to work out the rebels' plan?
Once you have, rewrite the message opposite.

Turn to page 95 to find out if you got it right!

Not long after she has seen the riot on screen, Katniss is hunting illegally in the woods when she comes across a woman and a girl from District 8. Twill and Bonnie describe how the uprising to wrest control of the main power centres back from the Peacekeepers was planned in the loud factories of District 8, and carried out when the whole population had to gather in the main square to watch Katniss and Peeta's interview with Caesar Flickerman (when Peeta proposed to Katniss to keep up the pretence of their romance). They successfully took hold of the Justice Building, the Peacekeepers' Headquarters and the Communication Centre as well as the railroad, the granary, the power station and armoury, until the Capitol sent in an army of Peacekeepers to restore order. The whole district was put on lockdown for a week, with the only television broadcasts showing the executions of the suspected leaders of the rebellion. When they were told to return to 'normal', the factory where the plan originated was bombed. This killed Twill's husband and Bonnie's entire family, so they ran away.

They tell Katniss that they are heading to District 13, an idea she finds ridiculous because everyone knows the 13th district is nothing more than rubble – a harsh reminder of the price Panem's people paid for the first rebellion against the Capitol, isn't it?

A private letter sent from one rebel to another

To Mockingjay 142,

Have you heard the rumours going round about the possible existence of District 13? I know what you're thinking – sounds crazy, doesn't it? But if you stop and think about it there are a few things about that place that simply don't add up . . .

Firstly, there's the fact that District 13's main industry was supposed to be graphite mining. Yes, this is what we've all believed for years *because the Capitol told us to*, but according to my sources there were only a few small mines there, and their population was fairly big. So what were the rest of them doing with their time? Some people are saying that 13 must've really been a nuclear power station. If that's true, it would mean that the Capitol couldn't afford to completely wipe them out for fear of a nuclear attack, and they could have bargained for a truce. Can you imagine? There could be a whole other district beyond the Capitol's control. What's more, they could have access to weapons that would help us win the rebellion!

Of course, it's all speculation, but there was one thing that they pointed out, which really made me think they have a point. You know when they show us footage on the news that's supposed to be filmed live in District 13? I swear they have been using the same old clips in the background for years. If you don't believe me, watch the corner of the screen next time. You will see the same shot of a mockingjay flying across it every time. I noticed it myself after they told me and it got me thinking – if what they're showing us isn't really what's in District 13, what is there to hide? Apparently 13 had the resources to survive underground, so there could be thousands of them there just waiting to be discovered.

As I said, at the moment this is all just talk, but a group of the men are planning to pack up and head to District 13 to see how much of it is true. It might seem like madness, but I'm thinking of going with them. We can all feel that change is coming, and maybe the people of District 13 can help make that change for the better. Anyway, let's meet tonight in the usual secret spot to talk about this. Don't mention it to anyone and burn this letter once you've read it.

From,
Mockingjay 127

Katniss quickly dismisses the idea of District 13 still being operational, as she cannot believe that they could have resources to hand and not even try to help the other districts, who have continued to suffer under the Capitol's brutal regime in the seventy-five years since the Dark Days.

After meeting Twill and Bonnie, she does not hear anything more about what might be happening in the other districts, not until her Hunger Games prep team come to style her for a photo shoot in which she has to model potential bridal gowns for her wedding to Peeta. From what she hears them saying about delays in district-produced goods reaching the Capitol, she starts to suspect that the rebellion has spread further than just District 8.

An article in the Capitol gossip magazine Capitol Chit-Chat *lamenting the delays in supplies that they are experiencing:*

Is it just us at *Capitol Chit-Chat*, or have the shops been out of *everything* lately? Not even our secret contact in the music biz could get his hands on the newest musical chips from District 3 – it was a serious downer at our bi-weekly office party! And you're going to have to work that much harder to look seriously fabulous this week (see our top fashion tips on page fourteen!), 'cause last time we checked everybody's still out of those ribbons and accessories you really *need* to finish off your outfit – I mean, what are they doing in District 8 anyway? (On one or two occasions we've even had to resort to recycling outfits we've *already worn*!) And don't even get us started on the serious seafood shortage. (We've heard there are storms in District 4 or something, but you'd think they'd at least manage to get our all-time fave prawn cocktail up to the CCC offices – we're getting withdrawal symptoms!) So come on Prez Snow, we're desperate, when is this going to get sorted out? Because we just don't know how much longer we can go on without our necessities!

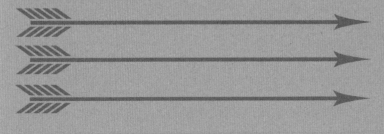

While the Capitol is dealing with unrest in many of Panem's districts, its crackdown on liberty has also spread to District 12. In District 11, Katniss considered their high barbed-wire fence lined with watchtowers full of armed guards excessive in comparison to District 12's lacklustre policing force. Though upon her return from the tour, this soon changes.

An official memo from the Capitol to the Peacekeepers of District 12.

President Snow's Office,
The City Circle,
The Capitol

For the attention of:
Mr Cray, Head Peacekeeper of District 12

It has come to our notice that for some time now, the Peacekeeping force of District 12 has been lax in enforcing many of the laws set out clearly in the Treaty of Treason. As a result, it seems that a liberal culture has become the norm in the district, allowing the existence of a thriving black market (which Peacekeepers themselves frequent!) and an acceptance of illegal hunting practices outside of the district borders. In particular, we are aware that citizens Katniss Everdeen and Gale Hawthorne regularly escape to hunt, exiting through the fence surrounding the district, which is not kept constantly electrified as it should be.

President Snow himself has expressed his dissatisfaction at the running of District 12 after a recent visit there. This letter is an official warning to you and your Peacekeeping force, who seem to have forgotten your duty. The people of District 12 are not your friends, they are your inferiors. Their lawbreaking behaviour will no longer be accepted, and neither will yours. We intend to implement a number of changes in District 12 to put an end to the inappropriate way of life that has been allowed to develop:

1) A large banner displaying the seal of Panem will be hung from the Justice Building, as a reminder of the Capitol's power.

2) The city square will be cleaned up and appropriately restored.

3) A whipping post, stockades and a gallows will be erected in the city square as a deterrent, and to be used to punish any form of lawbreaking carried out in District 12.

4) The fence surrounding the district will be kept permanently electrified.

5) The black market 'The Hob' will be burned down.

There will also be a new and increased Peacekeeping force sent out to the district, who will act professionally at all times and remain a constant presence in the city square. They will be armed with machine guns to prevent any unrest. This letter serves as a notice to you and any of your colleagues in District 12 who are deemed unreliable and a potential threat to the security of Panem – you shall all be moved to other districts shortly. Your official replacement, Romulus Thread, will arrive tomorrow to take his position, and he intends to set to work straight away, whipping District 12 back to shape. We trust that he will encounter no problems.

The Law Enforcement Department,
President Snow's Head Office

REVOLUTIONARY REPEATS

Katniss is surprised by President Snow's confession that her behaviour in the Hunger Games could be enough to start an uprising in the districts of Panem, which seem to be so firmly under the Capitol's control. Perhaps if she had access to our history books she wouldn't be!

Just look at the evidence of these two famous cases:

18th-Century FRANCE

RULED BY: King Louis XVI and his extravagant Austrian wife Marie-Antoinette.

MAJOR GRIPES: Widespread hunger and malnutrition caused

by years of poor harvest, rising food prices and poor transport to distribute food.

DISAFFECTION FUELLED BY: 1. Ruling classes' apparent unconcern for the sufferings of the people. Marie-Antoinette probably never said 'Let them eat cake!' in response to hearing about the shortage of bread to feed her people – but the famous phrase certainly captured her general attitude! The frivolous young queen was completely out of touch with the sufferings of the average Frenchman. 2. Expensive wars taking money from a starving populace. 3. New ideas about equality were causing people to question religion and the privileges of the nobility.

RESULT: Revolution in 1789. (It was inevitable, wasn't it?)

RUSSIA at the turn of the 20th century

RULED BY: Tsar Nicholas II (heavily influenced by a certain malevolent figure named Rasputin) and his unpopular German wife, the Empress Alexandra.

MAJOR GRIPES: Like France, widespread hunger was a problem and the gap between rich and poor was immense.

DISAFFECTION FUELLED BY: 1. Again like France, Russia had a weak ruler in Tsar Nicholas, who had an unpopular foreign wife. Nicholas also had an even more unpopular figure at his side (in this case his advisor Rasputin). Rasputin has gone down in history as a conman at best (and something altogether more sinister according to some reports!). What was certain was the population loathed him. 2. As in France, new ideas about equality were starting to spread through the educated classes and it was only a matter of time before they were communicated to the masses.

RESULT: Revolutions (two of them) in 1917.

You can probably see that the situation in Panem is not too different from how it was in both France and Russia before their revolutions. People in the districts are poor, hungry, overworked, oppressed and unhappy. This is made harder by the fact that there is such a contrast between their dreary lives and the extravagant way of life in the Capitol. When you think about it like this, it's no surprise that all it took was the act of Katniss and Peeta standing up to authority by refusing to kill each other for the tension in Panem to tip over the edge into an all-out rebellion!

CRACKING THE CODE!

The rebels have changed the first and last letter of each word round to stop the Capitol from reading their plans if they happen to get their hands on the message.

Here is their plot unscrambled:

People of District 8, for too long we have submitted to the Capitol's evil regime. Katniss and Peeta showed us that the Capitol can be challenged, and now it's time to follow their lead. Let's take back control of our own district!

Our plan is simple – we rise up and seize control of the main centres in District 8. The Peacekeepers won't be prepared for it and, if enough of us take part, we can overcome them easily. Let's see how they like that!

Next week the Victory Tour passes through here. As we are all required to attend, we will use it as a rehearsal for the revolution. Everyone will be placed in a team and that team will be assigned a building. During the ceremony, each team can position itself near its specified building to practice how it will work when the time comes for the proper uprising. Then, at the next mandatory public event, we can put the plan into action for real!

Listen out in the factory for further arrangements.

QUARTER QUELL

When Katniss won the 74th Hunger Games, she never expected to be able to put the experience entirely behind her; the Victory Tour, speculation about her relationship with Peeta, years of having to mentor future District 12 tributes and a lifetime of horrific memories ruled out any possibility of that ever happening. But she did at least think that she had left the arena behind for good.

Katniss is too young to have lived through a Quarter Quell before. This especially torturous version of the yearly Hunger Games takes place every twenty-five years (every quarter of a century) and always incorporates some new and particularly cruel element, designed to punish the people in the districts just that little bit more for their past rebellion. Katniss' only knowledge of the Quells comes from what she has heard about previous ones. In the 25th Hunger Games, to hammer home the message that their children were being taken as a result of their own actions, the people of each district had to vote on which children in the community would become their tributes for that year. In the 50th, the year that Haymitch won, twice the usual number of tributes (four per district, forty-eight overall) were reaped as a reminder that two rebels died for each Capitol citizen in the uprisings.

A few months before a Quarter Quell, the President picks a prepared envelope from a box filled with assorted others written by those who originally devised the Hunger Games, and reads out the special challenge that the year's tributes will have to face in honour of the Quell. Quarter Quells are even more brutal and cruel than the annual Hunger Games, but this knowledge doesn't prepare Katniss for what President Snow reads from the card. He announces that, for the 75th anniversary of the end of the Dark Days, to remind those in the districts that even their strongest representatives cannot overpower the Capitol, one male and one female tribute will be picked from among the existing Hunger Games victors of each district. As the only living female victor from District 12, the ruling means that Katniss will definitely be going back into the arena and either Peeta or Haymitch will have to join her.

Though the Hunger Games in their very nature are designed to remind the people in the districts of the Capitol's absolute power over them, Katniss cannot help but wonder if President Snow has engineered this plan specifically to eliminate her. After all, as a symbol of rebellion she has become a threat to him but as a new Hunger Games victor she is too popular for him to simply kill. The new rule conveniently ensures that she has to go into the arena and face almost certain death. So this is the perfect way for President Snow to get rid of her without revealing his motives, and to prove his dominance again, right?

Wrong. The Hunger Games are always unfair, but the idea of putting those who have already been through that hellish experience once back into the arena to relive it all over again is a bitter pill for the former victors and the people of Panem to swallow. President Snow might think the 75th Hunger Games will provide the answer to his problems in the districts, but in the end it may cause him more trouble than he could have ever imagined . . .

PRE-GAMES

The reaping gives Katniss and Peeta a chance to get a first look at their competition, made up of many old faces they recognise from previous Games. On reaping day in District 12, Effie draws Haymitch's name as the male tribute to enter the arena alongside Katniss. But it comes as a surprise to no one, least of all Katniss and Haymitch, when Peeta instantly volunteers to take the latter's place so that he can protect Katniss in the arena.

Upon their arrival in the Capitol, Katniss realises straight away that the Quarter Quell will play out very differently to the game she participated in the previous year. At the opening ceremony, where Katniss and Peeta dazzle everyone once again in costumes that glow like embers, she notices how all the victors interact with each other freely because they have spent years side by side as mentors in previous Games and are old friends. (She also notes how some of the stylists for the other victors have tried to capture the success of Cinna and Portia's costumes by incorporating flaming accessories into their own tributes' outfits. However, these are mostly so little in keeping with the rest of their costumes that they just look ridiculous. The past victors from District 10, for example, wear cow costumes (to represent their livestock industry) with flaming belts that make them look like they are cooking themselves!

The camaraderie extends to the Training Centre, where all the former victors eat together at lunch. As the most recent winners, Katniss and Peeta are at a disadvantage when it comes to forming bonds with the others but Haymitch urges them to try to make friends. Many of the other victors approach them and, after witnessing Katniss' impressive shooting skills in action, most of them put in a request with Haymitch to be their allies. Even though Katniss and Peeta reluctantly begin to like quite a few of their competitors, they decide it will be easier to just work with each other.

When the time comes for the victors to showcase their skills to the Gamemakers, Katniss and Peeta are unsure what to do. Without telling the other, they both end up taking a risk by performing a controversial act. Peeta – inspired by a comment Katniss made in the waiting room – paints a picture of Rue covered in the flowers Katniss placed on her dead body, while Katniss hangs a dummy painted with the name of last year's Head Gamemaker, who was killed after letting both Katniss and Peeta live. Their attempts to hold the Gamemakers accountable for the cruelty that takes place in the arena shock Haymitch and Effie and earn them unprecedented training scores of twelve points each. However, neither Peeta nor Katniss falls into the mistake of thinking that these high scores signify approval; the Gamemakers have certainly awarded them to make the rebellious District 12 tributes major targets for their rivals.

But it isn't only Katniss and Peeta who are setting out to rub the Gamemakers up the wrong way, something that becomes obvious in the round of interviews with Caesar Flickerman the night before the Games start. Throughout the interviews, the other victors' anger at being thrown back into the Hunger Games arena becomes clear as they subtly cast a bad light on President Snow and the Capitol. Some remark how sad it is that the Capitol audience will lose the victors they have grown to love; others question whether the victors returning to the Games is legal and why the all-powerful President can't stop something so unfair. They whip the audience up into a frenzy, with people crying and demanding change, which only becomes intensified when Katniss appears in the wedding dress she was supposed to wear for her wedding to Peeta. President Snow requested that she don the dress for her interview but the audience's outraged reaction soon makes it obvious that this was a mistake.

Katniss laments the fact that no one will be able to see her wear it at her wedding and then starts to spin in it, as Cinna instructed her to. To her surprise, and the shock of the crowd, the white dress catches fire and turns into a black feathery dress with white patches on the sleeves – making her a mockingjay, the symbol of rebellion in the districts.

It seems that no victor could possibly make a bigger impact on the Capitol audience, until Peeta takes the stage. As he did the year before, he shares some banter with Caesar before making an announcement that will shock and thrill the audience (and surprise Katniss!). In his last interview with Caesar, Peeta proclaimed undying love for Katniss; this time, he claims that he has already unofficially married her in a traditional District 12 ceremony. Then he drops the real bombshell by claiming that Katniss is pregnant, sending the audience wild. Not even the bloodthirsty Capitol citizens can help but think that to send Katniss back into the arena, risking not only her own life but that of her unborn child, is an unspeakable crime.

Katniss and Peeta hold hands and the other victors rise to join them, some eagerly, some more reluctantly, until all twenty-four of them stand together. Such a display of unity between the districts that the Capitol has striven to keep separate is unheard of and Katniss knows that the sight of it must be having a big impact throughout Panem.

So, the victors forced to be tributes again in the 75th Hunger Games stage their own mini-uprising before the whole of Panem, causing trouble for President Snow before they have even entered the arena. How long will their defiance last though, once they are sent into the arena with only a half-inch layer of blue jumpsuit to protect them?

ARENA

As soon as the tributes are lifted into the Hunger Games arena, Katniss realises that the layout is very unusual. It is shaped like a perfect dome, with force fields keeping the tributes trapped inside. The tributes arrive in the arena on metal plates that rise up through glass tubes. When the glass retracts, the contestants are left standing in a ring around the Cornucopia. Between the tributes and the horn, is salt water, divided into twelve sections by thin strips of land, with two tributes per section. The water poses major problem for a lot of the victors: most people in Panem can't swim as hardly any of the districts have sea or large water reserves to practice in. Fortunately, the belts on their outfits turn out to be flotation devices so they can at least bob in the water. The Cornucopia stands on a small central island with the supplies piled up inside it. Behind the tributes, encircling the water on all sides, is a sandy beach that becomes a thick jungle and stretches to the outer edge of the arena. The sky above it all is a uniform pink.

There is a variety of food in the arena, from nuts and animals in the jungle to fish and shellfish in the water. Some of the victors discover that they can cook their food by bouncing it off the force fields. The only source of fresh water in the arena comes from inside the trees in the jungle.

It is only on the second day of the game that Katniss comes to understand the bigger significance of the arena's layout. She comes into contact with Wiress, who has been sent into shock by the death of her fellow tribute Blight and keeps repeating the phrase, 'tick, tock', which the others dismiss as nonsense. However, as twelve bongs ring out, like a striking clock, Katniss begins to put the pieces of the puzzle together. She remembers twelve bongs striking the night before; she thinks of the arena, divided into twelve segments; and she begins to understand what Wiress is trying to say to her – the arena is a clock. Each segment is programmed to set off a different method of torture, devised by the Gamemakers, according to the time of day. The twelve bongs signal noon and midnight, when the cycle begins. She quickly tells the rest of her alliance and they try to work out what each sector of the clock holds:

Twelve to one – lightning. A tall tree in this section is hit by lightning after twelve bongs sound.

One to two – blood rain. Hot wet blood falls like rain from the sky, getting into the eyes and mouths of the tributes.

Two to three – fog. This corrosive fog creeps along in a way that is definitely not natural and causes burning blisters when it touches skin, as well as nerve spasms.

Three to four – monkey muttations. These genetically-altered monkeys look harmless but the slightest glance can provoke them to attack – as the tributes soon discover.

Four to five – jabberjays. The Gamemakers have used jabberjays to replicate the screams of the victors' loved ones.

Five to six – unknown.

Six to seven – 'beast'. This unknown muttation, which Peeta names as a 'beast', tears one of the former victor's bodies into five pieces.

Seven through ten - unknown

Ten to eleven – tidal wave. At this time, a huge wave is triggered, which washes right down to the beach and claims one victor's life.

Eleven to twelve – unknown muttations. Katniss supposes these muttations to be some kind of insects or beetles with pincers that could probably strip humans to the bone, as suggested by the loud clicking sounds coming from this area, which seem to swell when people are close by.

MAP OF QUARTER QUELL ARENA

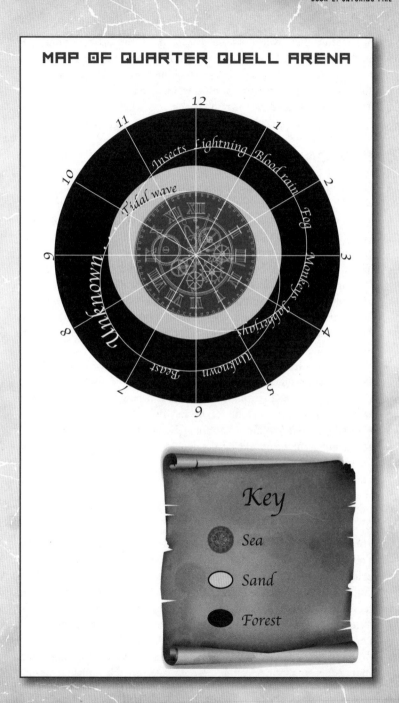

Key

Sea

Sand

Forest

Soon after they work out the meaning of the arena layout, the Gamemakers confuse the victors again by spinning the Cornucopia island around very fast and disorientating them. However, they are able to get their bearings again by waiting until the tidal wave from the tenth sector crashes down the beach.

DAY ONE

Despite their demonstration of solidarity at the pre-Games interviews, when the victors enter the arena it instantly becomes a case of 'every man for himself'. Once they have got over the initial shock of landing in water, the Game kicks in.

Katniss dives straight into the water and swims to the Cornucopia where she picks up a bow and arrows from the pile of weapons. There she encounters Finnick from District 4, whom she is about to kill until he points out that Haymitch has given him his own bracelet, and she knows this is her mentor's way of telling her to team up with him. Katniss and Finnick fend off the other contestants who have started to reach the Cornucopia, Finnick retrieves Peeta and his district partner Mags from the water and the four of them get away from the Cornucopia as quickly as possible.

They head into the jungle with an extra bow, more arrows, two knives and an awl (a tool for boring holes in wood), as well as Finnick's trident and net. Unfortunately, others are not so quick and get caught up in the usual Cornucopia bloodbath, dying at the hands of the Career Tributes (Gloss and Cashmere from District 1; Brutus and Enobaria from District 2). By the end of the first day, the body count is eight, with the losses as follows:

DISTRICT 5 Male

The District 5 male victor never gets a chance to show the skills that helped him win the Hunger Games because he is the first to be killed in the Quarter Quell. He meets his end when Finnick Odair spots him creeping up behind Katniss on the Cornucopia island. Finnick, who is trying to form an alliance with Katniss, automatically protects her by throwing a trident into the District 5 male's chest.

The little of his character that does come across before the game starts suggests that he wouldn't have made it much further than this anyway. Although he turns up at the Training Centre, he is not in good shape as he has obviously turned to alcohol to cope with his involvement in the Games. He throws up in the Training Centre, tries to eat poisonous bugs, and generally seems like he doesn't really know what is happening around him.

DISTRICT 6 Male

The male District 6 victor, like his female district partner, is rather old and addicted to a narcotic painkiller called morphling, presumably using it as a way of blocking out the reality of Panem and the Hunger Games. His addiction leaves him extremely thin, with sagging yellow skin and large eyes. He is also very childlike, spending most of his time at the Training Centre before the Games painting his partner's face with bright colours. It is surely this vulnerability that leads to his early death in the Cornucopia bloodbath, probably at the hands of the Career Tributes.

WOOF, DISTRICT 8 Male

Woof is one of the oldest victors in the Quarter Quell. He has begun to lose his hearing and focus and sticks with his district partner Cecelia in the Training Centre. Woof is placed in the same sector of water as Katniss in the arena but does not appear to adjust to his surroundings as swiftly as she does. It is not surprising that he is one of the casualties at the Cornucopia, given his age and his frailty, and being pitted against much younger, stronger competitors.

CECELIA, DISTRICT 8 Female

Cecelia's reaping stands out as one of the most affecting as she leaves three young children behind her, which makes for sad viewing. She remains a sympathetic, maternal figure although she never gets to display more of her personality because she is killed in the Cornucopia bloodbath.

DISTRICT 9 Male and Female

Both the victors from District 9 die in the Cornucopia bloodbath. They are never mentioned specifically by Katniss, perhaps because they didn't turn up to training or because they do not appear to be dangerous rivals or worthy allies.

DISTRICT 10 Female

All we ever learn of the District 10 female before the Quarter Quell starts is that, at the opening chariot procession, she is forced to wear a cow suit (representing District 10's industry of livestock farming). The suit, which features a fiery belt (clearly an attempt on her stylist's part to copy Katniss and Peeta's flaming costumes) is ridiculous enough to catch Katniss' attention. Unfortunately, she never has a chance to improve on this silly first impression because she is killed at the Cornucopia on the first day.

SEEDER, DISTRICT 11 Female

Seeder is a victor who Katniss immediately feels an affinity with. This is not only because she is physically familiar (with olive skin and straight black hair like a Seam resident, only her golden-brown eyes marking her as different), but also because she is connected to the District 11 tributes from the previous year, those who Katniss felt closest to apart from Peeta. Seeder shows herself to be a friend straight away when she hugs Katniss after the opening procession and reassures her that Rue and Thresh's families are safe after the trouble that Katniss and Peeta accidentally started during their visit to District 11 on their Victory Tour.

Although Seeder is around sixty, she still looks strong and has not turned to alcohol or drugs like many of the other former victors. She is at the top of Katniss and Peeta's list of desired allies before they decide that they don't want to be part of a group in the arena. It is not known exactly how Seeder dies, or at whose hands, but it is possible that the Careers saw her as a threat and targeted her. However she was taken out of the Game, her death is lamented by Katniss.

On the first day, another victor dies too – Peeta. Luckily, he is only technically dead; he hits a force field and his heart stops but Finnick manages to revive him. Their whole party is also weakened by thirst when they can't find any water in the arena aside from the salt water surrounding the Cornucopia. Fortunately, they are sent a spile as a present and manage to work out how to use it to tap water out of the jungle trees.

DAY TWO

Although the death toll at the Cornucopia bloodbath wasn't as high as it is some years, the Gamemakers' deadly interventions mean that the rate of deaths doesn't slow down on the second day.

BLIGHT, DISTRICT 7 Male

When Katniss is keeping watch for the rest of her group in the early hours of the second day, the cannon signals another death. She doesn't take much notice, but even if she had known it was announcing Blight's passing, it probably wouldn't have made much more of an impact on her. Blight didn't make a big impression during the preparatory stages of the Games, having been absent during the training sessions.

After the game starts, Blight escapes the Cornucopia with his district partner Johanna and the District 3 victors Beetee and Wiress. Blight and Johanna saved the pair from District 3 in an attempt to win Katniss over because Haymitch said Katniss wanted them as allies. The group are in the jungle when it starts to rain. At first they think this will bring relief from their dehydration as they have not been able to find any fresh water, but the 'rain' turns out to be blood, which gets into their mouths and eyes. Unable to see, Blight walks into a force field and dies.

Johanna's casual attitude to losing Blight suggests that he didn't have many useful skills. Maybe he was old, another addict or he was just lucky to win his year's Games.

MAGS, DISTRICT 4 Female

At around eighty, Mags was alive before the Hunger Games started and was one of its earliest victors. Despite her old age, she is a fearless woman. She proves this first in the Quarter Quell reaping, where she volunteers to take the place of a young woman from her District (Annie Cresta). Being from the fishing district, she shows great skill at making fishhooks from whatever materials are available and also has vast knowledge of the Hunger Games from her many years of mentoring other District 4 tributes. This knowledge helps her to recognize some edible nuts that provide a food source for her alliance.

Mags cannot communicate very clearly through words but her carefree attitude and keen sense of humour still come across. She walks with a cane outside of the arena and is at a physical disadvantage in the

Games, having to rely on Finnick to carry her when they need to move quickly. However, it is ultimately Mags' courage that leads to her death.

When her alliance is attacked by an artificial poisonous mist, they try to run away from it as fast as they can. Finnick carries Peeta, who is still weak from hitting the force field, and Katniss takes Mags. Eventually, though, the gas begins to cause their muscles to spasm and Katniss can no longer cope with the burden. Finnick is not able to carry both ailing tributes in his debilitated state so Mags bravely sacrifices her own life to give her friends a chance of escaping the fog. After kissing Finnick goodbye, she walks into the jungle and allows her body to be consumed by the deadly mist.

Mags' death is taken hard by the rest of the group, especially Finnick, who she mentored through his first Games and who had come to regard her as family.

As Katniss, Peeta and Finnick recover from the loss of Mags and the effects of the poisonous fog (which can be lessened by swimming in salt water), they notice a group of monkeys gathering in the trees near them. The monkeys turn out to be muttations and soon another life is claimed.

DISTRICT 6 Female

Like her male counterpart, the District 6 female's defining feature is that she is a morphling addict. She is in her sixties, incredibly thin and ill-looking with protruding eyes. She behaves in a childlike fashion, presumably because of the effects of years of drug abuse, and is fascinated by paint and bright colours. Though her district partner is slaughtered at the Cornucopia on the first day, the female morphling survives this. It seems that she retreated in the jungle away from her competitors because she is not seen again until the second day when Katniss, Finnick and Peeta are being attacked by ferocious monkey muttations.

As they struggle to battle against the horde of creatures attacking them, Katniss runs out of arrows and calls to Peeta for one of his. As Peeta is distracted, one of the mutts leaps towards him, dodging the knife Katniss throws at it. She is just about to run in front of Peeta to protect him when the District 6 female jumps out.

Although Peeta immediately stabs the monkey to death, its fangs have already pierced deep into her chest. He carries her out to the beach and strokes her hair while she gasps heavily. Peeta talks about the different colours he uses in his painting, knowing this will comfort the morphling, and she responds by painting a flower on his cheek, using her own blood, before drawing one final breath.

The three allies stay out of the jungle and remain on the beach, where they soon see three figures approaching them. These turn out to be Johanna, Beetee and Wiress. Finnick runs over to his old friend Johanna, who explains how they lost Blight to the blood rain. Katniss reluctantly joins the others and tends to the injured Beetee and traumatised Wiress. It is during this time that Katniss works out the clock set-up of the Games with Wiress' help. As she explains this to the others, it soon becomes clear that something is wrong as Wiress falls silent . . .

WIRESS, DISTRICT 3 Female

In her forties with a small build, ashen skin and black hair, Wiress doesn't appear to be a threat and is quite friendly towards Katniss in the Training Centre. Unsurprisingly, given that District 3's industry is electronics, Wiress and her district partner Beetee are inventors. She is clearly very smart, having created a stitching device that gauges the density of fabric and automatically selects the right thickness of thread needed, and her intelligence is probably what won her the Hunger Games. It is also Wiress who points out to Katniss the 'chink in the armour' – a small square of rippling air that signals a force field. Unfortunately Wiress' short attention span, which leaves Beetee finishing many of her sentences, has earned her the nickname 'Nuts' among the other victors (with the pair of them being dubbed 'Nuts and Volts').

This impression doesn't get better during the Quarter Quell. After being saved from the Cornucopia bloodbath by Blight and Johanna, Wiress is in the jungle with them when the blood rain begins to fall, causing Blight's death and completely unhinging Wiress herself. Afterwards, she cannot form coherent sentences and continuously repeats the seemingly nonsensical expression 'tick, tock'. It takes a while for the rest of her party to realize that Wiress has actually worked out how the arena works. Beetee remarks that Wiress is intuitive and compares her to a canary used in coal mining, which is brought into the mine as a test of how safe it is (if the canary stops singing, it means the air is contaminated). Unfortunately, just moments later this comparison proves to be all too accurate when Wiress, who has been sent to clean Beetee's wire at the water's edge, stops singing her funny childish song.

The others turn around to find that the Career Tributes from Districts 1 and 2 have crept towards the Cornucopia behind their backs, planning to launch an attack – and Gloss has already cut Wiress' throat.

CASHMERE AND GLOSS, DISTRICT 1 Female and male

Though they won their respective Hunger Games tournaments separately, in the Quarter Quell brother and sister Gloss and Cashmere come as a deadly duo. Judging from when Katniss remembers watching them win, they are in their mid-to-late twenties and are still good-looking and strong: the classic Career Tributes. They both attend the training sessions and invite Katniss to work at making hammocks with them, but the two parties don't mix well. Cashmere and Gloss come across as civil but unfriendly, while Katniss can only focus on the fact that she killed the District 1 tributes the year before, who they must have mentored. The District 1 victors show hints of defiance during the pre-Games interviews, when they make appeals to the people of the Capitol about the cruelty of the Quarter Quell ruling, but once inside the arena they fall back into traditional roles and form a Career Pack with Brutus and Enobaria from District 2.

When the Game starts, Gloss is one of the first tributes to reach the Cornucopia and he gets an arrow in his calf courtesy of Katniss as she tries to cover herself and Finnick while they collect supplies. As they retreat from the central island, the Careers swoop in and take their pick of the weapons. They undoubtedly put these to use straight away at the Cornucopia bloodbath, where it is almost certain that the Career Tributes did most of the killing.

Gloss and Cashmere reappear on the second day, when the Careers decide to attack the other group of victors that has formed, consisting of Beetee, Finnick, Johanna, Katniss, Peeta and Wiress. They stealthily approach this pack from behind, but the others are alerted to their presence by Wiress' silence when Gloss slits her throat open. In a turn of events remarkably similar to the death of his former protégée Marvel in the 74th Hunger Games, Katniss shoots Gloss in the temple. (Marvel was also shot in the head by Katniss, in retaliation for the murder of another vulnerable female ally – Rue.) A moment later, Johanna throws an axe into Cashmere's chest so the brother and sister exit the Quell as they came into it – together.

The attack of the Career Tributes happens very quickly and is interrupted by the spinning of the Cornucopia island, which causes

Katniss' group to lose their bearings in the arena. They must get on with things quickly however, as they soon have another problem to face. When Katniss and Finnick enter the jungle to collect water, they accidentally walk into a sector of the clock where jabberjays scream in the voices of the tributes' friends and families. They have to suffer this for an hour as an invisible barrier traps them. After a long and eventful day, this torture drains the former victors, but at least they have so far survived the horrors of the jungle, unlike some of their competition.

DISTRICT 5 Female and DISTRICT 10 Male

These two former victors don't make much of an impact during the Quarter Quell. Despite surviving the initial battle at the Cornucopia, both are killed on the second day. One dies between ten and eleven am when the engineered tidal wave comes crashing down and his or her body has to be lifted out of a tree. The other is killed between six and seven pm by what the others can only guess is some sort of beast, as the hovercraft has to lower its claw five times to pick up the pieces of his or her body.

DAY THREE

By the start of the third day, with the number of tributes left heavily depleted and the knowledge that they will have to turn on each other soon hanging over the survivors, Katniss suggests to Peeta that they end their alliance with the rest of their pack. Peeta persuades her that they should stay with the others until the Career Tributes are dead and then separate. Brutus and Enobaria still present the biggest threat to the group and so everyone agrees when Beetee comes up with a plan to stop them.

He proposes that they set a trap for the Careers using the spool of wire that he has clung on to throughout the game, which he reveals is his own invention and is highly conductive. They guess that the Careers must be hiding on the edge of the jungle, just out of the way of the horrors that lurk inside it but close enough to the beach to eat some of the seafood in the water and spy on the rest of the victors. To target these two, Beetee proposes that they lay the wire throughout the trees at the edge of the jungle (which will still be wet from the wave), dropping one end into the water and connecting the other to the tree in the twelve-to-one lightning sector. When this sector is activated, the electrical power from the lightning tree will pass down the wire and electrocute anyone within this area.

No one apart from Beetee really understands the strategy, but they all agree to it because they don't have a better idea of how to eliminate the Careers. They set to work carrying out the plan, with Beetee conducting some minor experiments to test his theory. Then he sends Katniss and Johanna to lay the wire as they move through the trees quickest.

While the girls are out in the jungle, the wire is cut by someone above them. Before Katniss can react, Johanna hits her over the head and deeply wounds her arm. As she lies on the floor, dazed and injured, she hears Brutus and Enobaria pass. She assumes that Johanna, and possibly Finnick, must have tricked her all along and knows that she must find Peeta. As she traipses back through the jungle she sees Finnick calling out for her and Johanna but is unsure whether to trust him. As the cannon announcing another death sounds, she is sure that the others will regard the night as a free-for-all killing spree now that their plan has fallen into chaos . . .

CHAFF, DISTRICT 11 Male

Chaff was the winner of the 45th Hunger Games. In his mid-to-late forties, standing two metres tall with dark skin and an arm that ends in a stump (he lost his hand during his first Hunger Games and refused to get an artificial replacement from the Capitol), Chaff is one of Haymitch's old drinking buddies, the pair having become friends during their years as mentors for the young tributes of their districts. When Chaff is reaped, Effie's comment that he can't stay out of a fight suggests that he might have volunteered to participate in the Quarter Quell, or at least that he has a reputation as a brawler.

Katniss doesn't initially warm to Chaff, as he is loud and abrasive and deliberately sets out to shock her by planting a kiss on her mouth when they first meet after the opening chariot procession. However, as she gets to know him better in the Training Centre, she realises that he is quite funny and self-deprecating when sober.

Unlike his district partner Seeder, Chaff survives the Cornucopia bloodbath but does not cross paths with Katniss' alliance. As the third day draws to a close, when the Game has been thrown into confusion,

Chaff demonstrates his strong spirit and courage by taking on the bloodthirsty Brutus. Sadly, this is one fight that he loses.

BRUTUS, DISTRICT 2 Male

The aptly named Brutus is a typical Career Tribute. Whereas most of his rivals were dismayed at the announcement of the Quarter Quell and horrified by the idea of having to compete again, Brutus was keen to get involved in the action and volunteered to take part. Brutus and his district partner Enobaria are the first to turn up to training and even though he is now middle aged, Brutus appears to have kept fit. Brutus is clearly determined to win and, after seeing Katniss' impressive archery skills, even requests to be allied with her, but she turns down the offer. During the interviews, Brutus stands out from the rest of his fellow victors because he doesn't condemn the Games and he is reluctant to hold hands with the others in a display of rebellion against the Capitol.

Once he is in the arena, Brutus joins forces with the other victors from District 1 and 2, as they must have planned all along. He rushes to the Cornucopia straight away and shows sharp instincts by holding his belt out as a shield against Katniss' arrow and then darting back into the water to avoid her. When Katniss and Finnick are at a safe enough distance from the Cornucopia, Brutus joins the other Career Tributes there to choose his weapons. He then goes on to use them to brutal effect in the opening battle that kills a third of the victors.

Brutus comes into contact with Katniss and her allies again when the Career Pack try to ambush them. Although their approach goes well, they are soon detected and Gloss and Cashmere are killed almost instantly. Brutus throws a spear at Peeta, which Finnick blocks, and the District 2 victors are left hiding behind the Cornucopia. They have to abandon their attack and run away from the Cornucopia, but the other group is hot on their heels when the Gamemakers intervene by spinning the Cornucopia around quickly, leaving those on it disorientated, while Brutus and Enobaria are given the chance to escape.

On the third night, Brutus and Enobaria thwart Beetee's plan to electrify the beach area by cutting the wire that Johanna and Katniss are unravelling. Shortly afterwards Katniss, who is bleeding heavily after Johanna's attack, hears Brutus call out to Enobaria that she is as good as dead and they leave her there to die. A few minutes later, as the frantic remaining victors run around the jungle, Brutus slays Chaff. His triumph doesn't last long though, as Peeta then kills him.

A greatly weakened Katniss makes it back to the lightning tree to help Peeta, but she finds Beetee there instead, knocked out on the floor. He is holding a knife wrapped in the conductive wire, which Katniss works out he must have tried to throw into the force field above him. The other victors are still roaming the jungle so when Peeta calls out to her, she calls back, hoping to draw potential attackers away from him. This works and Finnick and Enobaria soon run towards the lightning tree, though they fail to see Katniss who is camouflaged by skin ointment. On the verge of blacking out, Katniss prepares to shoot an arrow at Enobaria's neck (to try to give Peeta as few obstacles to victory as possible) when she remembers Haymitch's final piece of advice to her before the Games – he told her she must not forget who her real enemy is.

The full meaning behind the words finally makes sense as Katniss understands it is the Capitol, responsible for orchestrating the cruel and twisted Hunger Games, that must be stopped. She recognises the true significance of Beetee's plan and doesn't aim her arrow for Enobaria, but instead wraps some of the wire around it and sends it into the nearby force field, sending a volt through the wire laid throughout arena which blows the whole place apart – with six victors still alive . . .

ENOBARIA, DISTRICT 2 Female

Enobaria won the 62nd Hunger Games and is now around thirty. All that Katniss can remember about the former victor is that in her first Games, during some hand-to-hand fighting, she tore another tribute's throat open with her bare teeth! This gruesome act sums up Enobaria's cut-throat attitude towards the Games (literally!). In fact, after exiting the arena the first time around, she even had her teeth altered so that they are shaped like fangs and lined with gold to make them indestructible, which has made her a style icon in the Capitol.

With her district partner Brutus, Enobaria is first at the Training Centre and does not appear outraged or upset by the prospect of entering the Games again, unlike most of the other victors. She is also unsure about joining hands with her rivals after their interviews with Caesar Flickerman, confirming the stereotype of District 2 residents being those most loyal to the Capitol. Predictably, Enobaria joins the Career Pack and is one of the first to reach the Cornucopia and choose weapons, which she surely unleashes on some of her fellow victors.

When the Career Pack attacks the other group of victors at the

Cornucopia island on the second day of the Games, Enobaria hurls a knife at Peeta but Finnick blocks it so that it pierces his leg instead. This altercation leaves Enobaria and Brutus without any other allies as both Cashmere and Gloss have been killed. They seem to be in serious trouble as Katniss, Peeta, Finnick and Johanna start to chase them but, just at this moment, the Gamemakers intervene by spinning the Cornucopia around and give the remaining Careers a chance to escape.

The fierce District 2 victors still present the greatest threat to the alliance formed by Katniss, Peeta, Finnick, Johanna and Beetee. Although they keep out of sight, they presumably stay in the outskirts of the jungle – out of the way of any of the Gamemakers' traps or muttations and yet close enough to the beach to catch food from the water and keep an eye on the other victors. When Beetee sets his plan in motion and sends Katniss and Johanna out to unravel his wire through the jungle, they are found by Enobaria and Brutus. After Johanna attacks Katniss, the Careers leave her for dead and seem to go after Johanna instead.

At some point, Enobaria must part ways with Brutus because he is alone when he runs into Chaff. Enobaria makes her way to Finnick in the jungle and runs with him to the lightning tree at the sound of Katniss calling to Peeta. Moments later, Katniss prepares to shoot an arrow into Enobaria's neck – before she decides the force field is a better target. A narrow escape indeed!

BEETEE, DISTRICT 3 Male

Beetee, who is small with ashen skin, black hair and glasses, is characterised by his intelligence. As someone from District 3, whose industry is electronic goods, he is an expert with technology. Like his district partner Wiress, he is an inventor, and shortly before the Quarter Quell he produced a tiny musical chip on which it is possible to store hours of songs. Beetee is older than Wiress so is probably in his fifties or sixties. He is close to her and seems able to follow her thought processes even when she gets distracted, often finishing off her sentences. Beetee won his original Hunger Games by using wire to set up an electrical trap for his rivals, which has earned him the nickname 'Volts' among the other victors.

Katniss immediately takes to Beetee from the early stages of the competition, as she appreciates his calmness and intelligence at the Training Centre compared to some of the more ferocious or outspoken victors. At the Cornucopia, Katniss briefly considers taking Beetee and Wiress into her alliance but decides she doesn't have the time to get them from the water and protect them from the Careers. Luckily for Beetee, Johanna and Blight from District 7 seem to take on this responsibility instead. Despite Beetee receiving a knife wound in his back as he goes out of his way to pick up a spool of wire from the pile of weapons, he escapes the Cornucopia with his new allies.

After losing Blight in the blood rain sector, the others meet up with Katniss, Finnick and Peeta, who help clean Beetee up and attend to his wound. Sadly, Beetee then loses his district partner at the hands of the Career Tributes, but Katniss does manage to grab Beetee's wire from Wiress' body before it is lifted out by the Gamemakers.

The very thin pale golden wire which conducts electricity is Beetee's own invention. This unlikely weapon proves to be vital to Beetee, who devises a plan to eliminate Brutus and Enobaria from the competition by trapping them on an electrified beach. The other victors trust him as he obviously knows what he is talking about (and none of them can keep up with his quick mind!). As the Career Tributes sabotage the plan and everything falls into chaos, Katniss travels back to the lightning tree and finds Beetee lying on the floor, barely conscious. He is holding a knife wrapped in his special wire, a sight which Katniss takes a few moments to process.

When she does, she realises that Beetee was trying to throw his knife into the force field near the tree. His proposed plan to electrocute the Careers with the lightning from the first clock sector was just a front for his real intention to damage the arena with the energy from the force field. As he can no longer fulfil this mission, Katniss does it for him.

FINNICK, DISTRICT 4 Male

Twenty-four-year-old Finnick Odair won the 65th Hunger Games when he was just fourteen. As a District 4 tribute he was in the Career Pack and was helped by his mentor Mags. Due to Finnick's extraordinary good looks, he was a hit with the audience and favoured by sponsors who sent him food, medicine and weapons. In fact, Finnick was sent possibly the most expensive gift someone has ever received in the arena – a trident. With this tool, something he was very familiar with as his home is by the sea, Finnick was able to eliminate his opponents easily after catching them with a net he wove out of vines. Since then, tall, strong Finnick, with his golden skin, bronze-coloured hair and

sea-green eyes has remained one of the most popular Hunger Games victors ever. He is always in demand at every Hunger Games and seems to have a string of lovers in the Capitol.

Katniss is very wary of Finnick before the Quarter Quell starts. Although he tries to approach her at the opening ceremony and throughout their time at the Training Centre, she finds his flirtatious nature off-putting and doesn't trust the former Career Tribute at all. When they are pushed up into the Hunger Games arena, Finnick is the first person to make it to the Cornucopia (as expected, he has a distinct advantage when it comes to swimming because he's from District 4). There, he tries to convince Katniss he is an ally, first by showing her the bracelet Haymitch gave him, and then by saving her from an attack by the District 5 male victor. Against her instincts, Katniss decides to team up with Finnick and lets him rescue Peeta and his own district partner from the water before they all retreat into the jungle.

Katniss is still wondering how to get rid of Finnick when he does something that leaves her completely indebted to him – he saves Peeta's life. In the jungle, Peeta hits a force field which stops his heart until Finnick manages to revive him. From then on, Katniss sees a different side to Finnick, especially when he loses Mags to the toxic fog in the jungle and is deeply upset. When the monkey mutts attack, it is clear that without the combined effort of Peeta, Katniss and Finnick none of them would have survived. They even manage to share a joke as they rub grey-green ointment into their skin to alleviate the itch of the fog and scare Peeta with their hideous appearance. Katniss realises Finnick is not as conceited or shallow as she first thought.

At the sight of Johanna's party wandering onto the beach, Finnick is the first to approach them, showing no hesitation because Johanna is an old friend. When this new alliance is attacked by the Career Tributes, Finnick saves Peeta again by blocking a spear Brutus throws at him and taking Enobaria's knife in his leg to stop it piercing Peeta. He gets caught up in the jabberjay trap with Katniss and this experience reveals that, despite his apparent affairs with rich Capitol women, the person Finnick is really in love with is another District 4 former victor – Annie Cresta. The pretty dark-haired girl, who became slightly unhinged after her district partner was beheaded in the Games and only won because the whole arena was flooded and she was the best swimmer, is the person Mags volunteered to take the place of at the reaping.

As he is still athletic, handy with weapons and has good knowledge of seafood, Finnick is a great asset to their alliance. He also tries to relieve the tension between Katniss and Johanna. Finnick is separated from the girls during Beetee's plan but when Katniss is bleeding heavily in the jungle she hears Finnick calling for them. At this point, she assumes that Finnick and Johanna must have had a secret, deeper pact all along and are a threat to her. The last Katniss sees of Finnick is when he runs through the jungle towards her at the sound of her cries to Peeta, arriving on the beach with Enobaria just before she shoots the force field.

JOHANNA, DISTRICT 7 Female

Johanna Mason won her first Hunger Games only a few years before the Quarter Quell, meaning she is in her early twenties. Back then, Johanna's strategy was to pretend to be weak, causing her opponents to underestimate her. In fact she is smart, strong and deadly with an axe (well, District 7's industry is lumber!). Johanna, who has brown eyes and short spiky brown hair, is the only living female victor from District 7 so, like Katniss, she knew she would enter the arena from the moment the Quell ruling was announced. Apart from her talent for axe-throwing, Johanna makes an impression on Katniss and Peeta before the Games even start by stripping off the tree costume she wore during the opening ceremony as they wait together for an elevator, and continuing to chat casually to them throughout the ride. While Peeta finds this funny, it makes Katniss feel uncomfortable (as he tells her, this was probably Johanna's plan) and from that moment on the two female victors do not see eye to eye.

At the start of the 75th Hunger Games, Johanna and her district partner Blight save District 3 victors Beetee and Wiress from the clutches of the Career Tributes by taking them under their wing and helping them to escape the Cornucopia. Johanna later explains that she only took on the two weaker, older tributes in order to secure Katniss as an ally; Haymitch had warned her that Katniss would only agree to this alliance if Beetee and Wiress were also part of it. Together, the four victors from Districts 3 and 7 traipse through the jungle but face the same problem as Katniss' company – they can't find any water. So when rain falls on them they are relieved, until they realise that the thick drops are of blood, not water. Nobody can see a thing and Blight walks into a force field and dies instantly. These leaves Johanna covered in blood with Beetee, who is wounded, and Wiress, who is completely in shock, to look after.

Luckily, she finds Finnick, Katniss and Peeta a few hours later. Johanna and Finnick are old friends from the Hunger Games circuit so the two groups merge, although Katniss is not very enthusiastic about this. She thinks it will only be a matter of time before she kills Johanna, or the other way around. However, Johanna proves to be useful soon enough, when she hurls an axe into Cashmere's chest as the Careers ambush Katniss' group at the Cornucopia. Katniss and Johanna remain frosty with each other but Katniss recognises an underlying bond, comparing their relationship to sisters who don't get on. They share a dark sense of humour, and Katniss gains some respect for the older girl when she shouts out about the rebellion. This risky act of defiance against the Capitol shows Johanna's bravery and her comment afterwards that there is nobody left who she loves makes Katniss sympathise with her a little.

However, Johanna seems to completely change and prove Katniss' first impression right when Brutus and Enobaria creep up on the pair of them while they are laying Beetee's wire in the jungle. Before Katniss can react, Johanna has hit her over the head with the metal cylinder the wire was wrapped around and then stabs Katniss in the arm. She tells Katniss to stay down before running off into the jungle. Baffled and almost knocked out by this surprise attack from her supposed ally, Katniss can only think that Johanna and Finnick had a pact to turn on the others, and that Johanna has finally decided to show her true colours whilst she is alone with Katniss. After Johanna runs off into the darkness Katniss does not see or hear her for the rest of the Game.

KATNISS AND PEETA, DISTRICT 12 Female and male

Like Cashmere and Gloss, Katniss and Peeta enter the Quarter Quell as a team. However, there is one obstacle to their alliance – the fact that they are going in with conflicting game plans! After Peeta tried to protect her in the 74th Hunger Games, Katniss wants to pay him back by ensuring that he returns home alive once again, but of course Peeta is just as determined to save the girl he loves, even if the cost is his own life. What's more, each thinks they have entered into a pact with Haymitch to help the other survive when in fact he has agreed to both plans!

Again, the two are cast as tragic star-crossed lovers, and this time they are playing up to it even more by pretending that they are married and Katniss is pregnant. Although Haymitch wanted them to make friends at the Training Centre, and they began to like some of the other victors, they both decide that it would be easier for them to only rely on each other. This resolve is tested right at the start of the game, however, when Finnick Odair and his district partner Mags ally themselves with the District 12 victors. As Katniss and Finnick were the first tributes to reach the Cornucopia, they manage to pick up some weapons before the Career Pack starts a battle.

The new alliance walks into the jungle to try and get as far away from the others as possible, and when Katniss looks back she can see that the bloodbath has taken place, which dismays her all the more because she witnessed the friendliness between the victors before the Games. Later that day, Peeta walks into a force field and his heart stops. As Finnick tries to resuscitate him, Katniss is frantic with worry and very emotional even after he survives. She realises just how much she values him.

The group stay by the force field to allow Peeta to rest. They gather some nuts and Katniss catches a rodent, which they cook by bouncing chunks of meat off the force field. However, they are still dehydrated as they have not managed to find a source of fresh water in the arena. When they are sent a tool which looks like a metal tube, none of them know what to do with it until Katniss remembers that it is a spool they can use to tap water from inside the jungle trees.

When Katniss is on night watch, she spots a cloud of fog drifting towards her that she knows isn't natural. The party move to escape the fog but with Mags and Peeta so weak that their friends have to carry them, their progress is slow and they are caught by the mist. As they start to lose control of their muscles, it becomes even harder for Finnick and Katniss to carry the others, so Mags lets go to give her younger allies a chance to get away. These three escape the fog and recover on the beach where they form a larger alliance with Johanna, Beetee and Wiress. Katniss begins to suspect that some of the other victors are protecting Peeta when the female morphling addict from District 6 jumps between Peeta and a monkey mutation, while Finnick stops any weapons from hitting him as the Careers try to attack at the Cornucopia. She is not sure why, but suspects that this might have something to do with Peeta being such a good public speaker, which would make him the perfect spokesperson for the rebels.

After Katniss is subjected to an hour surrounded by jabberjays – when she hears the recreated screams of Prim, Gale, her mother, Madge and Gale's family – Peeta comforts her. Later that night, he shows her his tribute token. It's a golden locket adorned with a mockingjay to match hers and inside he has placed photos of Katniss' mother, Prim and Gale to try to convince Katniss that she has a lot left to live for and it is better that he dies, rather than her. They kiss, but this time it is not for the cameras and they only stop when Finnick wakes up and interrupts them. The next day, as they dive for seafood, Peeta finds a pearl and gives it to Katniss. He can tell from her expression that his plan has not worked the way he wanted it to and that Katniss still intends to save him.

However, both their plans are put at risk on the third night when they are forced to separate to fulfil Beetee's plot. Katniss does not want to leave Peeta behind and her suspicions appear to have been confirmed when Johanna turns on her. She is terrified at the thought of what could be happening to Peeta out in the jungle and drags herself back to the tree in the twelve-to-one sector to find him. Little does she know that Peeta is deep in the foliage searching for her, where he encounters and kills Brutus. At this point, Katniss has lost a lot of blood and believes she will die, so her only motivation is to make sure Peeta lives. Katniss hears him calling to her and calls back in an effort to bring the other victors in her direction rather than his. She does manage to attract Finnick and Enobaria, and prepares to kill them both to enhance Peeta's chances when she realises that what she should be fighting for is bigger than just her and Peeta, so she attacks the Capitol instead.

As the arena explodes around her, a hovercraft appears above Katniss and picks her up. Her concerns about what she has done are confirmed when she sees Plutarch Heavensbee, the Head Gamemaker, is inside. This is all she can take in before she blacks out from the amount of blood she has lost from her injured arm. She wakes up in a hospital bed with Beetee in a bed beside her. Katniss assumes she is in the Capitol but as she creeps through her new surroundings, trying to find Peeta and kill him before he can be tortured, she realises that she is somewhere else entirely.

She walks in on Plutarch Heavensbee, Haymitch and Finnick talking. Haymitch explains to her that there had been a plan to break the victors out of the arena since the announcement of the Quarter Quell. The tributes from Districts 3, 4, 6, 7, 8 and 11 were all part of it, as was Plutarch (who is secretly a member of a group trying to overthrow the Capitol). Their central aim was to save Katniss, as she has become the face of the rebellion, and also Peeta, who they knew she would want to protect. For this reason, some of the other victors sacrificed their own lives. Plutarch made sure that the special wire was in the arena so that Beetee could use it, and the bread that the victors were sent on their last day in the arena was a code for when they would be rescued – the bread came from District 3 and there were twenty-four rolls, meaning that they would be picked up on the third day at midnight.

Unfortunately, not everyone in the arena could be rescued by the rebels before the Capitol intervened – only Katniss, Beetee and Finnick were picked up by the hovercraft, meaning that Enobaria, Johanna and Peeta were left behind. Katniss learns that Johanna was actually on her side the whole time: what seemed like an attack, as she tore at Katniss' arm, was in fact Johanna removing the Capitol's tracker chip; while in abandoning Katniss on the forest floor, she was attempting to draw the Careers away from her. Those who were rescued are heading to District 13, which Katniss learns does indeed exist. She is also told that most of the districts are now revolting. Haymitch leaves it to Gale to approach Katniss later and reveal that after the 75th Hunger Games ended, the Capitol retaliated against the rebel plot by bombing the whole of District 12, destroying it completely.

A SIMILAR SACRIFICE

Showcasing the unthinkable – pain, suffering and human sacrifice – the Hunger Games make for horrific reading in today's society, but this was not always the case. In some parts of the world, human sacrifice was once a necessary part of life and practised on a far greater scale than in President Snow's Panem. This is certainly true of the Aztecs, who settled in the mountains of Central Mexico, circa AD 1300. A deeply religious people, the Aztecs believed they owed their very existence to the gods, fierce beings who sacrificed themselves for the sake of humanity and demanded to be repaid in kind – with human life. Hence, vast numbers of innocent people were thrown from, or slaughtered on top of huge pyramid-shaped temples in some of the most sadistic religious ceremonies imaginable. Animals, food and treasures were sometimes also offered up; there were different rituals for each god. Aside from the religious significance of these ceremonies, scholars have also suggested that this was a crucial way for the Aztecs to keep populations under control – just as President Snow strives to do with his yearly reaping.

CINNA'S CREATIONS

When Katniss comes to the Capitol to take part in the Hunger Games, she does not expect to make any friends, but there is one person that she forms a special bond with – her stylist, Cinna. Cinna stands out from everyone else there because of his simple fashion sense (especially for a Hunger Games stylist!) and the emotional support he gives her. In fact, from the start Cinna is truly convinced of Katniss' ability to survive, and believes in her when she doesn't even believe in herself.

What makes Cinna truly special, though, is his talent for creating clothes. More than mere outfits, his designs are always intelligent and meticulously planned to create a very specific impression. Before she is thrown into the Hunger Games, Katniss doesn't give how she looks much thought, but once she becomes a tribute she learns how important appearances can be. Though you shouldn't judge a book by its cover, everyone in the Capitol certainly does!

Despite the 74th Hunger Games being his first year as a stylist, Cinna manages to come up with amazing outfits that grab everyone's attention. Here we look at the costumes that show just how creative and gifted the wonderful Cinna is . . .

GIRL ON FIRE

The opening ceremony of the 74th Hunger Games was Cinna's first chance to make an impression with his work, and he certainly made a big one! This chariot-ride procession through the Capitol city centre is the first time the audience gets a proper look at who will be competing, so it is essential that the tributes stand out if they are to be remembered by the audience, and get the backing of sponsors who could supply them with life-saving gifts in the arena. They are supposed to wear something linked to their district's industry, which means that tributes from coal-mining District 12 have spent years wearing hats with headlamps or coal dust and not much else. But Cinna and Peeta's stylist, Portia, tried a different tactic – setting them on fire!

Clad in identical black unitards, shiny knee-high leather boots, capes and matching head-dresses fluttering with synthetic fire, Peeta and Katniss became the coal itself and set Panem alight! Though the District 12 tributes are usually ignored by the crowd because they come at the end of the procession, that year all eyes were on them as they provided a dazzling finale to the ceremony, and had everyone chanting their names. The other tributes were not impressed at having the limelight taken away, but what a way to start Katniss' transformation from anonymous Seam girl to 'the girl who was on fire'!

TRAINING TUNIC

Even when Katniss is not on screen, Cinna puts a lot of thought into her clothes, as proved by the outfit he dressed her in when she went to the Training Centre to prepare for the Games. The functional tight black trousers, long-sleeved burgundy top and leather shoes were light and practical for physical activity at the Training Centre work stations. Moreover, the simple style of the garments was similar to the clothes Katniss wears at home, and this made her feel more relaxed about entering a stressful environment full of her rivals. It allowed her to show her competitors a glimpse of who she really is, without any fancy adornments. Interestingly, Peeta's stylist Portia again dressed him in an identical outfit to Katniss', so the District 12 tributes, who were the only matching pair, entered the Training Centre looking like a team. As this way of thinking is unheard of in the Hunger Games arena, it must certainly have given their opponents something to ponder!

DRESS OF FLAMES

The pre-Game interview that is held the night before the tributes enter the Hunger Games arena is their final chance to impress the audience, with the well-practiced help of veteran host Caesar Flickerman. This is their last shot at coming across as charming, mysterious or intimidating and ensuring that they are unforgettable. So the stylists have a huge responsibility to make sure it is their tributes that the audience will be looking out for once the Game begins. Although he made Katniss' training outfit quite plain, Cinna went back to his spectacular best with her pre-Game interview outfit!

Continuing the fire theme, he put Katniss in a long silken gown covered in reflective red, yellow, white and blue gems that made it look like she was wearing tongues of flame when she moved. Even her nails were painted with flame motifs, while her hair was weaved into a braid with strands of red and her skin was stencilled with patterns and dusted a shimmering gold. Her eyes were painted dark to make them look bigger, with lashes that sparkled, and her lips stained a crimson red. Even Katniss didn't recognise herself when Cinna and her prep team were finished with her!

CANDLELIGHT VICTOR

After Katniss won the 74th Hunger Games, Cinna had to produce a dress for her victory interview with Caesar Flickerman. He knew that President Snow was angry at how Katniss and Peeta had bent the Hunger Games rules so that they could both survive, and that the pressure was on Katniss to prove that this wasn't an act of rebellion against the Capitol in her interview. So the image he created for this moment was carefully constructed to make her seem as harmless and vulnerable as possible. Although the design was no less skilled than his previous ones, Katniss' look was much more innocent. She wore a sheer yellow sleeveless dress with flat sandals, and her hair was loose with a simple hair band to hold it. This outfit, which was knee-length and made from material that seemed to glow, followed Cinna's 'girl on fire' theme but, rather than the red-hot fire of her pre-Games outfits, this time she represented a more gentle 'candlelight'.

The dress was also fitted with padding to round out Katniss' bone-thin body, and her makeup was applied to make her face look fuller (Cinna had to push for this to be achieved through clothing and makeup; the Capitol doctors wanted to perform plastic surgery on a drugged-up Katniss) – after all, we can't expect someone to come out from the Hunger Games arena after weeks of near-death experiences looking their best! All in all, Cinna achieved his aim, as Katniss ended up looking like a harmless girl of fourteen – quite remarkable for someone who'd just fought to the death to win the Hunger Games!

WINNER'S WARDROBE

Even after Katniss left the arena, she was still in the public eye for Capitol television shoots and her victory tour with Peeta, which meant that she still needed a stylist! Cinna more than rose to the challenge with a range of beautiful clothes, from the casual white shirt, flowing black trousers and woven grey, green and blue sweater outfit Katniss modelled on television when she presented her obligatory 'talent' as a victor (because victors no longer have to attend school or get a job, they must showcase an activity they have taken up to pass their time. Katniss' was supposedly designing clothes, but in reality it was Cinna who did all the work on her behalf!) to the pretty pale-pink dress and silver wrap combo she wore for an official dinner in District 11. Of course, no Cinna wardrobe would be complete without a few gorgeous gowns! He didn't disappoint, creating a gleaming full-length silver number for Katniss to wear at the District 12 Harvest Festival, a deep blue strapless velvet one decorated with diamonds for her appearance in District 2, an orange frock patterned with autumnal leaves when she went to District 11 and a fine green silk dress for her visit to District 5, which Annie Cresta later wore for her wedding to Finnick Odair.

GLOWING EMBER

When Katniss was put back into the arena for the 75th Hunger Games, Cinna had to come up with another coal-related costume for the opening ceremony. Luckily, he joined forces with Portia again and they were able to produce yet another show-stopping design!

On the face of it, the fitted black jumpsuits and black metal crown which Katniss and Peeta wore were nothing special but, at the press of a button hidden by their wrists, that all changed! The material had been hooked up to a power pack which made it light up, turning golden at first and then changing to a burning orange-red so that the wearers looked like burning coals in a fire.

The way that Cinna styled Katniss and told her to carry herself suggested that the impression he was creating was no longer one based solely on looking good or catching the audience's attention. Her dramatic makeup – painted arched eyebrows, sharp cheekbones, dark smoky eyes and purple lips – combined with the shadows that the crown (which turned flaming red like her suit) cast on her face made Katniss look much harsher than before. Cinna was sending out a clear message through his work: he no longer wanted to present Katniss as a sweet girl, but as a fierce threat. The outfit, and his instruction for her not to wave or smile at the audience during the procession, perfectly reflected Katniss' anger at the injustice of her having to face the horrors of the Hunger Games arena again, just one year after she thought she had escaped them for good. It also made her feel more ready to face her intimidating rivals. There's no doubt that this fiery look showed everyone that Katniss was not a contender to mess with!

MOCKINGJAY BRIDE

Arguably, Cinna's finest creation was the dress he made for Katniss' pre-Game interview before the Quarter Quell. After her engagement to Peeta was announced, Katniss had to model six bridal gowns, with the intention that the one which received the most votes from the Capitol audience would become her wedding dress. Although the public wedding never took place (both parties were heading back into the arena instead), President Snow still requested that Katniss wear the most popular dress for her interview appearance – a white gown made from heavy silk and covered in pearls, with a low neckline, tight waist and sleeves that trailed down to the floor. This move was intended to embarrass her, reminding everyone in the districts who saw Katniss as a figure of rebellion that she was still firmly under the Capitol's control. However this plan backfired as, by the time Katniss came on stage, the audience had already been worked up into a frenzy by the other victors' protests against the new Quarter Quell ruling, and they were simply horrified by the tragic sight of Katniss as a hopeless bride. The atmosphere of hysteria was taken up another notch when Katniss did what Cinna asked her to and spun around to show off her beautiful outfit. The dress burst into synthetic flames and turned into a black feathery version of itself, with white patches on the long sleeves making her look like a mockingjay bird, surprising everyone – not least Katniss herself!

This was the pinnacle of Cinna using his designs to comment on the politics surrounding the Hunger Games. While Katniss had accidentally sparked a feeling of unrest in the districts by refusing to adhere to the

Hunger Games rules, Cinna's statement was very deliberate. He knew that the rebels were using the image of the mockingjay (inspired by the brooch Katniss had worn in the Hunger Games arena) as the symbol to mark their uprising, and that the sight of her dressed as a mockingjay would only strengthen their fighting spirit. Although Cinna must have known that such an outright challenge to President Snow would surely have terrible consequences for himself, by not including Katniss in the plan he spared her this fate. A thoughtful, true friend until the end.

MOCKINGJAY WARRIOR

Even after Cinna was taken away by the Capitol, he never stopped being Katniss' stylist. In fact – demonstrating the same faultless intuition as always – he made preparations for any eventuality, and designed in advance a custom-made outfit for her to wear during the rebellion that was both practical and artistic. The black uniform – with its layers of body armour, helmet and weapons hidden in the boots and belt – was not only perfect for going into combat but also tailored to look good on camera for the rebel propaganda TV spots, which Katniss was required to film as the face of the rebellion.

In a continuation of the image he presented at the 75th Hunger Games interview, Cinna sewed white folds under the sleeves to replicate the wings of a mockingjay. Proving that he really had thought of everything, Cinna even included a secret pocket on the left shoulder of the uniform to hold a deadly pill that Katniss could take if she was captured by the Capitol, and reach with her mouth even if she was tied up. The sight of the sketchbooks of designs Cinna had left for her – and the knowledge that the stylist friend who she'd trusted wholeheartedly supported her becoming the figurehead of the uprising – made Katniss feel sure that it was right for her to take on this role. Cinna's awe-inspiring creations marked Katniss out as special from her first moments in the public eye, and his confidence that she would take on the responsibility of becoming the Mockingjay proved that, even though Cinna had lost his life, he never lost his faith in Katniss.

DISTRICT 13

For seventy-five years, the people of Panem have believed that their nation consists of the Capitol and twelve surrounding districts alone. Though there was another district before the Dark Days, the Capitol bombed it into oblivion to punish the rebels, destroying everyone and everything in it. Displayed in sporadic news reports shot within the ghostly district, footage of the scarred, rubble-strewn landscape serves as a grim warning to would-be rebels in other districts – dare to cross the Capitol and there's only one possible outcome for you and your loved ones. Or so the citizens of Panem have been led to believe . . .

When Katniss met Bonnie and Twill from District 8 in the woods, she thought that their idea that District 13 could exist was ridiculous. How could a society with resources and weapons just stand by and let the Capitol oppress everyone in the districts? Even if it did exist, would the people who allow the rest of Panem to suffer under President Snow's merciless rule really be any better than him? As she is swept up in the rebels' plot, Katniss is about to find the answers to some of her questions because, in fact, District 13 was never wholly destroyed.

Unfortunately for the Capitol, District 13 held their nuclear weapons development programme and there was a large underground facility built there. This meant that, when the rebels took control of the district, they were able to bargain with the Capitol. Although the Capitol had other nuclear weapons at their disposal, the fact that District 13 had the underground resources to survive and enough power to fire back meant that it was in the best interests of President Snow to call a truce. The agreement was as follows: Snow would make a public show of blitzing the place to rubble, but allow its people to live on secretly beneath the surface, where an entire underground society continued to develop.

Yet, if the Capitol thought that was the last they would hear from District 13, they were wrong. In the decades since the Dark Days, this opposing power has been growing and waiting. With a second rebellion underway, what better time for District 13 to resurface in support of the other districts? As it is the only place completely out of the Capitol's control, the secret district has become a centre for the rebellion. People on the run from other areas of Panem are now heading there, including the survivors from District 12. But District

13 has had to adopt a very strict way of life to survive on its own for all this time, so the newcomers need a thorough induction to adapt to the structured communal lifestyle. Why don't you join them on their orientation talk to get an insight into how things work in the underground world of District 13?

'Welcome to District 13. As you already know, our community survives underground. This may be a little strange for most of you and will take some getting used to, but don't worry, you will have time allocated in your daily schedule above ground when you can exercise and get some sunlight in our large fenced training area. Plus, you can find everything you need within our many corridors. We have enough living compartments for each family; they are all white and clean and each is laid out identically with exactly the same government-issued furniture. Compartments located on the top floor have a small window to the outside world. Our other facilities include an education centre, a hospital, a kitchen and dining hall, and the underground farms which supply our food, as well as the Special Defence Quarters, a lower-level bunker for emergencies, and the Command Centre where President Coin and her team meet, which most of you don't need to worry about. Our largest room, the Collective, is where we gather for any official public announcements or events. You can get to anywhere using our network of lift paths, which move sideways as well as up and down, or one of our several staircases.

GOING UNDERGROUND

District 13 is a revelation to refugees from the other districts – not only because it exists when they thought it had been ruined, but also because the whole place runs underground. However, Suzanne Collins' subterranean civilisation is not the first of its kind. The underground society is a common trope in dystopian and sci-fi fiction. For example, as early as 1895, H.G. Wells published his novella *The Time Machine*, in which the protagonist travels to the year 802,701 AD and discovers that the human race has split into two species. The fragile, elegant Eloi live a life of ease on the earth's surface but have limited intelligence, while the ape-like Morlocks live underground and work for the Eloi, but also hunt and eat them. (Can you see the resemblance between these two races and the silly people in the Capitol, who are kept in luxury and never question anything, compared to the downtrodden poor in the districts who produce everything for them and, in the case of those who have fled to District 13 at least, are sometimes literally forced underground?) A few years later, E.M. Forster wrote the 1909 short story, *The Machine Stops*, describing a future where the whole world lives underground and functions through 'The Machine', a technological system that is used to perform every single act, with face-to-face contact among humans being very rare. The idea of an underground society became more popular in the 1960s when the threat of nuclear war meant that this seemed a natural advancement of the self-dug trenches used in previous wars in order to deal with the new, more powerful types of bombs. If nuclear war ever does break out, would we too have to go underground to survive?

'With regards to your schedule, every morning you will receive this by inserting your right arm into a device in your bedroom wall, which will temporarily tattoo your day's agenda onto your forearm in purple ink. This might sound slightly alarming, but don't worry: the ink is not permanent and will come off in the evening when you wash. To a certain extent, your daily routine will depend on your age; those young enough will be taught at the education centre, while adults will be trained for work, which may include helping out in the hospital or kitchen. Your schedule tattoo contains an ID number which you must present to the sensor outside each room before you begin your activity. This way we can know that you are keeping to your routine.

'All our air and water is purified. You may find our meals have a little less flavour than you're used to, but I can assure you they are very healthy – we make sure of that. Food here is strictly rationed. Your dietary needs will be assessed based on your height, body type, age, health and the amount of physical labour you undertake. In short, you will be served the exact number of calories your body needs. Some of you who are malnourished will be given extra food until your state of health is considered acceptable. It is very important that you do not take more than your assigned share of food. If you don't finish your meal, you must leave it in the dining hall. Any hoarding of food or taking extra will be deemed as contrary to the principles of District 13 and you will be punished.

'This is one of our most important rules: there shall be no waste.

This does not only apply to food, but to all resources, including clothing and paper. Our frugal ways may seem excessive to some of you, but you must adjust. Without such tight rationing, District 13 would not have been able to survive for as long as it has. You will be supplied with everything you require. Everyone will be issued with clothing: grey trousers and a shirt. Please make sure your shirt is kept tucked in at the waist. Those in the army will also receive a military uniform – a dark grey jumpsuit.

'Everyone over the age of fourteen will be enter into our military and be addressed as "Soldier", as we're all now part of the war against the Capitol. If you enter higher military ranks you must attend training every morning, where you will begin with stretching, strengthening exercises and long-distance running. As you progress, you will learn how to assemble guns and practice using them at our shooting range. In addition, you will be given lectures and books on military tactics. If you show enough promise you may even be moved into our Simulated Street Combat class, deep in 13, where there is a replica Capitol street for soldiers to carry out practice missions in simulated war conditions. Once you are ready, you will take a four-part exam consisting of an obstacle course to test you physically, a written exam about tactics, a test of how good you are at using weapons and a simulated attack. If you pass, you will join one of our squads and be sent into combat in the districts, at which point your hair will also be cut short. Those of you who are privileged enough to be considered particularly important to the cause will receive a communicuff – a band to be worn around your wrist which can receive printed messages.

'Here you can feel safe from the Capitol's reach. Our ten-metre high district fence is always electrified, guarded and is topped with barbed wire. We have systems which can detect any approaching missiles and we maintain our own large arsenal of explosives, firearms, armoured vehicles and hovercraft. Some we inherited from the Capitol and merely updated; others we have manufactured ourselves. Now we have the expert help of Beetee from District 3 to design new and even more effective weapons for the rebellion. There is heightened security surrounding our most important rooms, such as Special Weaponry, where anyone who enters will not only have to have their schedule scanned, but also have scan checks on their fingerprints, eyes and DNA. They will need to pass through metal detectors at least once. We take no risks here, which is also why we have regular drills to practice how to react in an emergency situation.

'There are five levels of drill depending on how dangerous the emergency is, with level five being the most serious. For example, in a level-two drill for a minor disturbance, such as temporary quarantine in the event of a viral outbreak, you must return to your living quarters. However, in the case of a level-five emergency – which will be signalled by very loud sirens throughout the district – everyone will need to walk calmly down to the lowest levels of the district using the stairs. Here we have a special underground bunker equipped with beds, a kitchen, bathrooms and a first-aid station in case there is any need for citizens to stay there for a while. It is deep enough to be protected even from bunker missiles (which penetrate deep into the ground before detonating), and is reinforced with concrete and steel. If there is a level-five situation while you are here, you must scan your schedule to enter the bunker so we can account for everyone's whereabouts. Once safely installed, you must report to the area which matches your living quarters. For example, if you live in Compartment A you go to the area marked "A". You will be assigned a sleeping and storage space for your group. There you will find instructions on bunker protocol telling you where to pick up supplies.

'Lastly I must add that District 13 is pleased to include you in our ranks. Just by coming here you have been granted automatic citizenship and we look forward to seeing what you can bring to the war effort. Some of you may look at our extensive facilities and our advanced weaponry and wonder why we have taken so long to reach out to the other districts. Our history has not been easy; after the Dark Days our numbers were very small and we had no one left to help us. We have suffered hard times in the last seventy-five years, and seen our population depleted by a pox breakout that left many of those still alive scarred and infertile. Despite this, our careful rationing and discipline have allowed us to survive, and now we are ready to face the Capitol – and, with your help, grow and achieve even more than ever.'

STANDARD SCHEDULE
What would your daily life look like if you lived in District 13?

7.00 – Breakfast
7.30 – Kitchen Duties or Military Training
8.30 – Education Centre, Room 17
12.30 – Lunch
13.30 – Education Centre, Room 17

16.30 – Work Training or Military Training
18.00 – Reflection
18.30 – Dinner
19.30 – Return to room
22.00 – Bathing
22.30 – Lights Out

COIN'S COMMUNISM

After the revolutions of 1917, the Russian government sought to create a new way of life based on the ideology of communism. This was set up as an alternative to capitalism (the economic and political system adopted by most of the current Western world, whereby a small number of individuals privately own most or all of the property and industry, with the majority of the population working for a wage). In communist theory, the only way for capitalism to end is if the working class – who make up the largest section of society but are exploited by the richer class – start a social revolution. Then communism can be established, which means that there will be no more social classes; all property and industry will be jointly owned and all resources and work shared equally.

There are many echoes of communism in District 13 – the fact that everyone follows a very similar timetable, wears the same clothes, eats the same food and lives in identical compartments. Life in communist Russia was very structured and rigid, just like life in District 13, and even the fact that all adults are called 'Soldier' is a link to communism, as in communist countries it became customary for people to refer to each other as 'comrade' or 'citizen', so as to remove all distinguishing ranks and titles. Despite the good intentions behind communism, in Russia, as in other communist countries such as Cuba and North Korea, its flaws soon became apparent. When the original leader of the revolutions, Vladimir Lenin, died (only a few years after he took power), Josef Stalin replaced him and gradually his rule became a dictatorship. Should Katniss and the rebels be questioning whether District 13's lifestyle is really better than the one they already lead?

OLD ORDER VERSUS NEW ORDER

The Capitol has ruled Panem for as long as anyone can remember. Divided, poor, and harshly punished if they step out of line, to the people in the districts it seems that things will never change and that for generations to come they will be forced to watch their children die in the Hunger Games. But now, seventy-five years after the failure of the first rebellion against the all-powerful Capitol, revolution is rising in the districts once again and the fate of Panem is uncertain. At the forefront of the rebellion is a new power player, which has been waiting in the wings, gathering strength, and has just revealed itself to the rest of Panem: District 13. Now that they are squaring up to each other at last, how do these two sides compare? And who will win the bitter war that is set to change the future of Panem forever?

OLD ORDER

Represented by: The Capitol. The largest and wealthiest city in Panem, its citizens enjoy a rich and decadent lifestyle, knowing little and caring less about the struggles of the people in the districts. In the Capitol you only succeed if you put yourself first, individuality is cherished, and fame can bring you power.

Led by: President Snow. Coriolanus Snow has ruled Panem for over twenty-five years. He came to power at quite a young age by poisoning his opponents, and his unscrupulous methods have helped him to keep Panem under control ever since. Snow's method of ruling involves keeping the rich and powerful people of the Capitol happy, by ensuring they live in luxury, while suppressing the poor people in the districts. The districts themselves are kept divided (as travel between them is prohibited), downtrodden by the constant presence of Peacekeepers enforcing the Capitol's laws, and in terror of the yearly Hunger Games. The Hunger Games themselves are a model for the way in which Snow rules Panem; they are designed to emphasise the divisions between the districts, as well as the Capitol's power over them, and to provide entertainment for the Capitol. President Snow forces Hunger Games victors to carry out his agenda by threatening their loved ones. His main aim is to hold onto his power and squash any threat of uprising. He will do anything to achieve this.

Attitude towards Katniss: When Katniss threatened to commit suicide in the 74th Hunger Games, thereby forcing the Gamekeepers to accept two victors, President Snow recognised the influence that her rebellious actions might have in the districts (and the threat this might pose to his power). From then on, he was determined to prevent her from causing more controversy, and what easier way to solve the problem than to put an end to Katniss' existence? Fortunately for Katniss, her high profile as a Hunger Games victor prevented the president from making an obvious attempt on her life. As he had been able to do with previous victors, President Snow tried instead to minimize Katniss' threat by manipulating her public image, and he forced Katniss to play along by threatening to hurt her family. Snow told Katniss that she must continue her relationship with Peeta and even planned their wedding to make it seem like their refusal to kill each other was an act of mad love rather than a challenge to the Capitol. He wanted to remind her at every opportunity that he had all the power, while she was insignificant. But in the end he couldn't quite control her.

Fighting force: The Capitol government is determined to suppress the rebellion. It has a large, well-trained Peacekeeping force in every district and sends out reinforcements to try to stop the rebels at the first signs of unrest. The Capitol's airforces are on hand to attack rebels and to protect the city. The Capitol also employs skilled scientists who have spent years creating horrifying muttations and terrible weapons to attack their opponents.

Additional assets: Although he is not in Snow's camp by choice, Peeta becomes a significant figure in the Capitol's fight against the rebels. President Snow tries to exploit his power with words, and his influence over Katniss, by putting Peeta on television. Presumably, he promises to save Katniss if Peeta tries to publicly dissuade the rebels from standing up to the Capitol, and thereby causing the destruction of their society. With the help of Caesar Flickerman, and Peeta's natural way with words, the lines that he is told to say sound perfectly convincing. It soon becomes clear, however, that the Capitol is using more than just persuasion to manipulate Peeta. In fact, he has been 'hijacked' – his memories have been distorted by injections of tracker-jacker venom so that he can no longer distinguish the truth from the Capitol's lies, and he becomes hostile towards Katniss. President Snow's reason for doing this is partly to convince Panem that Kaniss is out of control – if Peeta believes it, surely it is true? – but even more importantly, he aims to hurt Katniss. President Snow has realised that she does truly care for Peeta, and he wants to target any weakness he can find in the girl who is vital to the rebels' efforts. Ironically, whilst Snow's treatment of Peeta does upset Katniss, in the end it makes her more determined to fight against the Capitol.

Strategy: President Snow has always tried to keep the districts too downtrodden to rebel. Once they do begin to fight back, his strategy is two-fold: he crushes regional uprisings with all the considerable force at his disposal; and he uses propaganda, as well as brutal example – like the destruction of Katniss' home, District 12 – to remind the people of Panem of the Capitol's superiority, and to intimidate them into backing down.

Allies: The only district that does not join the second rebellion is District 2. The people of this district have always enjoyed a favoured relationship with the Capitol, compared to the rest of Panem, so they do not see a revolution as being in their best interests. Most of the Peacekeepers are actually from District 2, rather than the Capitol, whose residents would find the lifestyle in the impoverished districts too difficult to cope with, so the citizens of this district feel greater loyalty towards President Snow than can be found elsewhere. They may even be scared of the rebels winning, in case they are punished for being so close to the Capitol. When the rebels try to take over District 2 they find it is a hard nut to crack, particularly as District 2's troops are hiding in an old mining mountain. However, Gale comes up with a way to overcome this obstacle by setting off explosions on the side of the mountain. The explosions start avalanches that block the entrances of the mine, meaning that the people inside are forced to use the old train tunnel out of the mountain to escape. When they do exit they are armed, but the rebels, who are also equipped with weapons, quickly surround them. Katniss tries to intervene to stop the seemingly inevitable battle, pointing out – to her own side as well as those from District 2 – that their common enemy is the Capitol. Her stirring words are interrupted when she is shot by someone from District 2. Fortunately, Cinna designed her armour well and she soon recovers. Back in District 13, she learns that her words did have some effect, as the workers from District 2 stopped fighting the rebels and turned on the Capitol's forces instead, signalling a change in their allegiance.

Propaganda: Obviously, for years the Capitol has been using propaganda to support its regime: coverage of the Hunger Games, President Snow's speeches, with their slanted version of Panem's history, 'news' reports from District 13 – to name just a few examples. When war breaks out, President Snow steps up the propaganda campaign. He uses the popular recent Hunger Games victor Peeta in interviews with Capitol-favourite Caesar Flickerman to try to play down the threat of revolution, and discredit Katniss and the rebels. This plan backfires when Peeta uses one of these interviews to warn the people in District 13 of an oncoming Capitol attack. Although his guards mete out swift punishment for his outspokenness, it could have saved many lives in 13 as it gave the people there time to retreat to a safe underground bunker out of the reach of the Capitol's bombs.

Weapons: Being the richest city in the whole of Panem, the Capitol has always had access to the best weapons and resources. They have top inventors at their disposal to create hi-tech guns, hovercrafts, bombs and fighter planes with which to attack the rebels. As years of Hunger Games have proved, the Capitol is also able to produce another type of weapon that is just as deadly as any firearm – muttations. In fact, when President Snow realises that his other attempts to kill Squad 451 as they enter the Capitol have failed, he turns to these tried and tested killing machines once again. A swarm of lizard/human hybrids are sent to hunt down the rebel unit through the sewers of the Capitol. Though they have been bred to hiss Katniss' name, they are prepared to rip the head off anyone else they come across and slaughter many of the Capitol's Peacekeepers, as well as the Avoxes who work in the sewers, in their quest to reach their target. They are fast, innumerable, and barely react to gunshots or arrows, so it is only when Katniss manages to detonate a bomb that they are finally stopped. By this time they have already culled most of Squad 451.

Of course, the streets of the Capitol are weapons in themselves. The whole city is planted with pods which the Capitol can activate – each one designed to trap or kill the target. Some of the pods have been there since the Dark Days but new ones have also been added. The effects of the pods are as horrific and varied as the surprises unleashed in the Hunger Games arena (indeed, Plutarch admits that he is responsible for creating quite a few of the pods himself). One might release toxic fumes when triggered, while another could spring a barbed wire trap or set off a bomb. The pods obviously present an obstacle to the rebels trying to invade the Capitol, but thanks to Plutarch and their Capitol contacts, they have a recent record of where most of them are hidden. The Capitol are sure to have activated new ones in the months leading up to all-out war, however, so the rebels cannot be guaranteed a safe journey through the city without encountering any of these unpredictable and highly dangerous weapons.

Strengths: At the start of the rebellion, the Capitol clearly holds more power than its opponents. The Capitol has fought and won a war before, which not only gives them experience, but also a good argument to dissuade the citizens of Panem against continuing the rebellion – after all, history just might repeat itself. Having kept control of Panem for seventy-five years, President Snow is an expert at subduing his people. The Capitol has firmly established Peacekeeping forces in every district and is able to respond to the initial uprising in District 8 very quickly and effectively by deploying its large army. The largest and wealthiest force in Panem by far, the Capitol's army have the best weapons and supplies at their disposal, whereas many people in the districts have nothing.

Yet another card in the Capitol's impressive hand is Peeta. As a well-liked Hunger Games victor, he can exert some of his influence to help President Snow in his propaganda. He can also be used as a bargaining tool when negotiating with Katniss and the rebel movement. President Snow knows that Katniss wants to protect Peeta and he hopes that this desire will persuade her to give up the rebellion (the same technique is used against Finnick, whose love Annie has also been captured and is being held by the Capitol).

Weaknesses: When President Snow told Katniss the Capitol's hold on power was fragile, she was surprised, but now she realises just how true that is. The main problem that President Snow faces is that his years of punishing the people in the districts are now coming back to haunt him. Finally, enough momentum has been created to push them to rise up and fight back. As a result of its bloody and unforgiving regime, the Capitol doesn't just face a few brave rebels but most of the people in Panem. What's more, the Capitol relies on the districts for everything and its citizens have never had to fend for themselves. As the war escalates, the number of supplies unavailable in the Capitol grows. The rebels know that if they win over all of the districts, then eventually the Capitol will be completely cut off with no means of providing for itself, leaving it extremely weak and open to attack.

Starting point of the rebellion: During the build-up to the war, President Snow tried to avoid a rebellion by increasing the size and strength of the Peacekeeping force throughout Panem, removing lax officials (such as District 12's Head Peacekeeper, Cray), and instructing existing Peacekeepers to toughen up their approach to even minor breaches of the law and come down hard on potential troublemakers. However, when Katniss blew up the Quarter Quell arena and effectively destroyed any chance of peace being restored with it, Snow decided to take more drastic action. Just fifteen minutes after the spectacular ending to the 75th Hunger Games aired throughout Panem, Capitol aircrafts were sent into District 12 to bomb the whole place to the ground, initially as a means of punishing Katniss. It was also an impressive of display of Capitol might as, with fewer than nine hundred citizens surviving, District 12 became Snow's warning to the rebels, just as District 13 had been since the Dark Days.

The Capitol also swooped into the Hunger Games arena just after the rebels and picked up Peeta and Johanna, who they held captive along with Annie Cresta, and any Capitol servants known to have attended Katniss and Peeta. They released Enobaria of District 2 as she was not connected to the rebel plot and remained loyal to the Capitol. **Highest point during the rebellion:** The Capitol's greatest successes in the battle against the rebels are fuelled by Snow's utter lack of scruples when it comes to displaying absolute cruelty and completely obliterating the opposition. When Katniss visits a hospital in District 8, President Snow doesn't know that she will be there, so the fighter planes that he sends in to blow it up are not for her benefit; they merely serve as a powerful reminder that he will show no mercy to anyone who defies him. This is also the message he is sending when bombs are dropped on District 13. Though the televised warning Peeta gives the rebels stops any real damage from being done, this move shows that the Capitol are not willing to back down to their rivals without a hard and bitter fight. President Snow displays his strength and power once more when he sends the lizard muttations after Katniss and her squad, without a thought for others who might cross their path. Though conventional means of attack have not stopped them, Snow is determined to thwart the rebels' mission using every possible method at his disposal. His mutts may not kill Katniss, as he had intended, but they certainly cause considerable damage to the rebel cause.

Turning point: From the Capitol's point of view, the real turning point in the war, when the rebels begin to gain the upper hand, comes when Beetee manages to override the Capitol's own television broadcast to show a film of Finnick revealing top-secret information about powerful people in the Capitol, including the President himself. Whilst this rebel propaganda is detrimental enough in itself, its airing is timed to coincide with a mission to rescue Peeta, Annie and Johanna. Although the rebels suspect that Snow may not be too sad to lose the Hunger Games victors (now that he has hijacked Peeta and programmed him to hate Katniss, he will surely cause maximum emotional and physical damage to the Mockingjay in District 13), the success of the rebels' TV battle is a cause for concern as it shows the Capitol is losing its firm grip on Panem.

Lowest point during the rebellion: When the rebels infiltrate the Capitol, the normally luxurious city falls into turmoil. The hidden pods which make up the Capitol's complex defence system are activated all over the city, war breaks out between rebel fighters and Peacekeepers, and the citizens of the Capitol are caught in the midst of it all as their homes and shops are wrecked. Amongst the invaders, President Snow knows Katniss and her allies are also there, trying to make it to the City Circle to finish off the President. Though he tries to halt them, Snow can't keep track of the Mockingjay as his precious Capitol is turned into a battleground, and he knows that this time he hasn't won.

Losses: Throughout the months of battle between the Capitol and the districts, many Peacekeepers were lost, while members of the Capitol's airforces must have perished when their planes were shot down by the rebels. With each of the districts that turned to the rebels' cause, the Capitol gained enemies and lost supplies, but the first severe loss to the Capitol's fight was District 2, which had always been a great asset to the Capitol and the source of most of their Peacekeeping force.

As the war draws to its bloody climax, Capitol citizens begin to lose their lives as well. When the rebels make it to the Capitol and the deadly pods are set off, there is carnage in the streets, with people dying everywhere and soldiers from both sides shooting anyone who moves. The model city, whose inhabitants are usually so concerned about looking good, is blown to pieces, with lives lost at every corner. The bloodshed reaches right into the City Circle, where outside President Snow's mansion a crowd of children have been kept, supposedly for their own protection, but in reality acting as a human shield for the President against the rebels' attack. While the children wait, a Capitol hovercraft appears above them and releases silver parachutes just like those used in the Hunger Games, which the children grab, sure that they have been sent gifts. However, the parachutes are a trick. They do not hold gifts but bombs, which detonate, leaving the City Square strewn with dead and injured Capitol children.

Outcome: Once the footage of President Snow's own aircraft dropping bombs on innocent Capitol children has been shown live all over Panem, the residents of the Capitol stop resisting the rebels and the war is over. President Snow is captured and is subsequently held prisoner in his mansion as he awaits trial and, almost certainly, execution.

COLD CONFLICT

The Cold War was a continuing state of ideological conflict and military tension between the United States and the Soviet Union (Russia and the surrounding countries which were also under its communist control), lasting from just after the Second World War to the early 1990s. Though the two world superpowers never actually fought each other directly, there was an ever-present threat of war and constant competition between the two in sports, economics and the advancement of technology such as space exploration and nuclear development. In *Mockingjay*, Suzanne Collins creates a parallel between this real-life stalemate between two nuclear powers and the one that the Capitol – a decadent and wealthy society which enjoys excess and luxury but exploits surrounding poorer communities (representing the USA) – enters into with District 13, a regimented, drab society under a strict government (like the Soviet Union).

But it is not just in the history books or the fictional world of Panem that nuclear power plays a large role. Today, most developed nations have nuclear weapons. Although there have been moves to reduce their numbers, no country feels secure enough to disarm completely, because as long as they have at least a few weapons, they act as a deterrent to other countries that might attack. The similarities between the universe of *The Hunger Games* and our own world is what makes the Collins' society all the more vivid and frightening.

NEW ORDER

Represented by: District 13. The only district to break free of Capitol control after the first rebellion, District 13 has fought hard to become self-sufficient and to build a new life for its citizens. The polar opposite of the pleasure-loving Capitol, life in District 13 might seem a little dull and regimented, but it works on strict principles of equality: each person gets only as much food as he or she needs, the burden of work necessary to maintain the district is equally shared, everyone lives in identical apartments, and social distinctions are levelled by the adoption of military ranks.

Led by: President Coin. Alma Coin is about fifty years old with sleek, shoulder-length grey hair and pale grey eyes. President Coin runs her district like it's a machine, with everything being strictly regimented and monitored. She is rather quiet and considers every decision carefully, especially if it involves deviating from her rigid rules. Along with the other rebel masterminds, she has spent years plotting the revolution down to the last detail. Coin is very direct and does not show much warmth or compassion, which can make her seem ruthless at times. Everything about her style of leadership is geared towards efficiency and achieving results. She is determined to overthrow the Capitol and to take down President Snow, and is willing for her side to pay a heavy price to achieve this.

Attitude towards Katniss: President Coin wants to use Katniss to fulfil her agenda just as much as President Snow did. She finds Katniss' unpredictability frustrating (especially as it is the opposite of the army-like order she has instilled in District 13!) and she makes it clear that she would rather have saved charming and easy-going Peeta from the Quarter Quell arena to lead the rebellion. Coin expects Katniss to take on the role of the Mockingjay but she never attempts to get to know Katniss or form a personal bond with her. When Katniss does agree to be the face of the rebellion, she sets a number of conditions, which Coin reluctantly accepts. In a perfect demonstration of the lack of trust between the Mockingjay and the President of District 13, Katniss forces Coin to announce her part in the bargain publicly, to prevent her from reneging on the deal. Although Coin does as Katniss asks, she makes it clear in her public speech that, as President, she holds the ultimate power and would kill Katniss if she thought she had to. To President Coin, Katniss is just a tool that could help her win the rebellion.

Fighting force: District 13 has spent the past seventy-five years transforming its citizens into an army, which is put through a rigorous training process designed to prepare its soldiers for the reality of warfare as much as possible. The army's ranks have swelled with the recent arrival of people from other districts, particularly the eight hundred or so citizens saved from District 12.

Distinct from the main army, Squad 451 is special unit of sharpshooters and includes some of the most impressive soldiers. The actual purpose of the team, however, is to act as the on-screen faces of the rebel invasion. It is because of this function that young, good-looking Hunger Games victors Katniss and Finnick are drafted into the squad. Although both have been disorientated ever since the climax of the Quarter Quell, with the loss of their loved ones Peeta and Annie weighing heavily on their minds, they are probably the most well-prepared for the challenges of war after their experiences in the Hunger Games arena. Gale is also a member of the 'star squad'. Apart from his prowess at shooting and his knowledge of traps gained from years of hunting, Gale is also highly respected in District 13 as he was the one who led over eight hundred people into the Meadow outside District 12's border when the whole place was razed to the ground by the Capitol. Led by Boggs, the rest of Squad 451 is made up of soldiers from District 13.

SQUAD 451

Another link to the Cold War is Squad 451, which is a clear reference to the book *Fahrenheit 451*. This dystopian novel by Ray Bradbury was written in the early years of the Cold War as a response to what he thought were the problems with American society at the time. It features an oppressive government, which controls the population's view of history and the truth through technology, just as President Snow and the Capitol use television propaganda to brainwash Panem into thinking that District 13 does not exist, and prevent people in the different districts from ever knowing about each others' lifestyles. In *Fahrenheit 451*, society also has dangerous forms of entertainment, which involve breaking windows and demolishing cars for fun. It seems fitting that Suzanne Collins borrows the number 451 for the name of the squad that will take on the mission to overthrow President Snow and the Capitol, thereby ending its oppressive way of life.

With their enemies from the Old Order firmly in their sights, here are the sharpshooters from District 13 who join Katniss, Finnick and Gale to make up Squad 451:

Boggs – The leader of the squad is a muscular man in his mid-forties with close cropped grey hair and blue eyes. With his rigidly straight back and permanently serious expression, Katniss initially thinks he is nothing more than Coin's right-hand man and cannot imagine that he has any feelings or emotions. However, she soon finds that she has misjudged him. When Haymitch asks members of the rebel command to think of a time when Katniss moved them with her actions, Boggs is the first to speak up, choosing the moment Katniss sang to Rue as she died. Boggs proves he is a decent man, considerably warmer than Coin, and often betrays flashes of dry humour. Most importantly, he always looks out for his soldiers. When Coin sends the still-unstable Peeta to join Squad 451, showing a blatant disregard for Katniss' life, Boggs is furious and vows to protect her. He shows his trust in Katniss when he gives over command of Squad 451 to her just before he dies.

Jackson – Boggs' second in command is a middle-aged woman, whose farsightedness is an advantage when she's shooting because she can see further into the distance than any of the others without the need for a scope. She is a natural leader and is reluctant to give up command to Katniss when Boggs dies. However, as a good soldier she knows there is no time for argument in war, and she quickly accepts the situation. In the end, Jackson shows her nobility by sacrificing her life for her team.

Leeg 1 and Leeg 2 – The sisters are in their mid-twenties and are so similar that it is difficult to distinguish between them; the only difference Katniss can find is the yellow flecks in Leeg 1's eyes. The pair are very close and Leeg 2 is heartbroken after Leeg 1 dies in the early stages of the squad's assault on the Capitol. She shows considerable strength to get on with the job and finally gives up her own life for the team and their mission.

Mitchell and Homes – The oldest members of the team, both men say very little but play a big role in the squad's assault on the Capitol. Mitchell dies protecting Katniss from Peeta after the latter loses his grip on reality and tries to attack her. Homes proves too that a good soldier never leaves a man behind, refusing to abandon Peeta to his fate even though his presence is a constant threat. Both men can hit any target from fifty yards.

Though Johanna Mason pushes herself through District 13's gruelling military training regime with Katniss, determined to join the rebel army after she is rescued from the Capitol, she fails at the last hurdle. The intense final exam is designed to target a candidate's weak spot and for Johanna this means water. During her captivity in the Capitol, Johanna was repeatedly tortured by being soaked in water and then subjected to electric shocks. When the street is flooded in the practice combat element of her exam, she has a flashback and has to be sedated. Though she can't be part of the mission herself, she makes Katniss promise that she will kill President Snow to pay him back for their suffering.

Additional assets: District 13 has long held the plan of overthrowing the Capitol, but they couldn't manage this alone. Amongst those who play key roles in orchestrating the rebellion are several who were once slaves to the Capitol's whims, including:

Plutarch Heavensbee – Plutarch was a spy in the elite society of the Capitol and has been secretly plotting the downfall of the ruling class for several years. As Head Gamemaker, he was central to the plot to break the victors out of the Quarter Quell arena, making sure that Beetee's special wire was amongst the spoils at the Cornucopia. When he met Katniss on her Victory Tour, Plutarch tried to let her know he was on her side by showing her his watch; as he ran his thumb over the face, a mockingjay glowed for an instant, signalling Plutarch's allegiance to the rebellion. The watch was also intended to give Katniss a clue about the clock-like Quarter Quell arena but, blinkered by her distrust of all the Gamemaker stands for, Katniss failed to understand his hints.

After openly declaring his allegiance to the rebels at the explosive conclusion of the Quarter Quell, Plutarch uses his management and creative skills to oversee the propaganda for District 13 with the help of his assistant, Fulvia Cardew. In particular, he is responsible for orchestrating Katniss' on-screen appearances for the rebels, and for creating her public persona as 'the Mockingjay'. Plutarch gives up status, wealth, and comfort in the Capitol to embrace the rebel cause and adjusts reasonably well to District 13's more basic lifestyle (only lamenting the lack of coffee). He shows he is a man of his word, keeping his promise to Cinna not to show Katniss the Mockingjay outfit he designed for her until after she had decided to accept this role of her own accord, although he knows that her friend's involvement in the scheme is likely to sway her. Plutarch always sees the bigger picture, and by fixing his gaze on the end result, he is able to overlook setbacks – even if these 'setbacks' are lost lives. His ruthless instincts made him a good Gamemaker; they also allow him to take part in the rebels' final plan to turn the Capitol's citizens against President Snow. Indeed, the drastic scheme, which results in the lost lives of numerous Capitol children, bears all the hallmarks of the Gamemaker's involvement, right down to the use of the silver parachutes that are a familiar feature of the Hunger Games. Plutarch's skills are recognised by President Paylor when she makes him Secretary of Communications in the government that is formed after the second rebellion.

Beetee – District 13 only planned to rescue the Hunger Games victors to make a statement but they soon proved to be valuable assets in their own right. While they may not have an attractive, camera-ready leader in Beetee, District 13 did land themselves a technical whiz! As soon as Beetee began to recover, he was taken away in his wheelchair to start creating new weaponry, including a range of incredibly versatile archery weapons for Katniss and Gale that are both showy and deadly. Beetee's strategies for attacking the Capitol are sometimes a little scary but they are certainly brilliant. Showing the cold calculation that made it possible for him to electrocute a number of fellow Hunger Games tributes when he was just a boy, Beetee is not above preying on human impulses to trap his quarry, and he and Gale devote considerable time to developing weapons based on snares. Around ten years before he arrived in District 13, Beetee redesigned Panem's programming network, which means he also able to help the rebels override the Capitol's television broadcasts with their own films. His skills prove vital in raising spirits and winning support throughout Panem; after only the first couple of films he manages to break onto the airwaves, the rebels take Districts 11 and 3.

Haymitch – Though he does not take part in operations out in the field, Haymitch plays a vital role in District 13's strategy, particularly when it comes to handling Katniss. Although each initially finds it hard to forgive the other for their part in allowing Peeta to be captured by the Capitol, Haymitch is still the only person that Katniss will listen to (although she ignores him sometimes too!) and he is able to guide and recast her actions to make her come across as the perfect Mockingjay. Haymitch and Katniss have been through so much together that, despite their frequent altercations, they have developed a close bond. This bond is strengthened by the loss of Peeta to the Capitol as they both love him and are determined to get him back.

Strategy: District 13's plan is to send their army into every district to secure victory for the rebels over the Peacekeepers and, when every district has been released from the Capitol's clutches, launch an assault on the weakened central city itself.

Allies: District 13 has the support of all the districts apart from 2. The other districts have already staged their own uprisings against the Capitol and are joining forces with 13's army to launch an even bigger attack. A key figure in the alliance is the District 8 leader, Commander Paylor. Paylor is in her early thirties but she already seems to have a great deal of military experience and is obviously used to holding a position of authority. Although she too answers to President Coin, she seems to have a fairly free reign to act as she sees fit within her district. She clearly plays some part in the final stage of the rebellion in the Capitol and it is her soldiers who guard President Snow when he is captured by the rebels. It is Paylor who gives permission to Katniss to talk with President Snow in the room where he is being held prisoner, perhaps hoping that he will reveal to her the real culprit behind the bombing of the children outside the President's mansion. After the rebellion, Paylor is elected President herself.

Propaganda: From watching the Capitol operate, the rebels in District 13 know how important propaganda can be. A rebellion in Panem has happened before but it burnt out, so this time around, to achieve success, they need to make sure that their message is kept alive. On their side, they also have a Head Gamemaker, who knows better than anyone how to sell something to an audience, and Beetee, who has experience of the Capitol's television system and can therefore hack into it and override it with rebel propaganda.

However, the central cog in 13's propaganda machine is Katniss. After trying to dress Katniss up and feed her lines to make her come across as the perfect leader, the rebels soon realise that she is at her most inspirational when she is in action. So they send Katniss into risky situations where she can shine and film it all. Katniss is shown shooting Capitol aircrafts, comforting injured citizens in District 8, returning to the ruins of District 12 with Gale, and making defiant speeches aimed at President Snow. The rest of Squad 451 are also featured in propaganda spots, or 'propos', to show that the rebels are a strong fighting force. Another regular face in the anti-Capitol propaganda is Finnick. Finnick hosts a series of short films entitled 'We Remember', each commemorating a dead Hunger Games tribute and aiming to connect with the people in the districts and remind them of the Capitol's cruelty. Finnick is also filmed revealing secrets about the corruption in the Capitol's high society and the underhand dealings of President Snow. Crucially, Beetee manages to play this film over one of the Capitol's interviews with Peeta so that everyone in the Capitol can hear the revelations and see that the rebels are gaining power.

To capture all of these pivotal moments, there is a TV crew constantly following Katniss and her squad. The crew has also come from the Capitol and consists of:

Cressida – With her head shaved and covered in tattoos of green vines, the director might sound like your typical, flashy Capitol resident. However, her diplomatic handling of Fulvia Cardew, and her willingness to go into action with Katniss in pursuit of a good shot, shows that there is more to Cressida than meets the eye. Cressida shows her faith in Katniss when she lies to Jackson for her, claiming to know about Katniss' supposed secret mission to assassinate President Snow.

Messalla – Cressida's assistant is a slim young man with multiple ear piercings and a tongue stud. Like the director, Messalla surprises Katniss by risking his own safety to film her in dangerous situations. When Squad 451 begin their final assault on the Capitol, the whole TV crew goes with them.

Castor and Pollux – The two burly cameramen are brothers, both with sandy hair, red beards and blue eyes. Pollux is an Avox, and worked for five years in the Capitol's sewers without ever being allowed to surface – it's hardly surprising that the brothers decided to join the rebel cause. That Castor did not disown Pollux after he committed a crime against the Capitol, but instead fought and paid to get his brother a job above ground, suggests his loyal character. Pollux's knowledge of the Capitol's sewers is turned to the rebels' advantage when they begin their assault on the Capitol.

Weapons: When the rebels won District 13 from the Capitol in the Dark Days, they inherited many of their resources. Over the seventy-five years that have passed, they have built upon the Capitol's aircraft, special weapons, and nuclear power and now have a large arsenal of their own. District 13 is now home to a fleet of hovercraft, as well as an extensive collection of firearms, explosives, armoured vehicles and archery weapons. Soon after arriving in District 13, Beetee sets to work, helping to develop even more impressive weaponry, including a personalised trident for Finnick and a bow for Katniss. The elegant, sleek black bow is mainly meant to look good on-screen, but is also designed to have perfect balance and respond only to the sound of Katniss' voice. When combined with Beetee's enhanced arrows (there are three types – some are razor sharp, some can set things on fire, and others are explosive – each is distinguished by a different colour shaft), the bow enables Katniss to shoot over one hundred metres accurately. Gale has also spent a lot of time in the Special Defence unit with Beetee, lending his snaring expertise to help come up with the most effective traps for the rebels to use.

Strengths: The rebel movement is so successful because it has the backing of nearly all of the districts, adding vital support and numbers to their army, and making them a force to rival the Capitol. Their cause is promoted further by the presence of the Hunger Games victors Finnick and Katniss, who are very popular figures in Panem. Katniss, in particular, is central to their schemes as she is the 'Mockingjay' – the figurehead of the rebellion who is supposed to embody everything it stands for and lead the way for everyone standing up to the Capitol. The rebels also have the benefit of District 13's hi-tech weaponry and Beetee's expertise.

Weaknesses: A huge obstacle to the rebels is the fact that most of the citizens in the districts have little more than fighting spirit to throw at the Peacekeepers. This means that they are severely damaged by carefully-planned Capitol attacks, as Katniss sees in District 8. Here, and all around Panem, many people aren't able to receive proper medical treatment as resources are so tight. District 13 has something of an uphill struggle to unite the districts and ensure that they are able to stand their ground.

Starting point of the rebellion: After Katniss and Peeta staged their unintentional protest against the Capitol at the end of the 74th Hunger Games, the severely oppressed people living in Panem's districts started to show signs of unrest. Some districts even staged riots, but the Capitol managed to restore order early on before things got out of hand. That is, until the climax of the 75th Hunger Games, when the leaders of an intricate rebel plot broke some of the former victors out of the arena in an act of public defiance broadcast to the whole of Panem. What better way to inspire the people in the districts to continue their fight?

Highest point during the rebellion: Despite the many setbacks they suffer, and attacks they encounter from the Capitol, the rebels' plan succeeds; they take control of the districts and eventually enter the Capitol. Many of their forces, including some members of Squad 451, make it right to the heart of the city, proving that President Snow and his army are not as indestructible as they once seemed to the rest of Panem.

Turning point: An important victory for District 13 comes when they win District 2 from the capitol's clutches. This district, which has always been the most loyal to the Capitol, was always going to be the hardest place for the revolution to succeed (apart from the Capitol itself, of course!), so winning over its citizens to the rebel agenda is a major coup for President Coin and her crew.

Lowest point during the rebellion: Though their power has steadily grown throughout the revolution, the rebel army still suffers plenty of setbacks. For example, though the Capitol's attack on District 13 is not as harmful as it could be, thanks to Peeta's warning, it demonstrates that the rebels are not out of President Snow's reach yet. The rebels experience a particularly low point even as they are within sight of success. As the rebel army moves through the Capitol, it pays a heavy price for each step it takes towards its goal; the Capitol's deadly pods and vicious muttations mean that only five of Squad 451 survive the invasion, and it is a hard struggle for these few to hold on amid the chaos.

Losses: Inevitably, a lot of the rebels take on a battle they can't win when they stand up to the Capitol. Most of the residents of District 12, including Peeta's family and Madge Undersee, pay for Katniss' actions in the Hunger Games arena with their lives. And Katniss sees first-hand the destruction of the hospital of already-wounded people in District 8, who didn't even pose a threat to the Capitol.

As the rebels make their way into the Capitol, they are greeted with the activation of pods, which kill people in ever more gruesome ways – some boiling them, others blowing craters in the street, all wiping out several rebels at a time. Nearly all of Squad 451 meets a tragic end as the team races towards the centre of the Capitol. Early on in their mission, Leeg 2 hits a pod which the rebels thought would release a swarm of muttated gnats, but in fact it shoots out metal darts, one of which pierces her head. The next day, Peeta is sent to replace her. As they film propaganda material, the squad accidentally sets off a pod they were not aware of, which explodes and blows Boggs' legs off. Before he dies, he just has time to hand his Holo with a map of the Capitol over to Katniss and warn her to continue pursuing President Snow, rather than following President Coin's orders. In the furore that follows the explosion that killed Boggs, Peeta becomes disorientated and lashes out at Mitchell, who falls back and is caught in another pod, this time a net of barbed wire. Later, as they are fleeing from the lizard mutts, Messalla runs into a pod that melts him. In order to buy their teammates more time and a chance of escape, Jackson and Leeg 1 fall back to take on some of the mutts, effectively sacrificing themselves.

Just moments later, only a few of the squad have managed to climb out of the mutts' reach when Katniss is forced to detonate her Holo to have any chance of stopping them, though she knows that some of her friends are still down there, including Castor and Holmes. As she does so, she witnesses Finnick being attacked by three mutts and, in the moment before he dies, she seems to see his last thoughts – images of the sea, Mags and, of course, Annie.

The fighting and killing all comes to a head when the children are bombed outside President Snow's house in the Capitol. Peacekeepers and rebel medics rush over to help the injured, including Primrose. However, they don't get the chance to treat anyone because they are running into a trap. A number of parachutes did not go off in the first explosion, being specially delayed to blow up anyone who rushed to the rescue of the children, and so Katniss is forced to watch her little sister die before her eyes.

Outcome: With the Capitol severely weakened by the rebel attack, the bombing of the children was all it took for the rebels to take over completely. The rebel mission was successful, though rebel troops are still combating a few small areas of Capitol resistance, and President Coin now has control of Panem.

ALL CHANGE IS GOOD?

To many of the downtrodden people of Panem, the appearance of District 13 – an armed, self-sufficient society that is willing to take on the Capitol – can only be a good thing. They are so used to the oppressive Capitol regime that they embrace any chance of change with open arms. But is all change really good?

Katniss is wary of District 13 from the start. She finds it very suspicious that they bargained with the Capitol after the Dark Days while the other districts suffered the consequences of the first rebellion for the next seventy-five years, despite the fact that 13 had plenty of weapons available. Her mistrust grows further when she finds her Hunger Games prep team, saved from the Capitol for her, tied up and beaten for taking too much food at dinner time. The revolution is meant to be about saving people from such treatment and yet it is taking place at the heart of District 13 itself.

This event prompts Katniss to ask the question: how different is this new order from the old one?

GALE OR PEETA

TEAM GALE

Type: Tall, dark and handsome – the brooding outdoorsy type!

First met Katniss: When he was fourteen and she was twelve, hunting in the woods.

Other crushes: Gale could have his pick of the girls from school, and he's certainly kissed a few, but he's never shown any true interest in anyone but Katniss.

Best physical features: Nature gave Gale a face that's always camera-ready.

Best traits: Family-orientated Gale is extremely loyal, brave and a great provider – what more could you want from a husband?

Worst traits: He has a short temper and can be very single-minded.

Most romantic moment: When he agreed to risk everything to run away with Katniss and told her he loved her.

Least romantic moment: During the rebellion, Katniss got to see Gale's ruthless side – and it wasn't always pretty!

Perfect date: If you really want to impress Gale, suggest a picnic in the woods. Gale feels most at home outdoors and he likes a girl who can catch her own meal, so after a spot of hunting you can sit down and roast your game together over an open fire.

Relationship with Katniss: They say that opposites attract, but Katniss and Gale are definitely the exception! Both teens grew up in the Seam and lost their fathers in the same mining accident. Despite attending the same memorial service, they first met properly whilst hunting in the woods. Realising they could work better together, they became hunting partners and have met up on the wrong side of the District 12 fence every Sunday since that day. They can relate to each other because they are both the eldest children in their families and feel a responsibility to provide for their younger siblings by catching game and entering their names into the Hunger Games reaping several times over for extra food. The two even look alike, with the dark colouring typical of Seam residents. Katniss thinks of Gale as her best friend; he is the only person with whom she can totally relax and share all her secrets.

Despite their similarities, there is one noticeable difference between the two. Out in the woods, Gale often flies into fits of rage over the Capitol and the running of Panem, while Katniss stays calm. Although she agrees that the politics of her nation are unfair and used to comment on the situation (before she knew any better), she has since learned to bite her lip, unable to see the point of protesting about anything she cannot change. Hours before the reaping, Gale tries to persuade Katniss to run away with him, promising that they could survive together in the woods outside of District 12. Yet, Katniss cannot contemplate abandoning Prim. Long before this day, she decided to keep her head down and simply get on with her life in 12. Though Gale's mind is on freedom, all Katniss can really focus on is looking after her family.

Handsome Gale receives plenty of attention from the other girls at school and has even kissed a few of them. However, he starts to realise that he has feelings for Katniss one day when they are trading their game in the Hob. Their Peacekeeper friend Darius starts bartering with Katniss for one of his kisses. He's only teasing, but suddenly possessive Gale realises doesn't like the way the conversation is heading. Certainly, he hates the thought of Katniss being with anyone else – all of which makes him realise that he sees her as more than just a friend. Although she denies any romance with her best friend, Katniss admits she would feel jealous of any girlfriend he got, but puts this down to not wanting to lose her trusted hunting partner. It occurs to her that everyone in the district must assume she will marry Gale eventually, but any chance of a straightforward life with him is lost when Primrose is reaped as a tribute in the 74th Hunger Games.

At the reaping, when Katniss volunteers to take Prim's place, it is Gale who carries the distraught little girl away from the stage. He understands that Katniss needs to be strong and protect her sister. Gale is the last person Katniss sees before she is whisked away to the Capitol. He gives her practical survival advice and promises he will care for her family while she's gone, but is taken away before he gets to tell her the most important thing – could he have been meaning to confess his love for her?

In the run-up to the Games, Katniss tries to establish a friendship with Peeta, but it is constantly overshadowed by comparisons with what she has with Gale – a relationship which feels much more natural to her. She misses him terribly and realises he has become closer to her than just a friend over the last year. Throughout the Games, her mind jumps back to Gale several times – often in relation to hunting, but also, Katniss can't help wondering what he'll make of her public displays of affection with Peeta. Meanwhile, outside of the arena, when Katniss makes the final eight, Capitol reporters are sent into District 12 to record pieces about Katniss and are inevitably pointed in Gale's direction. In light of her on-screen love affair, her handsome male best friend is instead portrayed as her cousin – it's lucky that they look alike!

When Katniss returns home, she doesn't see Gale alone for several weeks as she has to attend victory celebrations. Surrounded by reporters, she's given not a moment's privacy. Also, Gale has started work in the mines and Katniss and her family have moved to the Victor's Village. On her first free Sunday she goes to their usual meeting spot and waits for him for two hours, worrying that he has given up on her or is so angry about Peeta that she has lost him for good, when he finally turns up. They spend the day together hunting and talking as they used to. Reassured, Katniss thinks that everything can go back to normal . . . until – much to her surprise – he kisses her. Afterwards, they pretend it has never happened, but even so, Katniss knows they can never have just a simple friendship. They still see each other on Sundays to hunt, but they can't tell each other everything as they used to. Katniss knows Gale has been hurt by her public romance with Peeta. He's also too proud to accept any of her victory money, even if it is intended to help his family.

On their Victory Tour through the districts, Katniss has to resume her romance with Peeta. Haymitch makes it clear to her that this arrangement is not temporary – for the sake of audiences across Panem, President Snow will force her to be tied to Peeta forever – whether she wants to be or not, meaning she can never choose a life with Gale. Katniss resigns herself to this fact and when they reach the Capitol she arranges for Peeta to propose to her during their televised interview with Caesar Flickerman. However, when President Snow lets Katniss know (by means of a tiny shake of his head) that her act has not convinced him, it gives her the freedom to choose her own path once more. Back in 12, she meets up with Gale and explains everything to him. She implores him to run away with her and their families to escape the threat of President Snow. Gale agrees and tells her that he loves her, but she cannot say it back. Under less terrifying circumstances, who can say how she'd have answered him . . . but as it is, Katniss confesses she's been unable to feel anything for anyone but fear since the day Prim's name was drawn at the reaping. Gale is disappointed, but still wants to go until he realises that Katniss intends to ask Peeta and Haymitch to come too, and that there is an uprising in District 8. Once he's heard what's afoot in 8, Gale's determined to stay and start something similar in 12, where he feels he has a duty to fight for a better life – not just for his own family, but for everyone who lives there.

Shortly after Gale leaves, he is caught with a turkey (illegally poached from the woods) by the strict new Head Peacekeeper, Romulus Thread. Some time later, Katniss is drawn to the square at the centre of 12 by some terrifyingly unfamiliar noise. Pushing through a crowd of horrified onlookers, she sees what's caught their attention – Thread brutally whipping Gale for his 'crime' against the Capitol. With Haymitch and Peeta's help, Katniss intervenes and takes him back to her mother to be healed. Seeing him so badly injured makes her realise just how much he means to her. She thinks about how she'd feel if she was in his place, left behind in 12 and forced to watch him romancing another girl. Suddenly, she's overwhelmed by the feeling that she should be with Gale. She kisses the seemingly unconscious patient and, as he rouses slightly, promises him she will stay and fight against the Capitol with him.

Now that Katniss' mind is set on starting a rebellion, she decides she cannot possibly think of love or trying to figure out her complicated feelings for Gale. And this is how things are left between them when she is reaped to go back into the Hunger Games arena for the Quarter Quell. Gale puts aside his own issues to help her train for it with Peeta. Determined to save Peeta, Katniss is not expecting to return from the arena alive for a second time, and so she plans her last words to her best friend, wanting to tell him how important he has been to her and that she loves him in her own way. However, she never gets the chance as she is rushed straight to the Capitol before she can say goodbye to anyone.

But, though he may be out of sight, Gale is almost never out of mind. The very sight of her new servant provides a painful reminder of the boy she's left behind, as the Avox sent to wait on her in the Capitol is their old friend Darius. Last seen lying unconscious in the centre of District 12, the former Peacekeeper has paid dearly for his challenge to Thread's authority (disastrously, he tried to save Gale from the Head Peacekeeper's whip minutes before Katniss and Peeta arrived on the scene). This makes her feel almost as if Gale is present – in spirit if not in body – watching over her with Peeta. Another traumatic reminder comes when she accidentally strays into the jabberjay section of the Hunger Games arena and is tormented by Gale's screams. He is also one of the arguments used by Peeta to try to convince Katniss to fight for her own survival (rather than his) in the Quarter Quell – he honestly believes she could lead a happy life with Gale, without Peeta himself around to complicate matters.

Katniss goes into the arena believing that she will never see Gale again, but after the arena's been blown apart, Katniss is rescued by the rebels and proved wrong. Lying delirious in the hospital, she opens her eyes to be greeted by a familiar face. It is Gale, come to break the news of the destruction of District 12 in dulcet tones. He also accompanies her when she goes back to visit the ruins of her former home and is ready to reassure her, although he stays in the hovercraft. In District 13, Katniss and Gale spend much of their time together. With Peeta out of the picture, their friendship feels considerably less strained than when Katniss was being forced to fake a romantic relationship with her fellow tribute. Gale also seems to understand that there is no point in trying to push Katniss for anything more than friendship, since she is so damaged by what has happened and worried for Peeta. Despite their renewed closeness, they have different feelings towards District 13 and President Coin. While Katniss is suspicious of Coin's motives and District 13's methods, Gale fully supports the new rebel force. A fervent defender of their decisions, he feels that war against the Capitol calls for the kind of drastic action that will not please everyone.

This difference of opinion means a new distance starts to creep in between the two best friends. Katniss is appalled to discover her defenceless prep team, locked away in a hidden compartment in District 13 – bruised, beaten and shackled to the wall, simply because the hungry stylists attempted to steal a few slices of bread. Yet, Gale doesn't fully understand her outrage. In his eyes, this team of Capitol citizens deserves no better. In action, Gale and Katniss are the perfect team. He supports her when she visits the hospital in 8 and he is right beside her when they're shooting at the Capitol's planes. However, she begins to worry about his cold-hearted excitement at the prospect of deploying Beetee's weapons. Then there's his decision to keep one of Peeta's appearances on television from her – a move that angers Katniss very much. However, she decides to put her feelings aside on their visit District 12. Accompanied by the usual camera crew, they both relive their memories of the past.

In the wreckage of her house in the Victor's Village, Gale smoothes his fingers over the same wooden table where Katniss kissed him after his whipping. Seeing the tears in his eyes, Katniss can't help but kiss him again. Gale pulls away, however, remarking wryly that he only gets attention from Katniss when he's hurt.

Nevertheless, this doesn't stop Gale from risking his own life to protect Katniss and her loved ones. Thanks to him, both Prim and Buttercup are safely installed in District 13's underground bunker when the Capitol bombs being to fall. Gale also volunteers to be part of the crew who go to rescue the captured victors from the Hunger Games arena, leaving Katniss to worry about both him and Peeta.

Yet, after his safe return, Katniss' relief is short-lived. Unbeknownst to her, Gale has been using his hunting expertise to help Beetee develop snares and traps large enough to catch full-grown men and women. Katniss is disgusted to learn that they could be so inhumane but, once again, Gale maintains that they are just using the Capitol's own methods against them. The gap between them widens on their visit to District 2, the object being to help the rebels overcome the opposition there. In a rare moment alone, Gale admits that he's never stopped envying Peeta. As long as Peeta is sick (from Snow's hijacking), Katniss will never be able to let him go, meaning she'll never be able to be with Gale. Katniss responds by kissing him – perhaps because she's given up hope of ever getting Peeta back, perhaps because she's lonely. Either way, Gale recognises her confusion and pulls away. He says it doesn't count because Katniss is still unsure of what – or more accurately, who – she really wants. Soon though, Katniss has another reason not to kiss him.

Before long, Gale comes up with a plan to shut down District 2's mountain base, the Nut. An intricate network of disused mines, the Nut's rudimentary air supply depends on a number of vents in the mountainside. Gale proposes bombing the mountain, provoking a series of deadly avalanches and effectively sealing off these vital vents altogether. Horrified Boggs points out that – sealed within the mountain, the only exits blocked off by rebel forces – the civilians hiding within the Nut will suffocate within a matter of hours . . . none of which is enough to dissuade Gale from going through with it. He never intends for the Nut to be anything other than a death trap. Fortunately, the others decide to give the targets a chance to surrender, yet Katniss cannot believe that her childhood friend, who also lost his father in a mining accident, could formulate so cruel a plan. When they were younger in the woods, Gale would suggest worse things, but Katniss' experiences in the Hunger Games arena have taught her that empty words and concrete actions are two very different things. The bond between them is strong, however. Thus, they continue their friendship and it is Gale who reassures Katniss she is not a bad person when the hijacked Peeta accuses her of being manipulative and selfish.

As Katniss and Gale set off for the Capitol with the rest of Squad 451, Gale realises Katniss is waiting to put her own plot in motion. In fact, she's simply biding her time, waiting for her shot at killing President Snow. When the time comes, Gale promises to go with her. Together they infiltrate the centre of the Capitol. Facing attack from all sides, the old hunting partners must put all their differences aside to protect each other.

However, Katniss' mission never comes to fruition. Instead, her journey through the Capitol streets leads her to the City Circle, where children and teens are being sheltered from the carnage. In the moments that follow, Katniss is dealt a crushing blow. Overhead, a Capitol hovercraft circles, dropping silver parachutes of essential supplies into the crowd. Except that these are not the same silver parachutes Katniss recognises from the Hunger Games. Helpless, she watches as the parcels – lethal bombs disguised as gifts – explode in the children's hands. A team of medics rush forward to help them. Seconds later there's another round of explosions, but not before Katniss has locked eyes with Prim, at the heart of the blaze. After the death of her beloved sister – and the deaths of countless other innocent children – nothing can ever been the same between Gale and Katniss again . . .

During her recovery, Katniss strays into an unfamiliar part of the mansion, where she's surprised to find President Snow. With sadistic relish, he informs her that he was not the man to order the bombing of the children in City Circle; this is merely what the rebels wanted everyone to believe. Instead, it was Katniss' own comrades who hijacked the Capitol hovercraft. Though Katniss doesn't want to believe this, his words ring horribly true. Significantly, the bombing of the children was televised from start to finish. Katniss also remembers Beetee and Gale coming up with just such a plan in District 13.

The last time she sees Gale, he confesses that he couldn't say if he was the one to design the lethal bomb that killed Prim or not. What he does know for certain, however, is that his actions have blown the two of them too far apart for them to ever find a way back to their happiest days in the woods. Katniss realises this too; though she wonders if they could have made things work had they been able to continue their lives undisturbed in District 12. After the war, Gale moves to District 2, in pursuit of some fancy new job, and the two best friends never see each other again.

TEAM PEETA

Type: Blond-haired, blue-eyed prince charming!

First met Katniss: On their first day of school.

Other crushes: None. He may have looked at other girls, but he's been smitten with Katniss from the start.

Best physical features: His broad shoulders and dreamy blue eyes.

Best traits: Peeta is unfailingly loyal, kind, selfless and funny. A smooth-talker, he also has a magical way with words!

Worst traits: Peeta can be quite sensitive and easily hurt.

Most romantic moment: When Peeta confessed his love for Katniss in front of the whole of Panem. His retelling of the moment he first fell for her as they were hiding out in a cave in the 74th Hunger Games arena also had the 'awww' factor.

Least romantic moment: It's hardly Peeta's fault that he was hijacked by the Capitol to hate and mistrust Katniss, but trying to strangle your fiancée on sight is definitely not recommended!

Perfect date: Peeta would like nothing more than to treat his special lady to a relaxing date watching the sunset. He'd provide some sweet treats (home-baked, of course) and maybe even bring his easel to paint you.

Relationship with Katniss: Katniss and Peeta have always been in the same class at school. Indeed, Peeta fell for her on their very first day of classes after hearing her sing. Despite this, the two never really got to speak until facing each other in the Hunger Games. However, they did share one special moment when Peeta spotted starving Katniss outside his parents' bakery and deliberately burnt some bread (though he was punished for this) so that he could give it away to her. Though she never got a chance to thank him, Katniss has felt indebted to Peeta ever since because, in truth, his kindness came at just the right time. At her very weakest, fatherless Katniss had been on the brink of giving up. Peeta's generosity gave her hope – something extremely rare in the Seam – and the will to carry on. This is why Katniss' heart sinks when his name is reaped for the 74th Games; she doesn't want to kill the boy to whom she owes her life.

Despite feeling that Peeta might be kind, Katniss decides to distance herself from him as much as possible because this will make it easier to deal with if he dies in the arena. Though the District 12 tributes put on a united front in the opening ceremony and at the Training Centre, Katniss is careful not to trust Peeta or become too friendly with him. She feels her caution is justified when Peeta requests to be coached separately, although they'd both agreed to be coached together at the start. She feels almost betrayed by him – an impression that only intensifies when he confesses his love for her to Caesar Flickerman the night before the Games.

Extremely embarrassed, Katniss suspects Peeta is trying to make her look like a fool. She rages at him until Haymitch points out that Peeta has given her a new edge. If she's desirable in Peeta's eyes, then that makes the girl on fire worth a second look. Once again, it seems like Katniss owes him but, given the fact that they're just about to enter the arena, there's little she can do to even up the score. Later that night, sleepless Katniss wanders out of her room and up onto the roof. Beneath the chill night sky, she happens upon Peeta. He tries to explain to Katniss how he wants to die as 'himself' in the arena, rather than turning into a mindless savage. Yet, Katniss cannot relate to his argument, wondering how this could possibly be Peeta's only aim. All she can focus on is her own survival.

Anyway, as far as she is concerned, Peeta loses all self-respect as soon as they enter the arena, joining up with the ruthless Career Pack almost immediately. This is a major shock to Katniss, who assumes Peeta must have been pretending to be the kindly baker's boy all along. The unscrupulous Career Tributes are hated in District 12 and Peeta's allegiance with them makes Katniss hate him too . . . until he does something that confuses her completely.

After Katniss drops a nest of angry tracker jackers onto the unsuspecting Careers below her tree, she can't immediately flee the scene. Struggling to salvage a bow and arrows from Glimmer's corpse, she comes face to face with Peeta. Yet, rather than kill her straightaway, he urges her to flee the area. Seconds behind him, Cato is slashing his way through the undergrowth. Disorientated Katniss has also suffered some tracker-jacker stings, but as far as she can tell, Peeta just saved her life once more. This is Katniss' final thought before the venom takes full effect and she blacks out . . .

When the Gamemakers change the rules, stating that two tributes from the same district can be joint victors, Katniss makes up her mind to seek out her district partner. Spying on the Careers, Katniss overhears Cato bragging about how badly he cut Peeta. Alarmed, Katniss tracks down her wounded district partner and tries to treat him, though she finds the sight of his septic wounds quite gruesome. Despite their dire situation, the teens joke with each other and, as Katniss comforts Peeta, they even share a kiss. Very quickly, Katniss works out that these displays of affection are a hit with the audience because they are sent a pot of broth by their sponsors just moments later. Given this, Katniss starts to relax around him as they hide out from the Careers in a cave, swapping stories about themselves. She is determined to help her new ally, though he has obviously contracted blood poisoning. Though he begs her not to go (so much so that Katniss has to drug him before she leaves), Katniss is more than willing to risk her own life to pick up medicine for him at the Gamemakers' feast.

Together, they make it to the end of the game but, just as they're waiting for a hovercraft to materialise and take them home, the Gamemakers reveal their cruel final twist: the new rule is null and void. There can only be one surviving victor in the Games. As Peeta's hand moves to his knife, Katniss' instinct is to attack him first. A split-second later he tosses his weapon into the lake, yet Katniss' arrow is ready to fly – straight to Peeta's heart. Realising that he never intended to kill her, she is ashamed and admits that she can't bring herself to finish him either. Luckily, quick-thinking Katniss is able to formulate an alternate plan involving Peeta's poisonous nightlock berries . . .

In desperation, the Gamemakers rethink their latest ruling and both star-crossed lovers are both pulled out of the arena alive. Before they are reunited, Katniss learns that President Snow is furious about their stunt and they must act like they did it because they were madly in love. So Katniss continues to play out the romance, but Peeta isn't acting. When he realises that her affection has been a strategy all along, Peeta is deeply hurt. Ironically, at the same time Katniss herself is desperately confused. She feels guilty about being with Peeta, even though she can't define her relationship with Gale clearly and is left wondering how much of her time with Peeta was faked. At this point, all that she can be sure of is that she is genuinely sad to feel him slipping away from her.

After they return home, things between Katniss and Peeta remain strained. This can't continue on their Victory Tour, however. President Snow even pays a visit to Katniss' home to warn her that she must continue to seem besotted with Peeta if her moment with the berries is to be perceived as an act of mad love rather than defiance. So, in front of the cameras they continue to act like infatuated lovebirds. Behind the scenes, Haymitch warns Katniss that she will never be free of the romance that the Capitol audience have become so invested in – she will certainly end up marrying Peeta whether she wants to or not.

Peeta apologises to Katniss for resenting her behaviour. After all, he can appreciate she never set out to deceive him; she was just trying to keep them alive. However, he is soon angry with her again when she finally chooses to open up to him about President Snow's warning. After this revelation, the two agree not to keep things from each other. In future, they'll be friends. When Katniss suffers nightmares (so vivid that they cause her to cry out in her sleep), Peeta, who finds it hard to sleep too, hears her and goes to comfort her. From then on they sleep together every night, causing rumours on their train. In the Capitol, Katniss suggests that Peeta propose to her to keep President Snow happy. Peeta is upset because he wants their engagement to be real rather than pretend, but he goes ahead and pops the question during their interview with Caesar Flickerman. Nonetheless, the couple's best efforts are not enough for President Snow.

After they return home, Katniss starts making plans to run away and Peeta agrees to leave with her without a second thought. However, when Gale is whipped to within an inch of his life Peeta understands without Katniss having to explain that the plan is off. Not much later, Katniss injures her foot climbing over District 12's fence. Under the new Head Peacekeeper, it's alive with electricity once more. Rather than risk discovery after an illegal hunting spree, Katniss has no choice but to drop over the top. While she is recovering from the fall, Peeta visits her every day. He brings her favourite cheese buns and helps her add to a family book in which Mr Everdeen began recording survival tips. It's the first time that they get to spend together doing something which isn't related to the Hunger Games in any way.

This freedom from the tournament which brought them together proves short-lived when the reading of the card for the Quarter Quell is announced. Katniss' first reaction is shock and fear, but once she's managed to pull herself together a little, she visits Haymitch to ask him to do something for her – to help make sure that Peeta comes out of this arena alive. Of course, Peeta already went to see Haymitch the moment the ruling was aired to ask him to protect Katniss. Unbeknownst to the younger victors, their mentor agrees to aid them both. With their missions to save each other in their minds, District 12's former victors train for the competition as if they are Career Tributes. When the reaping comes around, Haymitch is the male victor who is reaped to go back into the arena but, as predicted, Peeta volunteers to take his place, so he can look after Katniss.

This year Haymitch wants them to team up with some of their rivals, but they decide they will work better as a pair. Indeed, they seem to share one mind when they both pull impromptu risky stunts in their shows for the Gamemakers. They share a bed again and spend one of their last days before the Games sitting on the roof together sharing a picnic and watching the sunset. Despite the worries weighing down on them both, they are able to have one perfect day together and when Peeta says he wishes he could freeze that moment in time forever, Katniss agrees with him. During their interviews with Caesar Flickerman, both add to the other victors' protests by lamenting the fact that their relationship will never have a future, but Peeta causes an even bigger stir when he announces that Katniss is pregnant! This year, his interview confession doesn't anger Katniss; in fact she thinks of it as the perfect way to make the Capitol look worse.

In the Quarter Quell arena, the District 12 tributes somehow become part of an alliance – an arrangement that turns out to be to their benefit when Peeta walks into a force field on the first day. Katniss is devastated to realise that his heart has stopped and, even after Finnick has managed to resuscitate him, she is an emotional wreck. As the competition progresses Katniss notices – to her confusion – that the other victors seem to be protecting Peeta. Her own motivation for saving Peeta is simple (she genuinely cares for him), but she can only imagine what's in it for the others. Perhaps they consider him vital to the rebels' cause as he is so eloquent and persuasive . . .

While Katniss is thinking about Peeta, he is constantly thinking of her. After Katniss is tortured by jabberjays, Peeta comforts her, choosing this moment to reveal to her that his tribute token – a golden necklace with a mockingjay pendant – is actually a locket containing photos of her mother, Prim and Gale. Peeta uses this trinket to try to convince her that she should be the one to win the Games, instead of him. Though it will be hard for her to cope with losing him, she could still lead a happy life back home in District 12. As for him, he couldn't be happy without her in his life. Even though Katniss doesn't agree with what Peeta is saying, they end up kissing and this time it is not for show.

The next day Peeta finds a pearl in an oyster shell and gives it to

Katniss; as he does so, he realises that he has not persuaded her. As Beetee's plan falls apart and Katniss is left bleeding heavily in the jungle, all she can think of is finding Peeta. He is calling out for her in turn. To give him the best chance of survival, she goes so far as to scream out loud, in the hope that she will draw the other victors away from him. When Katniss shoots her arrow into the force field later that night, she tries to reach for Peeta's pearl as a last comfort, certain that she is about to die.

The first thing on her mind when she wakes in a hospital bed is Peeta. She assumes that they have both been captured by the Capitol and goes looking for him. At the very least, she can save him from torture by killing him. But Katniss does not find Peeta. Instead she discovers that she has been saved by the rebels, while Peeta has been taken by the Capitol. Katniss is furious with Haymitch for his part in this turn of events and tries to attack him. As much as she blames him, she also blames herself for splitting up with Peeta in the Quarter Quell arena. This guilt and her worry over what the Capitol could possibly be doing to torture Peeta eats away at her.

So she is overjoyed to see him on television in Capitol propaganda, alive and healthy. Even as Peeta begs the rebels for a ceasefire, he is still protecting Katniss, insisting that she was never part of the rebels' plan. Katniss' decision to become the Mockingjay is also about protecting Peeta – her most crucial condition for this arrangement is that he will be spared from trial or execution by the rebels, though she knows they see him as a traitor for calling for an end to the rebellion.

Despite Katniss' initial joy at seeing Peeta onscreen, the next time he appears on television, he looks significantly worse; he is obviously having a very rough time in the Capitol. He is starting to appear less and less like himself and has an agitated air about him that Katniss has never noticed before. The rebels manage to interrupt one of Peeta's interviews with their own broadcast, but as the camera moves back to him, he warns District 13 that they could be dead by midnight. After this, the only thing that can be heard clearly is a blow and Peeta's cry as his blood spills on to the floor.

Peeta has given a warning to the rebels in District 13 that the Capitol is about to attack, but at what cost to himself? This is the thought rattling around in Katniss' head in the following days as she realises that President Snow is using Peeta to hurt her. In Finnick, she finds a confidant who understands her pain, as he has been subject to the same torment for years with Snow's threats hanging over Annie. All the two can do is play with old rope as they try to distract themselves from the many horrific possibilities of what could be happening to their loved ones. Katniss can't even record her propaganda shots as she is so worried about the effects her words may be having on Peeta and she breaks down instead.

When the rebels decide to rescue Peeta and Annie, it is a huge relief for both Katniss and Finnick. Knowing that Peeta has been brought back safely, Katniss is ecstatic and she rushes straight to the hospital to be there when he wakes. She finds him already awake and about to embrace her – except he doesn't want to hold her, he tries to strangle her! Peeta has been hijacked by the Capitol, injected with tracker-jacker venom that's made him associate only negative thoughts and feelings with his former love. Katniss tries to avoid him for a while after this and the few times that she does encounter him, he is angry and vicious towards her. He accuses her of being a mutt and, as he interrogates her about her romantic behaviour towards him as well as Gale, he paints her as manipulative and deceitful – bitter words that hurt Katniss all the more because she believes them to be justified. Seeing the boy whose unconditional love and reassuring presence she took for granted so corrupted makes Katniss appreciate just how much he meant to her before.

Katniss' attempts to stay away from Peeta are thwarted when President Coin sends him out to join Squad 451 in the Capitol. This decision convinces Katniss once and for all that Coin wants rid of her, because Peeta still poses a real danger to her safety. It takes Haymitch to make Katniss see that Peeta's hijacking isn't his fault and that she should try to help him rather than reacting in a hostile manner. Peeta doesn't know what effect he is having on her, because he doesn't know what is real anymore. So, Katniss and the rest of the squad try to help him remember as much as possible, putting his life back together piece by piece. In combat, however, Peeta is dazed. Apparently back in his hijacked state, he is on the brink of attacking Katniss. Mitchell attempts to stop him, but Peeta throws him off and into a Capitol pod. After this episode, Boggs and Peeta tell Katniss she should kill him, but she can't do this. She can't let go of the boy she cares about so much and she can't let President Snow win by coming between them.

After the war is won, Katniss first sees Peeta again at a meeting of former victors, called together to discuss the possibility of a final Hunger Games using Capitol children. Peeta is horrified and tries to persuade the others to stop it from taking place. He also stops

Katniss from swallowing her deadly nightlock pill after she has shot President Coin. It seems like the old dependable and moral Peeta is back, but now it is Katniss who is lost. She is broken and weary after Prim's death and goes back to District 12 a shadow of her former self. Then, one day Peeta turns up. With his help, and that of Greasy Sae and Haymitch, Katniss starts to build a new life. They commemorate all the people they have lost in a book full of memories and they comfort each other.

LITERARY LOVE TRIANGLES

While it's far from being the main plot of the series, Katniss' love for the two boys in her life is a very interesting storyline with lots of exciting twists and turns. Both the reader and the love interests long to know who she will pick, but there's a huge problem . . . Katniss is just as confused herself! And who can blame her? It's a tough choice . . .

Love triangles are common in many stories. After all, it's a great way to keep the reader guessing and turning pages. A love triangle which is very similar to the one in *The Hunger Games* can be found in Emily Brontë's classic novel, *Wuthering Heights*. In this story, headstrong and wild Cathy Earnshaw has to choose between two men – the swarthy gypsy she grew up with, Heathcliff, and a fair-haired, privileged local boy named Edgar. Like Gale, Heathcliff is linked to nature, not only in name but because he has spent years exploring the moors with Cathy. Heathcliff also kills animals (though when he does, it's in a rather creepier way than hunter Gale). On the other hand, Edgar represents culture and a better way of life for Cathy, plus he is absolutely devoted to her. In the end, Cathy marries Edgar because she likes him as well as the comfortable lifestyle that he can provide. Underneath it all, she still loves Heathcliff and ends up tormented by her choice. However, she doesn't live to regret her marriage long and dies giving birth to Edgar's daughter. Luckily, Katniss' dilemma doesn't end quite the same way.

Another link to *Wuthering Heights* is the fact that the love triangle affects the next generation of these families, just as Peeta's infatuation with Katniss mirrors his father's secret love for her mother.

Katniss and Peeta manage to find happiness together, after all the hardship and misery they have experienced. Eventually they marry and have children – a girl with dark hair and blue eyes, and a younger boy with blond curls and grey eyes. Though they can never forget the horrors they have been through, they each give the other the strength they need to carry on. Perhaps this ending is something we should have foreseen all along; after all, District 12's marriage ceremony involves cooking a loaf of bread in an open fire. And in this respect, the boy with the bread and the girl on fire are a perfect match.

When Katniss overheard Gale telling Peeta that she would eventually choose the boy she needed the most, she was deeply hurt. More than anything, how could Gale believe she'd approach the dilemma with such a heartless attitude, unmoved by any deeper feeling for either boy? In the end, though, Gale proves to be right. As Katniss herself admits, she needs Peeta's calming presence, rather than Gale's burning anger. As she seeks a way to move on, she feels her ending up with Peeta is what should've happened anyway, because only he can give her the hope that she needs to survive.

PANEM
PERSONAL ADS!

Throughout *The Hunger Games* trilogy, we watch both Gale and Peeta try to win Katniss' heart, but what if some of the other characters were trying to charm a partner? We can only imagine how they might go about things! Can you guess which Panem personalities are aiming to impress with these adverts?

1. I'm a mature man hoping to find a spark with someone who can keep up with my brilliant mind. Let's create something electrifying!

2. Creative mind seeks a muse to light his fire. I'll keep you in fashion and be there to support you, but be warned – I like taking risks and standing out from the crowd.

3. I'm a tall, bronzed, athletic guy with sea-green eyes. I've had a lot of dating experience but what I really want is a special someone I can look after. There might be plenty of fish in the sea, but I want to catch a girl who is a bit different from all the others.

4. Super stylish, ambitious, bubbly Capitol socialite seeks the perfect accessory: a new man on my arm! Must be well-presented, have impeccable manners and an eye for all the latest fashions. An appreciation for vivid colours would also be an asset. I expect there'll be a lot of interest, so you'll have to go all out to impress me – may the odds be ever in your favour, boys!

5. Rugged gent who doesn't play by the rules wants a bit of company. Do not contact me if you're: interested in slushy dates and discussing your feelings, a hygiene freak, shallow, stupid, talk too much or have an upbeat outlook. Someone who likes cleaning and cooking would be an advantage, as would someone who likes a drink (or two).

6. Independent woman seeks someone to have fun with, but nothing too deep (I don't like showing my emotions). I'm feisty, comfortable with nudity and handy with an axe if you get on my bad side! My date from hell = anything involving water.

1. Beetee; 2. Cinna; 3. Finnick; 4. Effie; 5. Haymitch; 6 Johanna

BECOMING THE MOCKINGJAY

Reaping day – and the heart-stopping moment when her sister's name is read aloud as the next girl tribute from District 12 – marks the beginning of a remarkable journey for Katniss Everdeen, taking her from being an unknown schoolgirl from the Seam, whose only concern is looking after her own small family, to the face of the rebellion against the Capitol, with the hopes of an entire nation resting squarely on her shoulders. Yet, in Collins' capable hands, this tremendous transformation seems entirely natural and believable. So, let's take a look at the events which mark Katniss' metamorphosis, leading up to the day when the revered Mockingjay can finally spread her wings . . .

THE MEANING OF A MOCKINGJAY

In a series filled with striking symbols (fire, pearls and bread to name but a few), the mockingjay is most prominent of all. Adorning the covers of Collins' novels, this bird remains vital to the rebel cause. So, what is it about this seemingly commonplace bird that's captured the hearts and minds of the people of Panem?

Firstly, the image of a mockingjay is what Katniss wore as her tribute token in the Hunger Games arena. A gift from Madge Undersee, this golden pin once belonged to Maysilee Donner. Madge's aunt and a dear friend of Katniss' own mother, Maysilee was reaped as a tribute back in the 50th Hunger Games. Yet, for Maysilee, the mockingjay was not so lucky. Despite putting up a brave fight (and saving Haymitch, Katniss' future mentor, from a vicious Career Tribute with one well-aimed poison dart), she died in the arena, pecked to death by a flock of candy-coloured bird mutts. When Katniss discovers the history of her token (and Maysilee's connection with so many of the important people in her own life), she feels that it holds even greater significance.

There is another reason why the emblem catches on so quickly though, rooted in the very origin of the species. Fittingly enough, a mockingjay is a bird that was never supposed to exist, a species created by natural mockingbirds mating with Capitol-created jabberjay mutts. The Capitol assumed that the all-male jabberjays would die out, just as they thought the rebels could be silenced. No one ever predicted that the jabberjays would be able to breed with natural species, but the birds' survival instinct proved stronger than anticipated. And so, the jabberjays live on through their mockingjay offspring.

So what's Katniss' link with the mockingjay? Well, for a start, Katniss' father could be compared to the mockingjay. Like the black-feathered jabberjay, Mr Everdeen's colouring was dark. He could also sing as beautifully as any bird (a talent which he's passed on to his daughter). The original purpose of the jabberjay was to provide the Capitol with information about the rebels' movements, helping Snow and his forces stay one step ahead. Similarly, Katniss' father provided her with all the information she needed to survive through his hunting tips and teachings about edible plants. Most importantly, jabberjays were left to die by the Capitol scientists who created them, whilst Mr Everdeen was killed in a mining accident, doing the job that was forced upon him by the Capitol. Just as the jabberjay lived on through the new mockingjay species, Mr Everdeen's legacy can be seen in his eldest daughter – a girl who takes after him in more than just physical appearance. Let's not forget that the mockingjays' mother-species are light-coloured mockingbirds and Katniss' mother stands out in the Seam for her fair hair and pale skin.

The thing that really defines Katniss as the mockingjay, though, is the fact that she is a problem of the Capitol's own making. Everything that has happened in Katniss' life which makes her so determined to fight to survive – her father's death, her family's poverty, Prim being reaped for the Hunger Games – has been brought about by the Capitol. In the same way that mockingjays were born out of the Capitol's failings with the jabberjay species, Katniss is a rebel that they have accidentally created through their mistakes. And just as the mockingjays found a way to thrive, Katniss survives against all odds.

When we first meet Katniss, far from being a fearsome rebel leader, she's just a poor Seam girl whose main concern is keeping her family alive. Although she resents the Capitol and the way that people in District 12 are forced to live, she learnt from a young age to keep her thoughts to herself because they would only get her in to trouble. It is Gale, not Katniss, who rages against the Capitol and longs to change the way things are. Hours before the reaping, Katniss cannot even contemplate Gale's idea of running away from the paths set out for them in District 12, refusing to hope that their lives could change for the better. However, Katniss does not have to seek change because her life changes dramatically the moment that Prim's name is picked out at the reaping – instinctively Katniss rushes forward to take her sister's place, an impetuous decision that changes the course of her own future irrevocably.

This act of self-sacrifice speaks volumes about Katniss. In that moment, the whole of Panem can see that she is impulsive, brave and strong. Haymitch hails her spunk and the people of District 12 salute her respectfully, demonstrating just how powerfully Katniss can command a crowd. However, this is hardly her intention; the only reason she steps forward as a volunteer is to protect her little sister. Similarly, in the arena Prim is all that keeps her fighting to win the Games; she has promised her younger sibling she will return and she's determined to honour her words. In the run-up to the Games, inciting a rebellion (or making an impression of any kind upon her nationwide audience) is the last thing on Katniss' mind. The night before they're due to enter the arena, Katniss and Peeta contemplate the possibility that neither one of them may be coming home alive. Pensive as ever, Peeta tries to explain to how he's anxious to keep his dignity in the Games. An ordinarily decent individual, he's determined not to abandon his principles – even in the arena. Rather than just being another piece in the Capitol's sadistic Games, he wants to prove that he can't be controlled and would rather die on his own terms than live on in a state of compromise. Yet, Katniss doesn't quite understand where he is coming from. A starving Seam girl, she's never really had the luxury of such thoughts; the only thing on Katniss' mind is survival.

However, she starts to appreciate the true meaning of Peeta's words with the loss of Rue. Beloved by her family and friends, Katniss understands only too well that the life of this tiny girl is precious. She can't bear the thought that her friend is about to be forgotten, casually dismissed by the Capitol audience and the callous Gamemakers who contributed to her death; she wants to make them feel fully responsible for the consequences of their decisions. After singing to Rue in her last moments, she covers her body with flowers and salutes her as she is lifted from the arena.

Katniss' focus (on her own fate) is further complicated when the Gamemakers announce a new ruling stating that two people from the same district can win. Katniss demonstrates her best side as she searches for Peeta and nurses him back to health, risking her own life to pick up the medicine needed to cure his blood poisoning. When she finally kills her greatest rival, the brutish Cato, she does so out of mercy rather than anger or a desire for victory. In fact, none of Katniss' kills in the arena are made in cold blood alone. Apart from Cato, she drops the tracker-jacker nest onto the Careers to give herself a crucial chance to escape and shoots Marvel in response to his murder of Rue. For someone to win the Hunger Games in this fashion is very rare, if not unheard of. As Katniss herself grimly observes, being 'nice' is not a trait that gets you particularly far in the arena.

Of course, the moment when Katniss first found herself being painted as 'the Mockingjay' came at the end of the 74th Hunger Games. Rather than battle Peeta to the death, Katniss concocted a different plan; she and Peeta would commit double suicide by swallowing poisonous nightlock berries. The idea was Katniss' alone. She suggested this not because she wanted to die, but because she suspected that the Gamemakers, desperate for a victor, would stop them before they could go through with it.

Yet, later, even Katniss questions her motives in this heated moment. Not wanting to face the people of District 12 in the aftermath of Peeta's death is undoubtedly a part of it. Then there's her growing affection for the baker's son . . . but there's some other element to her actions besides, a dangerous thrill of defiance that captures the minds of many people in Panem. For the first time in living memory, they've watched someone refuse to play by the Capitol's rules – and actually get away with it!

Katniss' actions may have been motivated by self-preservation more than anything else but, whilst standing up to President Snow and his regime was never her intention, she ended up doing just that, and her bravery set a shining example to the oppressed people of the districts. If a lowly Seam girl can beat the system and change the rules, then why not them? Though Katniss doesn't recognise the impact of her actions, this certainly isn't something that's escaped President Snow. Desperate to minimise the damage, he sets about forcing Katniss to take her already extremely public relationship with Peeta to the next level. If she can convince the nation that she was acting out of blind love rather than calculated defiance, then Snow might just allow her loved ones to live. Threatening the lives of Katniss' family and friends, the canny President scares her into playing along for a time. Yet, while he may have temporarily subdued the unwitting Mockingjay, it's no longer in his power to quash the growing rebellion that she's accidentally set in motion.

As Katniss embarks on her Victory Tour, she sees the effect of her presence in the districts first-hand, watching helplessly as a man is gunned down for honouring her in District 11. She feels the simmering anger of the crowds throughout Panem and experiences a crackdown on liberty in her home district. One of the first victims of the brutal new regime is Gale, whipped to within an inch of his life for poaching in the forest just as he always has done. While she was initially scared by the knowledge that other districts were revolting, gradually she begins to realise that Gale is right – Katniss is in a position to help this change in the air turn into something more permanent. Although the Quarter Quell ruling seems to be President Snow's way of preventing this from ever happening, in fact, it only makes Katniss more determined to defy him.

Tributes are meant to enter the Hunger Games with one objective – to survive. But Katniss doesn't enter the Quarter Quell hoping to win; this time, her aim is to protect Peeta. In just a year, her approach has changed from wanting to make it out alive for Prim to wanting to die to save Peeta. This selflessness is something that Katniss seems to have adopted from the boy with the bread himself, but there is more to it than that. Katniss knows that in fighting to keep someone else alive, she is breaking the rules of the Games and challenging the Capitol once more. It seems like a little of Gale's fighting spirit has rubbed off on her, after all. For the first time in the trilogy, Katniss seems able to step outside her own problems to look at the bigger picture. By choosing to die on her own terms rather than those set out by the Capitol, she can inspire everyone in the districts who believes in her to continue fighting for change.

It is not just Katniss' own decisions that impact upon her public image, however. Peeta makes her a more tragic, sympathetic figure by pretending that she'll be going into the arena pregnant. Yet, the most credit for shaping her public image must surely go to Cinna. From the start, Katniss' stylist has excelled at making her stand out in an array of beautifully-designed flaming outfits. When the Quarter Quell rolls round, he recognises the time has come for a different approach. In the 75th opening ceremony, he gives Katniss a harsh new look to represent the anger she feels at being tossed into the arena a second time. For her pre-Game interview with Caesar Flickerman, President Snow insists that Katniss wears the dress she was supposed marry Peeta in and, whilst she complies with his wishes, Cinna makes sure that the President's request backfires on him in the most spectacular style.

In the districts, those who have followed Katniss' lead and challenged the Capitol by staging uprisings of their own have been using the mockingjay – inspired by the pin Katniss wore as her tribute token – as a symbol of the resistance (ironically, Capitol socialites also adopted the mockingjay as a fashion statement, without any idea of its significance within rebel ranks). Knowing this, Cinna combines the bird motif with the 'girl on fire' theme he has built up with Katniss' previous costumes, to publicly transform Katniss herself into the Mockingjay. Although Katniss has no idea of the real function of her wedding gown, the fiery feathery creation that emerges onstage calls to mind a phoenix rising from the ashes . . . symbolising Katniss' own rebirth as a rebel leader – in the eyes of the public at least. While Katniss has no say over the ways that Cinna and Peeta manipulate the public's perception of her, she takes matters into her own hands when she blows up the Quarter Quell arena.

Though she can't predict the exact damage her arrow will do, firing it into the force field represents her most conscious attack on the Capitol yet. Whereas her display of defiance at the end of the 74th Hunger Games was merely a strategy for staying alive, this time she is making a deliberate decision to rebel against the establishment. Yet, how much credit can Katniss (the future Mockingjay) really take for pulling this off? After all, if Beetee's plan had run smoothly, she wouldn't have needed to shoot her arrow in the force field. The end result, however, would have been the same. Of course, Katniss should be credited with carrying out the plot anyway, but in the aftermath of the explosion, she realises that her entire role in the Quarter Quell was carefully orchestrated by the rebels – resulting in Katniss feeling used to say the least. Without realising it, she was at the centre of a secret scheme that the others were either protecting her from or just didn't trust her with.

In District 13, Katniss is again required to play a major part in the rebels' campaign. Everyone expects her to take on the role of the Mockingjay eagerly, but what Katniss herself requires is time to consider it further. In fact, her 'opposition' to the Capitol up to this point amounts to nothing more than a string of impulsive acts, without much thought behind them at all. Yet, their impact across the nation –

for better or for worse – has been huge. With the deaths of the people she killed in the Hunger Games – and all those hurt in the districts as a result of something she said in public – already weighing heavy on her conscience, Katniss realises only too well that becoming the official face of the rebellion will make her influence even greater and she's simply not sure she's ready to take on that responsibility.

WHY KATNISS?

There are moments throughout the series when Katniss wonders why people have taken her to their hearts as the Mockingjay. After all, she's surrounded by people she considers to be much more suitable for the role. Finnick Odair, for example, is incredibly popular and could surely influence vast numbers of people with a single smile and one strategically placed fishing net! Gale is a true rebel with a burning desire for change and a courageous fighting spirit. Above all there is Peeta, who is unfailingly good and selfless, and gifted with such a fantastic talent for articulating his thoughts that he could persuade anyone of anything. However, it is Katniss that the rebels choose to be their leader because they identify a fire inside of her that she can't see for herself. Years of having to fend for herself have made Katniss a survivor and others can recognise this quality immediately.

Nobody can deny that Peeta's intentions are just as pure as Katniss', perhaps even more so. Nevertheless, Peeta always plans his actions with the utmost care to try to bring about the outcome he wants. Katniss, on the other hand, reacts instinctively. Instinct prompts her to volunteer at the reaping and it's also what sparks her idea of swallowing the nightlock berries. After years of being made to watch people act in ways that are deliberately contrived, Katniss is a breath of fresh air for Panem's audience. Though Peeta causes a sensation by declaring his love for Katniss, he plays by the rules when he does so, announcing it during his allotted airtime with Flickerman; in contrast, when Katniss honours Rue's dead body and suggests committing suicide, it's safe to say that the rules – and what it means to break them – are the last thing on her mind.

Katniss is ruled by her feelings alone – this is what puts her in the Hunger Games in the first place – and she cannot control them the way Peeta can. Though she taught herself to hide her emotions while growing up, every now and again her mask slips to reveal Katniss' true self. It is these moments of emotional intensity that truly inspire the people of Panem. She is real and raw in a way that no one else on their Capitol-approved television screens ever has been. This is what makes Katniss so special and their perfect Mockingjay.

In the end, she decides that there's no way that the damage can be reversed. The rebels have gone too far to back down and thus, she agrees to be their mascot. Before she does this, she puts forward some conditions for President Coin. Though she is not happy with all of them, Coin accepts Katniss' terms with a single stipulation of her own; should Katniss fail in her mission as Mockingjay, her safety cannot be guaranteed by the rebels. At this point, Katniss realises that President Coin does not value her as an individual at all; she's just another leader trying to control and exploit Katniss to help her own cause.

The moment she takes on the mantle of the Mockingjay, Katniss becomes a product, to be sold by the rebels to the rest of Panem. They decide every aspect of how she comes across – from what she wears and says to how she should act. Despite having the best production team available, Katniss' initial television shoots are not successful. For whatever reason, she's simply not connecting with the camera and it takes Haymitch's intervention to figure out why. Every time Katniss has inspired or touched people in the past, she has been acting independently and in the moment, not reading from a script or following directions. So Plutarch sends her into more risky situations and Katniss starts to come alive in front of the camera. Though she is squeamish and scared when visiting the injured in District 8, there she realises how much people admire and respect her. Moments later the hospital is bombed. Undeniably impressive, Katniss' fire and rage towards the Capitol is a response that no one could have manufactured.

Even though she is now a raging success as the Mockingjay, Katniss is uneasy about some of the tactics that District 13 is using to fight the war. She doesn't approve of the snares created by Beetee and Gale in Special Defence and is horrified by the rebels' decision to start an avalanche to trap the opposition in District 2's mining mountains. Eventually Katniss realises her need to distance herself from District 13. As she travels with Squad 451 to the Capitol, she takes on her own personal mission to disobey President Coin's orders and kill President Snow herself. What's more, Coin's decision to send hijacked Peeta to join Squad 451 is enough to convince Katniss that the leader is trying to kill her. After all, from Coin's point of view, wouldn't she be more useful dead? There would be no danger of her pulling further unpredictable stunts and she would be a martyr whose memory they could use to promote their cause. Even Coin's own soldier, Boggs, warns Katniss not to trust the rebels just before he dies.

All Katniss' grand designs are put on hold, however, when she reaches the end of her mission. Instead of seeing President Snow die, she can only watch as Prim burns to death. Katniss is caught up in the flames too, and this time the 'girl on fire' routine isn't just a metaphor. More than her dress catching fire before the Quarter Quell, this harrowing experience represents Katniss' true rebirth. Now that the war is won, no one wants to use Katniss anymore and, even if they did, it would be almost impossible since she is so emotionally damaged by the loss of her sister. There is just one task left for her to carry out as the rebels' Mockingjay – she will be the one to assassinate President Snow.

Before she does this, Katniss learns from the ex-President himself that it was the rebels, not the Capitol who ordered the bombs that killed Prim to be dropped. She is also part of a meeting in which President Coin proposes one final Hunger Games tournament involving the children of the wealthy and powerful citizens who once ran the Capitol. The plan will only be put into action if the surviving Hunger Games victors agree. After all that Katniss has suffered in the fight for equal rights, she cannot believe that she has ended up right where she started. After careful consideration, she votes 'yes' to the plan.

However, when the time comes for Katniss to shoot an arrow at President Snow's head, it is not him she aims for. It is President Coin, the woman who promised a better way of life for Panem, but betrayed them all by bombing innocent civilians and planning to reinstate the sadistic Hunger Games – inflicting pain, suffering and death on a new generation of children. Katniss realises that, with Coin in charge, there will be no rebirth for her nation. Everything will essentially be as it was before. When she lets her arrow fly, her target is a true revolution, a future society in which the people of Panem can live in safety. As in all her best moments, this is Katniss listening to her heart, rather than following orders or playing a part. This is the moment where, without the aid of fancy costumes or instructions, she becomes the true Mockingjay.

BEING A VICTOR – WHO REALLY WINS?

Hunger Games victors are celebrated throughout their nation and held up as shining examples of warriors. In some districts it is seen as such a great honour to be a victor that people volunteer to go into the arena. However, behind the apparent glory of winning, what kind of existence awaits them outside the arena?

Throughout the trilogy, one theme that's constantly coming up is that of exploitation – what it is to be forced to play a role. The tributes must be dressed up and paraded in front of the Capitol crowds just to be sent to their deaths. Even if they put on a good enough show to be the last one standing, the game doesn't truly end for them there. Hunger Games victors are not winners; it is only President Snow who triumphs. Katniss begins to see this after her own victory, when she is forced to play up her romance with Peeta. Thrown into an arena full of victors in the Quarter Quell, the pattern becomes ever more apparent.

Many of Katniss' 'opponents' still use drugs or alcohol to block out the horrors they have seen, as well as the pressures of life in Victor's Village. At first, Katniss dismisses Haymitch as a drunken fool, but consider all that he's suffered over the past twenty-four years – as if living with the knowledge that his family and girlfriend were killed as a direct consequence of his 'outsmarting' the Gamemakers to win were not punishment enough, he's condemned to watch fresh tributes sent to the slaughter every year – and it's not so difficult to understand why he might turn to the bottle for comfort. Similarly, Finnick may come across as shallow and promiscuous, but that is because President Snow has chosen to cast him as such. In reality, Finnick is kind, genuine and utterly devoted to his one true love, Annie. Indeed, this 'weakness' is what has made him so easy for the President to manipulate. With Annie at stake, Finnick can only comply with Snow's demands, even if it means selling his body to wealthy Capitol residents. Even tough-as-nails Johanna Mason has suffered at the hands of President Snow. As her and Katniss start to form a friendship in District 13, Katniss can see how damaged the older girl is. The truth is that Johanna's been left with no one that she cares for.

But Collins makes it clear that it is not just President Snow who uses people. The rebels are just as keen to draw Katniss and Peeta into their Quarter Quell breakout plot – with or without the tributes' consent. They are manipulated into carrying out Beetee's plan and when it succeeds, Katniss is expected to be the on-screen leader the rebels want her to be. As she undergoes hair and makeup styling and is directed on what to say and how to appear, she feels like a tribute about to go into the arena again. However, in this respect Katniss fares considerably better than Peeta, who has to be hijacked to perform in his own propaganda slots. This torture takes a terrible toll on the good-natured baker's boy. Transformed into a pseudo-mutt-version of himself, he has to learn everything about who he really is all over again.

Interestingly, there is a parallel between these tormented victors and celebrities in our own world. Nowadays, it seems so easy for anyone to become famous (and sometimes just as easy for them to be forgotten). They could appear on a reality TV show, get caught up in a public scandal or follow the traditional route and become well-known for their career. Whatever the reason, when someone becomes a celebrity these days, it's tantamount to becoming public property. Subject to intense scrutiny, they'll obviously need agents to control their image. Often, they cannot escape the media glare, even when they want to. Of course, most stars choose to put themselves in the public eye unlike the hapless Hunger Games victors, resigned to a lifetime of playing a part through bad luck rather than their own choices. It is only when Katniss breaks out of the role created for her by others that she can truly be said to 'win' and even then it is a hollow victory after all that she has already lost.

Though she finds true love with Peeta, the most they can do is try to pick up the pieces of their lives by having children. And, though it takes Peeta fifteen years to convince Katniss to start a family, the fact that she does so at all shows how far she has progressed. Before the rebellion, Katniss refused to even contemplate the possibility of bringing a child into the world. But, with Peeta's help, Katniss has come to believe in the good in the world as well as the bad. And so, perhaps Collins' final lesson is one of hope. Katniss found something beyond her despair because she fought for it. She challenged what she was being told and in doing so built a better future for the next generation. Her story is testament to the fact that, though it will surely mean making difficult choices and sacrifices, we too can change the things that we don't like about our society for a better future.

WAR OF THE WORDS

During the war between the Capitol and the rebels, such a lot happens that it can be hard to keep track of who does what and what happens where! Can you figure it out to complete this crossword?

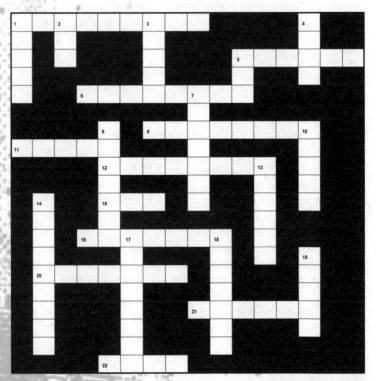

ACROSS

1. Who does Katniss find in the ruins of District 12 and bring back to 13 for Prim?
5. What is the name of Castor's brother, who is also a cameraman and an Avox?
6. Peeta is this after being captured by the Capitol . . .
9. Which member of Squad 451 does Peeta accidentally throw into a pod?
11. Katniss has to record lots of these for the rebels . . .
12. Which building gets bombed when Katniss visits District 8 during the rebellion?
15. In the war, District 2's old mining mountain proves to be a tough *what* to crack?
16. Which member of Squad 451 is farsighted?
20. What weapon does Beetee specifically make for Finnick?
21. Who does Gale help to come up with traps for the rebels to use against the other side?
22. Whose quick thinking helps some citizens of District 12 survive the Capitol's bombs?

DOWN

1. Who is the leader of Squad 451?
2. Which district is the last to be won by the rebels?
3. Who designs the uniform Katniss wears throughout the rebellion and her TV spots?
4. What is the name of the device that Squad 451 uses to guide them through the Capitol?
5. You don't want to run into one of these in the Capitol . . .
7. What is the word that the mutts President Snow releases into the Capitol sewers are programmed to repeat?
8. Who does not make it into the rebel army because of their torture-induced fear of water?
10. Who is the first member of Squad 451 to die?
13. The mutts that President Snow sends after Squad 451 are half-human and half-*what*?
14. What is the name of the pill that the members of Squad 451 are issued with so that they can commit suicide if they are captured by the enemy and facing torture?
17. Who directs Katniss' propaganda shots?
18. The Capitol agreed to a treaty with District 13 after the Dark Days because they had these kind of weapons . . .
19. How many different types of arrow does Beetee create for Katniss to use?

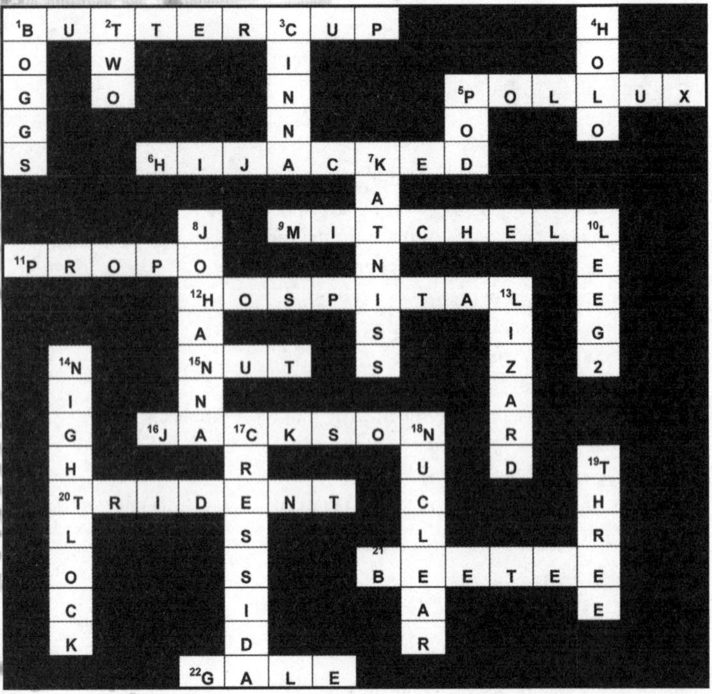
1 BUTTERCUP
2 TWO
3 CINNA
4 HOLLO
5 POLLUX
5 POD
6 HIJACKED
7 KATNISS
8 JOHANNA
9 MITCHEL
10 LEEG 2
11 PROPO
12 HOSPITAL
13 LIZARD
14 NIGHTLOCK
15 NUT
16 JACKSON
17 CRESSIDA
18 NUCLEAR
19 THREE
20 TRIDENT
21 BEETEE
22 GALE
1 BOGGS

HOW TO SURVIVE THE HUNGER GAMES

The ultimate guide to ending the Games alive!

PRE-GAME

If you want to give yourself a fighting chance in the arena you need to remember that the Game starts long before you're in there. Here are some tips for dealing with the preliminary stages of being a tribute:

BE CONFIDENT

You may be scared but you don't want your competitors to catch onto this and think you're an easy target, so when your name is reaped keep a brave face on. Sponsors will back people they think can win, so look like a survivor and you're more likely to end up one.

MAKE THE MOST OF THE TRAINING CENTRE

Whilst you don't want to show off too many of your skills to your fellow competitors, the Training Centre is a great opportunity to get a better idea of what their strengths and weaknesses are. You can also pick up some valuable skills and knowledge here – such as how to make snares, tie knots, and camouflage yourself, or learning which plants are deadly – which may prove invaluable when you're playing the Game.

ESTABLISH A GOOD RELATIONSHIP WITH YOUR MENTOR

So your mentor is a grumpy alcoholic who's forgotten what a shower is? You'd rather take your chances facing a horde of fanged monkey muttations than become friends with him/her? Well, tough. Your mentor is the person who will be responsible for securing deals with sponsors to get you much-needed gifts in the arena, like food and medicine, and the one who decides when you receive them, so you want to get on their good side. Most importantly, they are one of the few people who really know what it's like to be a tribute. They had the skills and sense to win their year and have been mentoring other tributes ever since, so they have a unique insight into how the Games work and what strategies are best. Listen to them and do everything they say, even if you don't like it. They know best!

HAVE A GAME PLAN

It's important to decide what kind of tribute you will be. Are you going to rely on your ability with weapons and physical prowess? Are you going to win by outsmarting your opponents? Will you intimidate them with your bloodlust like Cato or Brutus? Or take the opposite approach and deliberately let yourself be underestimated then prove everyone wrong, the way Johanna Mason did? Put your plan into action during the interview stage, but . . .

DON'T GIVE TOO MUCH AWAY

As much as you want to create a formidable impression, you don't want to reveal what your real talents or weak spots are. Steer clear of mentioning your weapon of choice or any special skills you have that could give you an advantage. If your opponents don't know how you operate they won't be prepared for your method of attack or able to sabotage your survival.

STAND OUT

Whether you're given a helping hand by your stylist with an attention-grabbing outfit, or you say something to shock everyone during your interview, you have to make sure you are noticed among all the other tributes. You need to go all out to impress the Gamekeepers (shooting at them is not necessarily the best option, but it worked for Katniss!), charm the public and win yourself sponsors. You want to be the one that people are rooting for once the Game starts.

IN THE ARENA

Now that you've done everything you can to ensure you're prepared for the arena, it's time to face the real challenge. Follow these golden rules and it'll be your name Claudius Templesmith announces at the end. Let the Hunger Games begin!

REACT FAST

Being dropped into the arena can be a shock at first. Your first instinct may be to assess your surroundings, but you don't have time for that. Try to grab some supplies from the Cornucopia, then get out of there as fast as you can before the inevitable bloodbath begins.

ACCLIMATISE TO THE ARENA

Now that you're safely out of your opponents' reach (for the time being), you can get a better idea of where you are. Arena landscapes can range from jungles to great expanses of water, but more often than not they are a combination of lots of different terrains. Try to work out what sort of environment you are in and where the sites of particular danger or benefit might lie, for example, woods could be a good hiding place, whereas in the open space of a sandy beach you'd be a sitting duck. Look out for any animals, muttations or plants that could be a threat or help to you.

FIND WATER AND FOOD

Many tributes are killed not by their rivals, but by starvation or dehydration. Avoid this fate by tracking down a water source early on and stocking up. If you're lucky you will have picked up some food at the Cornucopia, if not, get hunting or picking edible plants or berries (this is where your Training Centre lessons will come in handy). You can try to steal food from others but this carries risks – if they don't catch and kill you, you could still end up like Foxface and be accidentally poisoned!

FIND A GOOD HIDING PLACE

You might not feel much like playing hide-and-seek with your fellow competitors, but it's possible to win by waiting for the others to kill each other off. Although it's unlikely that you'll last the whole Games without being discovered, the chances are that the number of tributes left will have significantly depleted by the time you really have to start playing the Game. While you're hiding you may overhear useful information from other tributes, and it will also give you the opportunity to catch up on some sleep – but never become too relaxed in your hideout. Good places to hole up could include any caves or large trees, but beware that anywhere too obvious will probably also be spotted by others, and if you stay put too long the Gamemakers might find a way (fire or flood, for example) to get you moving!

BE AWARE OF YOUR OPPONENTS

It may seem obvious, but it's a good idea to be conscious of where the other tributes are in the arena. Most will be careful not to advertise their position, but you can look out for clues such as old fires and traps, and expect that places where food and water can be found will be likely stop-off points. Be particularly cautious of the Career Tributes, traditionally those from Districts 1, 2 and 4, who have been bred and trained to participate in the Hunger Games. They are often favourites to win the competition and usually form an alliance in the arena to pick the weaker contestants off, making them even more dangerous, so you would be wise to stay out of their way for as long as possible. Watch out for Claudius Templesmith's nightly announcements, so you can keep an eye on who's out of the Game and who's left to face.

MAKE ALLIES (BUT BE CAREFUL)

It's not just the Career Tributes that can become stronger by joining forces; you could also increase your winning potential by forming an alliance. In doing so, you would have extra skills and knowledge on your side, as well as increased protection from attacks. However, you should only become allies with someone you trust and always bear in mind that the Hunger Games only has one winner (usually!).

THINK OUTSIDE THE BOX

If you're not a Career or a Thresh-like giant, you may think that you're at a disadvantage, but there are plenty of other ways to survive. Though they may not seem important, your ability to climb trees or swim, your knowledge of hunting or just plain cunning could be the thing that keeps you alive. If you're lucky you'll also have some useful supplies or weapons, but if not be creative with what you do have. Finnick Odair managed to weave a net out of vine and trap his fellow tributes in it. A sleeping bag isn't a deadly firearm but it'll stop you from freezing to death. No one knew why Beetee needed wire, but he put it to pretty effective use, and the tracker jacker nest Katniss dropped on the Career Pack did as much damage as a sword could.

DON'T UNDERESTIMATE YOUR OPPONENTS

You may think you already know which tributes are your biggest rivals, but you don't want to get caught out wishing that you'd paid attention to the quiet little girl in the Training Centre. Someone may not have physical strength on their side, but put a bow and arrow in their hand and they could turn into an assassin, so don't give them that chance!

PUT ON A GOOD SHOW

Remember that first and foremost the Hunger Games are a form of entertainment being broadcast to the rest of Panem. The Gamemakers are always looking for an interesting narrative, and if you make the mistake of letting things get boring, they'll soon find ways to spice it up! Avoid the possibility of them starting a flood, igniting a fire or releasing a pack of ferocious animal muttations by keeping the cameras on you. Whether your story is a romance with an ally or a vendetta against a rival, find a hook to keep yourself at the centre of the Game. A camera-worthy tribute is also going to get more attention from sponsors, which could gain you food, medicine or even a weapon when you most need it.

STAY ALIVE!

Haymitch's original advice to Katniss and Peeta may have been said in jest, but the man has a point. Sometimes pure resilience is all that stands in the way of you and victory. Whether you have to eat raw squirrels, lie in mud for days or blow the arena apart, don't give up fighting to live until you hear the trumpets blaring and Claudius Templesmith shouting:

LADIES AND GENTLEMEN, I AM PLEASED TO PRESENT THE VICTOR OF THE HUNGER GAMES!

**Disclaimer: While these rules should give you a great head start on your fellow tributes, your success in the arena will also depend partly on luck. And don't forget that winning is often just the start of your role as a piece in the Capitol's games. However, that's still better than ending up as a wolf mutt.

Happy Hunger Games!
May the odds be ever in your favour!

HUNGER GAMES HEAD-TWISTER!

Now that you've learnt all about Panem – or just refreshed your memory – how well do you know the world of The Hunger Games?

1. What is District 8's industry?

2. What is the name of the red-headed Avox girl who serves Katniss in the Capitol?

3. Who is the only living female victor from District 7?

4. What are the names of Gale's siblings?

5. Which year of the Hunger Games did Finnick Odair originally win?

6. What are Katniss and Peeta's favourite colours?

7. Who became President of Panem after Alma Coin?

8. What was the name of the tribute Haymitch formed an alliance with in the 75th Hunger Games?

9. What was Tigris' job before running her shop?

10. What is the name of Plutarch Heavensbee's assistant?

11. Which district does Gale move to after the second rebellion?

12. What was the name of the male tribute from District 8 in the 75th Hunger Games?

13. What do the lizard mutts that follow Katniss and the rebels through the Capitol's sewers smell of?

14. What is Katniss' favourite thing about the Capitol?

15. Who sells alcohol illegally in District 12?

ANSWERS

1. Textile production

2. Lavinia

3. Johanna Mason

4. Rory, Vick and Posy

5. 65th

6. Katniss – green. Peeta – orange.

7. Commander Paylor of District 8

8. Maysilee Donner

9. Being a Hunger Games stylist

10. Fulvia Cardew

11. District 2

12. Woof

13. Blood and roses, like President Snow's breath

14. The lamb stew

15. Ripper

PERSONAL REVIEW

Here you can record your experience of *The Hunger Games*!

Your favourite character:

Your least favourite character:

Most kick-ass moment:

Saddest moment:

Funniest moment:

A character who didn't make it that you really wish had:

The tribute you'd least like to get into a fight with:

The tribute you'd most like to form an alliance with:

Best fight:

Best weapon:

Your favourite Cinna outfit:

Scariest muttation:

District you'd most like to be from:

Your favourite scene from *The Hunger Games* film: